PRAISE FOR *WHISPER TOWN*

"Patricia Hickman's WHISPER TOWN shows that love of neighbor, springing from a heart broken by Jesus, is ultimately the greatest triumph...A compelling page-turner."

—ERIC WIGGIN, author of *The Gift of Grandparenting*

"Hickman's prose rings with gritty authenticity and stark, lyrical description."

—LIZ CURTIS HIGGS, author of *Thorn in My Heart*

"Patricia Hickman's characters in WHISPER TOWN are so realistic, so endearing, you come away believing you must have met them somewhere, and if not, you wish you could. A most enjoyable read!"

—SYLVIA BAMBOLA, author of *Waters of Marah*
and *Return to Appleton*

"Yet a third marvelous visit to Nazareth, Arkansas...Ms. Hickman delights us with quaint humor and a cast of quirky characters, even while shining a keen light upon racism in the thirties."

—LAWANA BLACKWELL, author of *A Table by the Window*

"Patricia Hickman has given us a wonderful book about the many facets of love—a man for a woman, a father for his children, a pastor for his flock, and a caring individual for a needy one—without ignoring the cost of such love. Insightful, layered, and faith-filled, WHISPER TOWN is, quite simply, tops."

—GAYLE ROPER, author of *Winter Winds, Autumn Dreams*

more...

WHISPER TOWN

A NOVEL

THE MILLWOOD HOLLOW SERIES

PATRICIA HICKMAN

WARNER
Faith®

NEW YORK   BOSTON   NASHVILLE

Warner Faith

Time Warner Book Group
1271 Avenue of the Americas, New York, NY 10020

Visit our website at www.twbookmark.com

Warner Faith® and the Warner Faith logo are trademarks of Time Warner Book Group Inc.

Printed in the United States of America
First Edition: June 2005
10 9 8 7 6 5 4 3 2 1

Library of Congress Cataloging-in-Publication Data
Hickman, Patricia.
 Whisper town / Patricia Hickman.
  p. cm. — (The Millwood Hollow series)
 Summary: "The third novel in the Millwood Hollow Series about an unlikely hero and a ragtag trio of orphans in racially segregated 1930s Arkansas"—Provided by the publisher.
 ISBN 0-446-69234-4
 1. Clergy—Fiction. 2. Racism—Fiction. 3. Orphans—Fiction. 4. Arkansas—Fiction. 5. Depressions—Fiction. I. Title.
 PS3558.I2296W48 2005
 813'.54—dc22   2004027775

Text design by Meryl Sussman Levavi

*To my nephews and nieces, Elizabeth, Tim, Michael,
and little Patricia, who are so much more than a mix
of black and white, having had placed within you
the lampstand of conflicting cultures,
a candelabra of beauty, lovely in God's sight.*

WHISPER
TOWN

For we, being many, are one bread and one body;
for we are all partakers of that one bread.

1 CORINTHIANS 10:17

I

*E*VERY SUNLIT COMMUNITY CAN CAST A DIS-
concerting shadow. That is why a town celebrates its
own virtues with harvest festivals and greased pig competi-
tions, thereby casting its citizens in the best light, all flaws
dimished. Church in the Dell's yearly apple social lured the
happiest of saints and the worst of sinners into its cinnamon
and spice womb.

Jeb greeted people out on the lawn using his best minister's handshake: thumbs up, skin to skin. Talk of an unusual
nature sifted through the ordinary chitchat, spoken three times
in succession from the lips of three different church members
before he eventually latched onto the gist of the matter.

A commotion down in Apple Valley, where, on good authority, rumors had circulated not more than a summer ago of
how the daughters of the county commissioner had lost their

virginity, now had tongues wagging with a new vigor; the whole operation of this recent rumor mill affected the chatter even more vibrantly than the commissioner's daughters' scandal.

A hush settled over the church lawn and, what with Florence Bernard's lighting of candles along the path, even the boys inclined to rowdy exuberance took to whispering. The apple orchard hid secrets, awful stories, mothers said, that caused the schoolchildren to walk around instead of going through Apple Valley. A shadow had slipped over Nazareth and no amount of conjuring could lift its spell. The rumors shadowed the evening like the darkening horizon, the color of brine gone bad.

Florence Bernard and Josie Hipps acted as hostesses directing visitors to the tables. Hot spiced apples, crumb pies, cobblers, apple dumplings, hot cider, and squash and apple soup enticed guests into the tent set up by the Church in the Dell elders, where tables and chairs borrowed from first this one and then that one presented a plain yet inviting asylum for the church social.

Mellie Fogarty made a point to tell every woman who came through the tent's entry that her roses had come in good this year. Every table displaying a Fogarty centerpiece proved her right.

Angel Welby, with her hair pulled back to emphasize her emergence as a fifteen-year-old woman, offered herself as a centerpiece to a circle of boys from Stanton School. Jeb floundered more often than not in what he perceived as his awkward paternal offerings to his less-than-receptive charge. It was in his estimable opinion that his duties as fledgling shepherd to the Church in the Dell flock had a greater chance of fulfillment than his fatherly offerings to the Welbys, and that being evidenced with the passing of days.

Angel's hair had darkened and her eyes had blued in the spring of her adolescence. She had never been a girl who would divulge her thoughts to anyone, let alone a preacher to whom circumstances had forced her to yield her life and siblings. So Jeb watched her grow, wild as wood roses, and rendered helpless to tend her soul with any measure of goodness. Angel grew fast among the weeds, her lot as a poor girl born to a momma whose mind had been swept away with the Depression.

Florence brought Jeb a bowl of soup with a slice of sopping bread. "Taste Josie's soup, Reverend, and then tell her how good it is before she drives me nuts with worry."

Jeb sipped from the bowl and then raised his thumb to Josie, who waited nervous as a rabbit beside the cider pot. "Tell her it's the best squash and apple soup I've ever tasted," he said to Florence, and then whispered, "except for yours, Florence."

Florence thanked him. She let out a sigh and said, "I'll be back shortly with something sweet. Anything in particular tickle your fancy, Reverend?"

Jeb knew better than to play favorites, so he said, "Bring me what you like best, Florence."

His answer satisfied the middle-aged divorcée. She went out in search of a new conquest: a farmer widowed two years who might be easy pickings for the best apple pie chef in Nazareth.

Jeb milled among the men, who talked about the measly harvest and last month's dust storm. Ivey Long told him, "Got the plow horse hitched up to the hay wagon. I guess the children are anxious for a moonlight ride."

"I haven't been on a hay ride myself since I was yea

high," said Jeb. "The church appreciates you driving your wagon, Ivey."

Jeb heard the pleasant sound of the handsome schoolteacher behind him. Fern Coulter brought the sweet scent of a woman into the tent. He straightened his tie and smoothed his slicked-back hair around his ears. "Fern, you look fine in that dress." He offered her cider and she accepted it.

The rumors twisting like a cyclone through downtown the last few days had not dampened their feast of apples. Jeb would wait and bring up the matter to Deputy Maynard, who would surely show up at the mere mention of free eats. If anyone could quell the rumors of a slaying in the orchard, George Maynard would know the truth and help dispel the outlandish stories of blood on the apple pickers' path.

❧

Jeb believed in the world he could not see, but he left the practice of dwelling on the unseen to lonely old women whose neck hairs rose up during full moons. He did not listen to the wind when the children claimed to hear whispers at night. Least of all, he did not pay heed to the bad dream that awakened him on the morning of the autumn's first apple social.

He had no choice but to be a reasonable man. The church he shepherded down here in the hollow needed a rational minister, one who treated each day like a new pearl collecting on the town's long string of bad days. Too many villains had emerged from hard times. Nazareth, Arkansas, held in its possession a short list of heroic souls.

In 1933, heroes had ebbed from the national canvas like the hacks on Wall Street, or else took to masquerading as tramps on railroad cars, and oftentimes as politicians who ped-

dled emotional causes for a little sway. A body had to look hard
into those places and imagine a hero existing beneath the sub-
terfuge of a swindle. The long and short of it was this: a loaf of
bread bought votes. Myths arose primarily from the ink of pulp
fiction, meaning that for a dime, heroism could be rolled up
and tucked inside a ten-year-old boy's shirt. Ordinary men quit
aspiring to valor what with its high cost and all. Empty stomachs spawned nostalgia, but it was the kind that turned sensible people into monsters, and that led to unimaginable grief
considering the sad state of affairs for jobless heroes.

To inflame the bonfire of a national calamity, freedom
had been bought and paid for on good, compatriots' paper, but
not all Americans had redeemed their own personal bundle of
liberty. Not enough of them, at least, and not soon enough.
When the lean years of the Great Depression swallowed up
hope, the yearnings of the insignificant were relegated to the
end of the bread lines; this was a quagmire for Jeb whose reck-
less habit of trading in the tide of human sorrow got him into
trouble with the everyday people, those who, when in a tight
spot, gave little thought to even the least imaginable yearnings.

Jeb had requested no particular elements of his encum-
bered life, not a tin whistle's worth of the weight hanging over
his head. He had said more.than once it was his turn to be at the
receiving end of a lucky break. At the head of his want list: a
quiet Arkansas parish church to shepherd that could pay him a
steady wage, a pond where he could wet his line, and a wife to
bed; more specifically, an uncommonly good lady named Fern
Coulter,.who had supplied his library with an abundance of clas-
sical works. Each book he read had shown him his own lack,
causing him to reach beyond his sharecropper's state of mind.

Fern had come to him in the most gingerly fashion. Out

of all the women he had known back in Texas, none had wooed as slowly as Fern.

He laid blame at the door of their thorny beginnings and justly so.

In the first place, his most recent years consisted of a series of surplus hindrances kicking through the door, elements and people whom he did not want, ask, or need. These were children he looked after but had not in the least manner sired—Angel Welby, the biggest girl, who paid him the least amount of regard and respect for what little necessities he had provided, and her two younger siblings, Willie and Ida May. The Welbys took to him like pond leeches.

Angel admittedly had taken better to him when he was a con man than when he had bowed his heart to God and become a legitimate preacher. The oldest girl from the family of Welby—a clan whose elders never bothered to check up on their displaced progeny—favored the idleness of a life pretended over the strenuous efforts of a life devoted.

Jeb deemed the girl to possess few comely traits.

She had flowered handsomely in her youth, a teenage beauty; but her disposition had soured on her. Her habit of deriding Jeb at inopportune moments, such as at church functions in plain sight of respectable congregants, made him wistful for the day the girl's journey would lead her quietly back to her origins.

Jeb saw no sign of that happening any time soon. Summer had come and gone with no promise of change. He did not aspire to heroism, especially since a hero's wages plus a nickel would buy little more than his morning cup of coffee. He did not want his life to become the stuff of fables, but try as he might, the whole gallantry matter came knocking uninvited.

❧

The moon hung over the hollow so full it appeared that any minute it might burst. Children and youths scrambled to claim a spot on the hay wagon. Florence and Josie commandeered the clean up of tables and grounds. Jeb herded children and pining teen couples toward Ivey's wagon. "First rule, no hay throwing." He shot a warning glance to Angel's brother, Willie. "That means you, Willie Boy."

Willie pulled a buddy down from the edge of the wagon and claimed his place while the boy pummeled his arm. Willie poked him hard and traded licks while telling him he was soft as a girl.

Two boys pulled Angel into the wagon, youths far too old for her, at least in Jeb's estimation. Jeb took the spot next to them, if for nothing else but to keep an eye on matters, and realizing too he should save room for Fern. He glanced up the path and saw her picking her way around a stand of birch trees. She lifted her face and smiled at him. Jeb knew she intended the smile for him. He pulled rank on one of the boys next to Angel and cleared a Fern-sized space. He waved at Fern. "Wagon's filling up. Best you hurry."

"You coming too, Jeb?" Angel sighed. Her brows formed fallen crescents.

"Make way for the chaperone of your life."

Angel had the look of a cornered fox. "All the other old people are staying back at the tent, Jeb. You ought to stay and be sociable."

He said, straight into her ear, "Mind your tongue, Biggest."

Not so fast to admit defeat, Angel said, "I saw Oz Mills drive up in his fancy Packard. You'd better corral that teacher before she's snatched up by a higher bid."

"Fern, you coming?" Jeb asked. The banker's nephew Oz had taken over the family business when his uncle Horace Mills had moved his family to Hope when Oz's ailing father had taken to his bed. The brother bankers held tight while other financiers sunk into the Depression's quicksand. Oz and a pack of his college-swell friends swarmed like flies around Nazareth's last surviving bank.

"Sun's going down." Fern glanced over the heads of the children. "I'd better run back for my jacket."

"You can wear mine." Jeb pulled off his suit coat.

Fern reached for his coat, but then said, "I don't want to mess up your good coat. I'll only be a minute." She turned and ran back up the path.

The last of the youths clambered aboard and Ivey pulled out his whip.

"Hold up a second," said Jeb. "We're waiting for one more."

A cloud rolled across the moon and the last tincture of sunlight faded. The hollow blackened except for the lanterns on the wagon. Jeb anticipated the warm feel of Fern next to him in a jostling wagon. Eagerness rose inside him, an underground stream bubbling to the surface. Wooing Fern Coulter had been a tedious occupation over the last year, first winning trust from a woman that once thought of him as lower than algae. Inviting her to join him on the hay ride and hearing her low boylike voice say, "Why not?" had raised his hopes.

"Miss Coulter's not coming back, you know," said Angel. "She always finds an excuse."

"Tonight's different and you got your own friends to yammer at, Angel." Jeb put on his jacket and warmed his hands inside his pockets. He shifted from one foot to the next. Finally Fern appeared at the top of the hill. Behind her, stretching his long bones down the path, loped Oz Mills, the banker's nephew. His silhouette cut an intrusive figure even in the moonlight.

"Jeb, I'm so sorry," said Fern.

Angel whispered something near to sarcasm to one of the boys.

Fern talked rapidly. "Oz has come to tell me that my mother and father have shown up tonight a day early for their visit."

"Invite them to join us," Jeb said. He wouldn't look at Oz.

"This is awful, I know. But Daddy's not feeling well and he's back waiting at my house with my mother. I'm sure the long drive from Oklahoma's exhausted him. I should go and see about him."

Ivey gave the old horse a whistle.

"I'll see her back," said Oz. He helped Fern slip into her jacket. As she turned to head back up the path, Oz said, "You have fun with the kiddies, Reverend."

Angel set the boys to snickering at Jeb's expense.

⁂

The wagon ride turned into a grueling festival of screaming girls and hay-tossing boys. Jeb's woolen coat was prickly with straw and his imagination bristling with thoughts of Oz joining Fern and her family for coffee while he fended off attacks of hay. He jumped from the wagon, reminded Willie to see Ida May up the path, and then meandered back toward the tent site. He led the departing rabble by the light of a lantern and elbowed through into the sanctuary of the tent.

Deputy Maynard bellyed up to the remnants of pie salvaged for him by the ladies' food committee. "Don't you look the scarecrow?" Maynard laughed.

"Spare me the compliments," said Jeb. "Any coffee left, Josie?"

The families gathered up their children and headed back toward their trucks and wagons.

"Sorry I missed the festivities, Reverend. We got us a for-real investigation up at Apple Valley."

"I was hoping it was just gossip."

"Nazareth hasn't seen this kind of business since, well, since your arrest. Hey, what's past is past, I always say."

"The apple pickers told it right, then?" asked Jeb.

"Best as I can figure, someone come to some harm out in those orchards, but who it was is yet to be known. Nobody's filed a missing person on anyone. But we got a shirt that says that somebody took a beating. What's become of him is anybody's guess." He turned and told Florence what good pie she made.

Maynard said, "Don't like the sound of bloody-shirt stories, nosirree, nosir! Makes folks nervous. Seems to me like everyone's too scared to know what to make of it, or to talk about it."

"You saw the bloodied shirt, Maynard?"

"Got it locked up in the jailhouse."

"Anyone missing from around town?" asked Jeb.

"Not that anyone has reported. Or no one wants to fess up. Say, where's your schoolteacher gal pal?"

"Her folks showed up tonight. You believe someone in Nazareth knows what happened down in the orchard?"

"It's the best guess for now. Florence, how about slicing me another piece of your apple crumb pie?"

Jeb made an excuse and left the tent. The families congregated outside, laughing and talking about whose kids were going without shoes. Not a person from Church in the Dell could possibly know about a beating down in the orchard, not without blabbing it to everyone.

He said his good-nights to the departing families and gathered up the Welby brood.

The moon had disappeared entirely, overtaken by the evening clouds. He led the children around to the parsonage by the light of the lantern.

"Tonight was like heaven!" said Angel. "Not one, but two boys like me. Both of them gave me a ring." She slid the rings up and down the chain around her neck.

"You ought to at least pick one." Jeb cupped his hand behind Ida May's head, moving her ahead of him on the path.

"More fun this way. You get more stuff and all anyway."

"It's not about how much stuff you can get out of a boy, Angel," said Jeb.

"I'll give one of the rings back after I decide which one I like the best," said Angel.

"It's not like picking out a new dress. A body has to study the situation, keep an eye on the person, and see how they treat you."

"If that's true, you ought to stop trying to win Miss Coulter over then. She treats you like an old shoe."

"Fern is a complicated woman. Jewelry and flowers and such don't mean a thing to her. She wants to know more important things, like what a body's been reading or how much of your time do you give in helping out a neighbor in need."

"Every woman likes flowers and jewelry, I don't care what she tells you. She's still a girl and girls like to be given stuff. Men who don't know that are up the creek, far as I'm concerned."

Willie told Jeb, "I like Miss Coulter. She knows how to hunt and fish and I never see her walking around bragging about who give her what. I think you're wrong, Angel."

"Neither of you know nothing about women." Angel dropped the chain into her blouse.

"Dub, how come Miss Coulter thinks you're an old shoe?" asked Ida May.

"Fern can hunt and fish? Who told you that, Willie Boy?" asked Jeb.

"She tells it to her class. When some of the boys are having trouble with math, she uses her fishing line and asks things like, 'If Willie's trout is ten yards from him but is swimming a foot every five seconds, how far will he have to throw his line to reach that trout in fifteen seconds?'"

"Fern never said she fished," said Jeb.

Angel blew out a breath. "That don't mean nothing. Miss Coulter was raised with boys." She said it like Fern had been raised with wolves.

"Fern's not average. But she takes a long time to get to know." He figured Fern had a reason for never bringing it up. "You take this whole fishing-and-hunting matter. Not once has she told me that she does either one. Leastways, not that I can recall. She's never shown up in the deer woods, has she? I'll grant you, she doesn't brag about all of her abilities. She's uncommon."

"News flash, Jeb Nubey. She doesn't tell who she doesn't like," said Angel.

"She made Bobby Gray give up his hunting rifle once when he brought it to school." Willie directed his comments to Jeb. "But then she opened the barrel and told him he should clean his gun. After school she give it back to him and showed him how to carry it."

A gun blast reverberated, tree to tree, through Millwood Hollow.

Ida May latched onto Jeb's arm.

"Someone's out hunting possums, Littlest," said Jeb.

The ratchet of toads boomed out of the woods, but no other identifiable sound.

"Let's get inside," said Jeb. "Some fool teenager out there might mistake us for night prey and I don't want to be his next kill."

"I don't believe no stories about the apple orchards," said Willie. "People tell lies all the time."

Ida May asked what stories. Angel guided her around the church and onto the parsonage lawn. The Welbys made for the porch. Jeb locked them all inside for the night, checking out the window twice. He shut off the lights.

A rumor gave no man cause to waste good electricity.

2

YELLOW-WHITE LIGHTS MOVED THROUGH THE marsh at the edge of White Oak Lake, boys out frog gigging most likely. The lights undulated in the fog that stretched all the way down the stream that emptied out beneath the bridge at Marvelous Crossing. A torchlight moved down the stream and into the woods.

A bird called out in the night, a trilling song that made the darkness easeful. A goose flapped down, landing on the stream's shore, followed by tufted goslings that pursued the mother into the shadows.

Stillness eventually blanketed the woods and Jeb closed the window shades, satisfied that peace prevailed in spite of women's rumors.

Jeb stared at the ceiling from his bed until the soft yellow of lunar light trickling through his window allowed his eyes to adjust. He felt startled awake, as though someone had shaken him out of his slumber. But he heard nothing outside that would justify such a thing. An owl hooted and then fluttered off its limb to chase dinner. Jeb's eyes closed slowly. Then he heard a noise, like something soft and padding quietly through dewed-over grass. He bolted upright. Stumbling across the floor, he thrust one leg into his trousers and then the other. The children slept. He crept so as not to bring them spilling out into the hallway. Halfway up the hallway and out of his stupor, he mulled over the fact that he had not grabbed his hunting rifle. He stopped at the edge of the parlor entry and peered across the room. Only a tree limb shadowed the front window.

Jeb threw on the light switch, illuminating the naked bulb outside near the door. The churchyard was nothing but evening shadows. He reached for the table lamp, but his hand froze over the lampshade.

A cry came loud, harsh.

Jeb threw open the door. He took one step and his toe bumped against a basket. He knelt and pulled back a jumble of cloths. He fell backward and then came seated on the door's threshold, assessing the matter before him, a child—an undersized baby, it seemed—lying in a laundry basket. He dragged the basket inside, out of the chill.

The baby wailed again, its eyes squeezing out tears like a ripe lemon. Jeb lifted the child from the basket, handling it awkwardly, the same as when he'd pulled a bass from White Oak Lake last Saturday.

He came to his feet, holding out the squirming bundle as though it might bite him, and looked through the door glass, hoping to see movement in the woods or a lantern light.

All was still and quiet as though the night hardened like iron in the cooling shadows.

Jeb held the baby close, pulled out the waist of the diaper, and said, "She's a girl." He studied her round eyes, full lips. Her skin was soft like peaches but tawny and her eyes stared out like two of Willie's prize marbles.

"What's going on?" Angel appeared in the doorway, her thin legs showing through her translucent cotton gown.

The baby girl threw back her head and cried again. Jeb held her out to Angel.

"Where'd you get a baby this time of night?" Angel stretched out her arms and yawned like a boy, ignoring the outstretched bundle. She even kept back a ways, creating some distance.

"Someone left her out on the porch. Look through the basket, Angel, and see if she's got a bottle tucked in her things."

Angel rummaged through layers of blankets. She pulled out a note. "It says, 'We heard you was a preacher who takes in kids. Baby's name is Myrtle Sapphira.'" Angel's eyes lifted to study Jeb's reaction, almost like she half-expected him to say it was all a big middle-of-the-night joke. She continued reading the note. "'We give you all the things for her care. She was born recent.'"

"And, of course, they didn't sign it," said Jeb.

Angel shook her head. "Here's her bottle." She held it out to him by the nipple. "She don't look like a Myrtle. More like a June bug thrown on its back. Good night."

Jeb did not want the bottle. "Maybe you should give it to her." He tried to surrender Myrtle to Angel, but Angel kept her arms folded in front of her.

"Just hold her close to you in your right arm. Feed her

with the left." She stuck the baby's bottle in the crook of his arm. "I'm going back to bed."

"You're not leaving me alone with this baby!" said Jeb.

"She ain't mine to care for."

"Babies don't like me, Angel. Maybe if you made her a bed next to you—"

"Note says you're the preacher who takes in kids. June Bug, meet your new daddy." Angel waltzed out of the room.

Her laugh irked Jeb. "This is a big sin, leaving a newborn with the likes of me."

She stonewalled Jeb, slamming the palm of her hand against the framing. "I'm not taking care of another kid, Jeb!"

"We'll find a home for it in the morning."

"You better search down around Tempest's Bog then."

"Why there?"

"She's a Nigra baby."

"Nigra?" He stared at her round face and pulled back the blanket to see the black-as-coal curls around her temple. "Angel, I've got to get some sleep. I'm meeting the deacon board early and then I've got to get my Wednesday sermon ready." And then he had planned to be at the school by noon to see if Fern might join him for lunch.

"I've got a history test first thing, Jeb. I flunked the first one and can't mess up again."

"Stay home, then. It'll give you an extra day to study. I'll vouch for you with your teacher and you can take it the next day."

"Don't want no extra day. I'm going to bed now." She disappeared down the hallway.

Myrtle nuzzled Jeb's shirt pocket, searching for a latching-on place. Jeb tapped her bottom lip with the bottle's nipple

and her lips parted like a baby bass. He slumped down on the
sofa to feed a stranger's baby and to think up what he might
tell one of the churchwomen to get them to take on one more
mouth to feed. It was ten past midnight.

৵

The sun came early. Myrtle had slept for a few hours at a
stretch and then awoke for another feeding. When Jeb's eyes
opened, his head was propped against the hard sofa arm with
the baby girl asleep on his stomach.

Ida May and Willie stood next to the sofa, waiting for
Jeb's eyes to come open.

"Can we keep her, Jeb? She's a little dumpling, ain't she?"
said Ida May.

"That's all we need around here, another girl." Willie
grumbled and munched on hard warmed-up bread.

"Angel says someone left her on the porch." Ida May
fingered the blanket around the baby's head. "They must have
been bad off like our daddy or something to just drop off a
whole baby like that."

"What does she eat?" asked Willie. "She don't look like
she's got a good set of teeth yet."

Jeb held his finger to his lips. "She just fell asleep again.
Hush and go finish your breakfast." He had a headache and
his chest was damp with spit-up.

Myrtle lifted her head. Her eyelids fluttered and she
gazed out at them.

"Since she's awake, let me hold her, Dub," said Ida May.

He sighed and slid his thumbs under her tiny chest.

Ida May flopped the baby over into her arms.

"Can't hold babies like a rag doll," said Jeb.

"You ought to take her to the doctor, make sure she's well." Angel entered the room, dressed for school and holding her books.

"Aren't you full of advice?" Jeb sat up. He was still dressed in his work clothes from yesterday. "Lot of good you do me now."

"Willie, Ida May, go and get your books. I have to head for school." Angel sent them off to the bedroom.

"I don't want to go to school. I want to stay home and play with Myrtle," said Ida May. She whined all the way down the hall.

"She's kind of runty, ain't she?" asked Willie.

"Taking this baby to the doctor's a good idea. Maybe he's met the mother, knows how I might find some family members out there who lay claim to this girl baby. Angel, sure you don't want to come along, help me with holding her and all?"

"Jeb, I have to make a good grade on this test or I'm in hot water with Mrs. Farnsworth."

Jeb sniffed the air. "What's that smell?"

"You changed her, didn't you?" Angel stared at him as though she looked a fool in the eye. "I can't believe you left this baby all night in a dirty diaper. She'll get the rash, Jeb. You have to change her now."

"I never had no call to change a baby, Angel, you know that. It wouldn't hurt you none to grab a diaper out of that basket and help me out. At least give me the lowdown on how it's done."

Angel sighed. She set her books on the floor and retrieved a diaper. "Lay her on the sofa then." She opened the diaper and then grimaced.

Jeb turned to leave.

"Jeb, go and fetch a clean, wet washcloth. Maybe two, while you're at it."

Jeb ran into the kitchen and found a stack of clean linens, where Angel had stacked them on the kitchen table. He ran with one to the sink, wet it, wrung it out, and then hotfooted it back into the parlor.

"Now check her things and see if you can find a jar of ointment. She's going to need it."

Jeb dug through the basket. "I don't see any."

"Run fetch a jar from the kitchen then. It's in the cabinet where I keep the iodine."

"We're ready to leave," said Willie.

"Give your sister a minute, Willie." Jeb ran back into the kitchen to the pantry.

"Jeb, I can't be late!" Angel yelled.

Jeb knocked over a can of baking powder. He grabbed a box of cornstarch and then saw the ointment in the back of the cabinet.

Angel held out Myrtle's legs by the toes.

"I'm waiting out on the porch," said Willie. "Man can only take so much."

"Is this the stuff?" Jeb asked Angel.

Angel said, "That's a good idea. I forgot about using cornstarch."

Jeb glanced down and saw that he still held the cornstarch box in his left hand. "My grandma's old remedy," he lied. He couldn't remember back that far.

"June Bug's got a rash. That cornstarch should help it dry up." Angel finished up using ointment on Myrtle's red places and closed the diaper. "She's all yours." She grabbed her books and ushered Willie and Ida May out the door. Before closing the door, she said, "You'll do fine, Jeb. Just get her off to the doctor and he'll know what to do. Surely you can handle that."

Jeb looked down at the baby, who made sucking breaths as she wound up for another long wail. Her bottle was empty and Angel had left the soiled diaper on the rug. He ran to the door. "Angel, wait! I don't know what to feed her."

Angel climbed into the Ford of a friend. Willie and Ida May climbed in behind her talking their heads off. Angel waved at Jeb before they drove away.

Myrtle's cry took every bit of starch out of Jeb's morning plans. He checked his watch. The deacon's meeting had commenced ten minutes ago.

∽

Jeb had not carried around that feeling of being the town underdog for quite some time, but the feeling he got hauling around this baby did test a man's spirit. He had to change clothes once before ever having left the parsonage, and then just as he tiptoed through the church entrance with his large basket of baby, she awoke and let out the most awful scream.

Will Honeysack looked up from his chair, startled to see the Church in the Dell preacher carrying what looked like a load of laundry. "Morning, Reverend. We been waiting for you."

"Fellers, I got a dilemma. Look what someone left for me last night."

The deacons inspected the basket.

"Lord-a-mercy, Parson!" said Arnell Ketcherside. His chair almost tipped backward. "What you going to do?"

"I was hoping one of you boys would tell me." Jeb looked at Sam Patton. "You think your wife might take her in? Greta's been wanting a girl, what with the last two of yours being male."

"Reverend, this baby's a Nigra baby. You sure someone ain't pulling your leg?" asked Arnell.

"I'm afraid I couldn't oblige," said Sam. "Greta's still got one on the breast and the boy ain't even started school. She's about half out of her mind, as it is."

"Freda's been so busy at the store, she's about to shoot me as it is wanting a new floor in the back room. Both of us nearly fell through stacking up cans," said Will. "We been up late every night this week trying to figure out how to keep the store going."

"You know of anyone down around Tempest's Bog that might take her in? Or at least figure out who come up missing a newborn? The way I figure it, you can't hide secrets like that too long, not in this county." Jeb jiggled the basket the entire time that he spoke, trying to appease this angry little god.

Will sat back in his chair, clamped his hands on each knee, and then laughed. "I never seen a preacher get hisself into so many fixes as you, Reverend!"

"Boys, this is serious," said Jeb.

Myrtle had stayed up most of the night and then sprayed her breakfast all over his good tie.

"Reverend, ain't you ever been around babies before?" asked Floyd. "They don't sleep for the first year or so."

"I can't take going without sleep, Floyd. A man's not made for such things."

Myrtle's hand lifted and came over her face as though she fanned flies, but her eyelids drooped. She took a breath and then fell asleep.

Jeb crept to a pew and set the basket down. "Let's meet at the front of the church."

The men carted chairs up the aisle, following Jeb and creeping so as not to make a sound or bump a chair against a pew arm.

"First order of business," said Jeb. "Let's pray."

3

TUESDAYS BROUGHT WOMEN OUT INTO THE yards to do the wash and air linens on the clotheslines. As Jeb motored away from the churchyard, he had a silent conversation with a housewife he passed along the way, imagining how he might deliver Myrtle into the happy matron's arms and then, having done his preacherly duties, hop back into his Ford and drive away in search of more holy exploits.

Not a thought about his Wednesday-evening message had come to him all morning, his mind too dammed up with worry over what to do about Myrtle. He drove over Marvelous Crossing, past Fern's cottage beyond the pond, and then made the right turn down the lane that would lead to the house of the only doctor in Nazareth, Dr. Forrester.

When he pulled up and parked next to the picket fence, he tipped his hat at a teenage girl seated out on the porch. He thought he recognized her from Angel's class, but she did not appear to know him. "Dr. Forrester around?" he asked.

"My aunt's inside with her baby, my cousin Ben. He's got colic and keeps the whole house up all night. Be fine with me if they just leave him here."

"You say he's got colic? Can the doctor give a baby something to help it sleep?" Jeb hefted Myrtle's basket out of the front seat of the truck.

The girl shrugged and fell back into a stupor.

He waited outside the doctor's front door until Mrs. Forrester appeared and opened the door for him. Jeb felt relief when she smiled back at him.

"Reverend Nubey, what you bringing to us today?" She looked surprised.

Myrtle's eyes were open wide now and she nuzzled the blankets around her.

"Someone dropped off a baby girl in the middle of the night, Mrs. Forrester."

"Terrible times we live in, Reverend."

"Mystery to me why they'd drop a baby off on my porch."

"Does she have a name?"

"The note in her basket named her Myrtle. No last name."

The teenage girl's aunt came out of the doctor's house holding her baby. "Let's go, Shirley." The two females climbed into a buggy parked next to Jeb's truck.

"What's this all about?" asked Dr. Forrester.

"Someone dropped a baby off on the preacher's doorstep, Stu."

Jeb smiled at Thelma Forrester. She returned the smile but kept her distance.

The doctor invited Jeb inside. The house smelled like Mrs. Forrester had stewed persimmons. A row of family photos stared back from a piano top, a well-kept lot of grown children sitting with the Forresters' next generation posed around the adults in sailor-type costumes, the kind rich kids were forced to wear well into puberty.

"I'll make a fresh pot of coffee, Stu." Mrs. Forrester disappeared behind a green kitchen door. The parlor steamed up again.

"Doc, I got my hands full as it is with the Welbys and I don't have a woman around the house to see to this child's needs," said Jeb.

Dr. Forrester lifted Myrtle out of the basket. "You're hungry, aren't you?"

"All I had to give her was milk from the icebox."

"Cow's milk makes them sick, Reverend. What you need is a wet nurse."

"I need a home for this baby."

"Thelma, could you come and change this baby for the reverend?" Thelma appeared, her face red and damp. Dr. Forrester placed the baby in her arms.

Jeb watched her lift the baby expertly and whisk her into the next room. He slumped down into a chair. "I'm grateful to you, Doc. Angel changed her before school. Diaper handling is not my calling, so to speak."

"You thought about driving her out to Tempest's Bog, asking the families if they know of a girl who may have gotten herself in trouble? Could be this baby belonged to a girl too young to care for her."

"I'm headed that way, but truth be told, I don't have it in me to track down her family. Myrtle kept me up all night.

One end of her or the other, it seems, always needs fixing. She's troubled, I believe."

"She's a healthy girl. Newborns take their time about getting their days and nights straightened out. They don't know when it's time to go to bed, only when they're hungry or wet."

"You know of a foundlings' home or some such that would have women who could care for her?"

"Only orphans' home I heard of was up in Batesville. They shut it down in '31, from what I hear."

"Well, hang it, Doc! There's got to be a solution to this here dilemma other than the fact I need to go out in search of mother's milk."

Dr. Forrester pulled out a slip of paper and wrote a name on it. "Only wet nurse in town is a handful herself, but she could give you what you need. Had a baby out of wedlock and she's been hiring herself out to a couple of the town's wealthy mothers. Can't say as I know of a perfect wet nurse. They all tend to be a rough lot."

"You saying I have to pay this woman for her services to feed Myrtle?"

"She lives right outside town. Follow Main through downtown and then on out to Bellow's Pond. She lives in a shack with her other two children and her own baby. Name's Belinda Tatum."

"Here's your bundle, Reverend, all clean and fresh." Thelma slipped Myrtle into Jeb's arms again. "You've got a dozen diapers under those blankets. If I were you, I'd make a place for them other than right under her. She'll need a clean one again soon. You may as well drop in at the Woolworth's and pick up a couple dozen more diapers while you're at it."

"I wish you the best of luck, Reverend. You're the best-natured man I've ever met. I figure that when word of a good reputation spreads, things like this happen," said the doctor.

"You're an instrument of God." Thelma leaned over and stroked Myrtle's face. "Couldn't have asked for a prettier baby."

Jeb headed straight for Tempest's Bog. The rest of his day would not be spent in folding diapers or in dealing with a hard-to-get-along-with wet nurse.

He checked his watch. The noon hour had come and gone and he still had not gone to see Fern. Oz Mills had taken up permanent residence in Nazareth and that was a bother.

Myrtle sighed.

⁂

Jeb's memory of Tempest's Bog was a blur. He had been through the neighborhood once when he'd heard of a sick woman dying of the influenza. He'd never found her even after he had asked around, house to house, for a solid hour. Since then, he had not gotten any requests to visit Tempest's Bog. It was prettier than its name in the daylight with sunlight bleeding through the tree limbs like fairy highways. The sky overhead had blued up nicer than it had been at dawn when Myrtle had engaged him in the battle of wits that he had lost.

An old railroad station had been built right next to the crossroads. The sign on the station read TEMPEST'S BOG, the only indicator that he had officially come into the community.

Tempest's Bog was a place that had grown up like a sixth toe on the town's foot, as though it was a part of Nazareth for tax purposes, but otherwise a neglected appendage on the south side. Three men propped their chairs against the station's east office entrance. One whittled soft wood while the other two passed a beverage back and forth. It was tucked into a wrinkled brown bag stained from a lot of use.

Jeb rolled down his window. "Afternoon, fellers. Name's Reverend Nubey, Church in the Dell."

Two of the men would not look up, but the whittler, minding his p's and q's, said, "Same to you."

"You lost, Preacher?" one of the other men asked.

"I got something that don't belong to me," Jeb answered.

"If it's a bag of money, it belongs to me," the third man finally spoke up.

All three of them laughed out loud. One tucked his bottle into the side pocket of his brown overshirt.

Myrtle cried out. Jeb leaned over her and jiggled the basket. The rocking had lost its effect. She wailed until Jeb poked the bottle into her mouth. For now, the cow's milk would have to suffice.

He told the men, "Someone dropped a baby off on my porch last night. The doctor said I should try asking house to house."

"Horace, you know of anyone missing a baby?" one man asked the other.

The men all shook their heads. "We got several new babies on our road, but they all accounted for, best I can remember." The whittler stopped his whittling.

"Maybe it's best I ask around anyway," said Jeb.

"You can ask all you want, mister, but I'm telling you, we don't have no one missing a child."

"You saying she's colored?" one of the men asked Jeb.

Jeb nodded. He gunned the engine. It ground to a start

and he threw the truck into gear. The men stared after him as he drove down Tempest's Lane.

⁂

Jeb knocked on the doors of three houses, each time holding Myrtle up to the person's face when they opened the door. Some people sat out on their porches. When one group of men and women saw Jeb hauling a basket of crying baby down the street, they went inside and slammed the door closed. Jeb knocked anyway. He heard yelling from inside. Finally the door opened. A young girl, a teen of about fifteen, poked her head through the open door. She had combed her hair into tidy rows that started at her forehead and stopped at her neck. "What do you want?" she asked.

"You ever see this baby before?" Jeb asked.

She closed the door but then cracked it open. She could not take her eyes off Myrtle, who stared out of the pink blanket. "She's not mine, if that's what you're saying."

"Is your momma about?"

The door closed. Jeb thought he had been left alone for good until the door was forced open.

"Get gone, mister!" The woman had a wide girth and full lips that flowered open when angry.

"Ma'am, I'm sorry to bother you, but I'm just trying to find the mother of this baby."

The taut lines in her face relaxed. "Baby?" She studied the contents of the basket. Then she said to Jeb, "Where'd you get a baby?"

"My front porch."

"Who exactly are you?"

"Reverend Jeb Nubey, Church in the Dell." He would

have extended his hand but couldn't, so he tried his best to smile.

"Jackie, you get out here!" she shouted.

The teenage girl appeared, this time her face more sullen than before. "What I do?"

"You hear of any girl out having a baby? Maybe don't want her folks to know?"

Jackie shrugged.

"You lie and I can tell and God can tell, so you may as well come out with it."

"I'm not lying."

Jeb told her, "I've been all up and down the street asking and no one knows a thing about her. You wouldn't know of a family that would take her in, would you?"

"Whites don't want her, my guess?" The woman's mouth lifted at one corner.

"I'm not married and I've already taken in three youngens. Don't seem right for this little girl to be brought up without a proper momma."

A large man appeared behind the woman. "It's a girl, you say." He didn't smile at all and his face was without any expression.

Jackie whispered something to her mother that Jeb could not hear.

"Take her, Monette," said the man. He looked up at Jeb. "Leave her here. You can be on your way."

"Preacher, don't leave her!" Jackie grabbed the basket before Jeb could set it on the porch.

"Shut up, girl!" The man was angry. He grabbed her by the shoulder. "I told you to stop mouthing off or you'd get it!"

"Jackie, go on into the kitchen," her mother told her.

Jackie did as she was told but kept yelling, "He's not my daddy" and crying.

Jeb backed away. He held the basket close to him. The big man took a step forward onto the porch. Jeb turned and ran to his truck, jostling Myrtle. She whimpered.

He heard the man swearing at him from the front porch. From an upstairs window, the curtain came open. Jackie waved from behind the glass, as though she shooed Jeb and Myrtle away.

The sun had now fully bloomed into afternoon. It felt like summer. The bog part of Tempest's Bog heated up like mud stew.

Jeb drove them away from Tempest's Bog. "We're going to go and meet your dinner, little girl," he said. "She'd best be nice."

જ

"Who told you about me?" Belinda Tatum was a stout woman, at least as young as twenty. She was missing a bottom tooth. When she talked, she had a matter-of-fact tone, but she drew back her shoulders as though she expected a fight.

Jeb stuck out his hand. "Dr. Forrester sent me over."

"Oh, him. Sometimes the women around town talk about me. That's why I asked. I guess you want me to come over to your place?"

Jeb had not thought that far ahead. "I'd be grateful if you could. I don't know anything about babies or feedings."

"I come morning and night. I just weaned a kid from up north of town, so this is a good time."

"I'll give you my address."

"I charge five dollars a week and that's not negotiable."

Jeb felt the color drain from his face.

"It pays the grocery bill, and 'sides all that, Doc says I give the best milk in the county."

Jeb expected her to moo.

"You try and keep her on cow's milk and see if she don't get sick. Babies can't tolerate cow's milk, you know. You try putting her on dairy and see if she don't die."

"This is just until I can find her a good family." He handed Belinda the address.

"You're giving away your baby?"

"Myrtle's not mine. She was left on my porch."

"I got a cousin named Myrtle. Can I see her?"

"Here, come out to the truck."

Belinda followed Jeb out, her arms still full of her own wriggling baby boy. She peeked through the truck window. "Reverend, she's a Nigra baby."

"It's fine. I don't think she'll mind."

"You didn't tell me that."

"What difference does it make?"

"I can't do that at all." Belinda backed away from the truck.

"You seem like a reasonable person."

"Find some momma down in Tempest's Bog."

"I'll pay you extra."

"How much?"

"Six-fifty a week."

"Seven."

"Fine, then." Jeb reached through the window and picked up Myrtle. "How about a dollar's worth right about now?"

4

TOADS COULD BE HEARD MAKING A RUCKUS down the alley between Snooker's and the feed store, like creatures engaged in mating rites.

Farley Williams drove up on most nights from Tempest's Bog. He was the man who danced in the evenings from the time the sawmill closed until the bottoms of his feet ached. Every night his spot in front of Snooker's pool hall was left for him. It seemed he had always been there, like he was born on that place so he could dance a shuffling kind of step that someone overseas had taught him back in 1910, in a club down on some island beach. He would sing too, until his voice lifted so high and loud that it would send him into a kind of whirligig, a step he had added, he said, because no one could teach you that kind of thing. It came from somewhere else. The women from Church in the Dell said it was from Satan, but Farley would not say yea or nay. He'd just hold out his cup until the person asking what made him dance in such a way would give up the wait and toss in a penny and leave him alone. As long as he kept his gift a secret, people would pay for the chance to try and dig the truth out of him.

Jeb had coaxed Angel into watching Myrtle for an hour by promising her a movie ticket and popcorn for the Saturday matinee. He stopped in at Snooker's to ride some of the men about showing up at church for the sake of the womenfolk, but then he veered right back out of doors to talk with Farley. "You dance better than anyone I know," said Jeb.

"Hello, yourself," Farley answered. He stopped and leaned against the ledge of the large picture window to catch his breath.

"How's the missus?" asked Jeb.

"Tard and overwoiked." Farley said his vowels like a man Jeb once knew from Louisiana. "Too many mouths to feed. I hear you got an extra."

Jeb let out a sigh. "Word spreads fast."

"Josephine would string me up like a trout if I brought home another child, Preacher."

"How about if you agree to just keep your eyes and ears open? If you hear of anything, anyone who might know something about Myrtle, will you pass it on?"

"That I can do." Farley hit a fine C and then sang and clapped a bar or two before he cut loose with another dance.

Jeb dropped a penny in his cup and then two more.

❧

"I know a stranger when I see him." Fern must have seen Jeb's truck parked outside Fidel's. She appeared from the drugstore doorway the minute Jeb stepped off the walk.

"Fern, you're out late."

"My folks just left for Oklahoma. The house was too quiet, so I drove into town."

"How's your daddy? I'm sorry I didn't get the chance to visit with your folks this go-around."

"He says he's better. But my mother is frustrated. He's hard to look after."

"I'm glad you decided to come into town."

"I'm grading tests tonight. It's monotonous. I drove to Fidel's for coffee and hoping I could find some adult conversation. My lucky night. Join me?"

"Coffee sounds perfect." Once inside, Jeb helped Fern off with her sweater and ordered two coffees.

"Ida May told me about your midnight visitor. As a matter of fact, she told the whole school and half the church."

"Kids drop into my life like walnuts," said Jeb.

"The girls thought surely by the time they got home, you would have found a landing place for her. To hear Angel tell it, you even tried to keep her home from school to watch the poor little thing."

"I'm desperate. You know I drove all up and down Tempest's Bog and not one person knew a thing about her. It's like invisible hands dropped her out of the sky onto my porch."

"Where'd you leave her?"

"Angel's watching her, but she assures me that I shouldn't grow too accustomed to that. I even had to hire a wet nurse."

"Belinda Tatum? She was in my class a few years back. Shame about her."

"Well, she's Myrtle's only meal ticket. As a matter of

fact, she's coming tonight, so I should go, I guess. That girl gives me the willies. I don't want her around the kids without me present."

"Belinda's all right. I should head home."

A solitary light burned in the bank window. Oz had parked his Packard out front. He'd most likely be getting off soon, closing out the books for his uncle Horace Mills. If he saw Fern parked at Fidel's, he'd be down the street in the shake of a stick. "Fern, you ought to drop by the house tonight."

She hesitated. "I'd better get home to those test papers. Work never ends."

"I'll walk you to your car." Jeb snapped his fingers at the druggist.

"Right away, Reverend," said Fidel.

Jeb cupped his hand beneath Fern's elbow and guided her to the door. He saw the lights go out at Nazareth Bank and Trust. "Off we go, Fern." He helped her into her car.

⁂

"She's been screaming since right after you left, Dub." Ida May waited out on the porch. She cupped her hands over both ears. "Angel's a nervous wreck."

Jeb went inside and found Angel rocking Myrtle on the couch. "Jeb, she's hungry. Where's this Belinda woman you hired to keep something in this baby's mouth?"

"She's late, I reckon. Willie, you get your schoolwork finished?"

"Not with that caterwauling going on, Jeb. This babying stuff is not for me. I'm ready to join the railroad boys."

"Jeb, run fetch me a damp cloth, like the cheesecloth I keep over the butter. Sweeten it with a little sugar," said

Angel. Her face was washed out and colorless with strands of hair hanging over her brows and into her eyes as though she had just climbed out of bed.

"I know what you're thinking," said Jeb. He fetched the sugar cloth.

Angel held it to Myrtle's lips. She took to it right away but grunted between suckles in a manner that said that she would not be satisfied for long. "Can we give her milk, Jeb?"

"She's too young, Biggest."

A flood of light beamed across the parlor.

"Someone's here!" Willie jumped up and ran to the door. "This Belinda drive an old black Model A?" asked Willie.

"It's got to be her," said Jeb.

"Praise be to Jesus!" said Angel.

"It's about time you got religion, Biggest."

❧

Belinda stubbed her cigarette out on the porch railing. She blew out a trail of smoke that followed her all the way into the house. Before Jeb could offer her a private room, she began unbuttoning her sweater.

Willie turned around and headed into the kitchen.

"Angel, why don't you show Belinda to your room?" Jeb suggested.

Belinda did not follow Angel. "There's the matter of seven dollars."

"I'll pay at the end of the week," said Jeb.

"No can do. I need it up front."

"How do I know you'll show?"

"I'll show," she said, and pulled off her sweater.

Jeb pulled out his wallet. "I'll pay you half now and half at the end of the week."

"Deal, Preacher."

Angel lifted Myrtle to her shoulder, holding her close. "I'm going with you," she said.

"Suit yourself." Belinda took the money out of Jeb's hand and followed Angel down the hall. "Oh, and my grandmother is watching my brats tonight, but she can't always do that. Sometimes I have to drag them along."

Jeb seated himself on the sofa with his study notes. After a half hour he heard Myrtle's cry. He lost his place reading, got up to go see what was going on, then, thinking better of it, sat down again and picked up his book. He should have insisted that Fern bring her tests to grade at the parsonage. She might have had a better way with Belinda that he lacked. Besides, he was starting to feel lonely at nights after the kids went to bed.

Even in the dark, standing out on the town walk, she looked lovely, like the first time he laid eyes on her. Dogged if he had ever met a woman like her who took her time about deciding if she was going to have a serious go with a man or not. Things between them had seemed to glide along with a renewed pace for a while. She had begun to say things to him that let him know that she was beginning to trust him. She had shared with him more about her brothers in Ardmore and about her girlhood growing up in Oklahoma. This whole situation with her daddy's health had distracted her.

Once, she had disclosed how timid she had been as a girl in a house full of boys. Jeb could not picture her timid in any form or fashion. She had told him of a tree house built within the limbs of a giant cherry tree. "In the summertime I slipped out of the house in the mornings with my stack of reading and made fast for that tree. If I could be the first to it before my brothers awoke, I'd pull up the ladder my grandfather had made from rope. No amount of yelling on their part could get me to lower that ladder. Then I'd read all day until my mother called us home for dinner."

Jeb pictured her in his mind, reclined on a make-believe bed, stomach down and reading book after book. Then he imagined the way that life led him across her path and then made him work like a slave to get her. He had read a story like that in the Old Testament, about a man who had to work seven years to get the woman he wanted.

Now this whole matter about her daddy had left him feeling outside her circle of trust again.

"I'm done and I need another smoke." Belinda walked out, pulling her blouse down.

He glanced away, not willing to stare at Belinda's ample milk supply.

"I'll be back in the morning. Your oldest has a mouth on her. If you want to keep me coming around, you'd best tell her to watch herself."

Jeb held the door open. "Good night, Belinda." When he shut the door behind her, he let out a sigh. She had left behind the scent of tobacco. He had to find a home for Myrtle soon, if for nothing else but the clearing away of every trace of Belinda Tatum.

⁓

"The whole house is disrupted, Will." Jeb had gone out into the night for a walk and was surprised when Will Honeysack's car pulled over. Will yelled to him, "Get in."

"One day your life is taking on what seems to be a sense of

order and the next it all comes tumbling down around your ears. I think I'm finally getting ahead, making a little headway with Angel, or seeing Willie take a little more interest in his studies, and then boom! Down comes the whole sky around my ears."

"I asked Freda about the baby girl. She says you got a problem on your hands."

"Tell Freda that I said thank you. I don't think I knew until now what it really must look like to be an orphan. I mean, I know the Welbys were abandoned. But at least we've had some contact with family. They know from whence they came. Myrtle has no past, no one to tell her how she was born or what her daddy looks like."

"It's a dilemma."

"The families at Tempest's Bog won't take her in, the families around town won't even consider it. Doc Forrester says all the foundlings' homes he once knew about have been shut down like the whole world has closed its doors to the orphan."

Will gave his words a thought as they crossed White Oak Lake. "Most people don't like to think about orphans, Reverend. They don't know what to do, so they just don't give it a thought."

Jeb was unsure whether or not he would have given thought to it either—if Myrtle had not been dropped off on his watch.

Will backed into a private road and then pulled out to deliver Jeb back to the parsonage. "I told Freda I had forgotten my newspaper, but I really couldn't stop thinking about you and what you might be doing tonight."

"You're a good friend, Will Honeysack."

"Not as good a man as you, Reverend."

5

JEB WAITED A HALF HOUR PAST TIME ON Thursday morning for Belinda to show her face. She dragged her two small sons out of the car along with her baby. With one hand she crushed her played-out cigarette against the oak tree that Jeb's mentor, Reverend Gracie, had once planted in the front yard. With the other she settled her baby on her hip and herded the other two toward the house. If she read in Jeb's face how testy she made him, she either did not have the sense to let on or did not care.

"I'm going into town to see the deputy about Myrtle," he told her. It had taken all day Wednesday to prepare his evening message. What with performing a juggling act between reading and then pacifying Myrtle, he had not had the benefit of a spare moment to tend to the business of passing her off to more nurturing arms.

Myrtle had awakened again this morning at two, four, and again at six. He had paced with her on the front porch a solid hour waiting for Belinda's old car to chug into the yard.

Jeb drove away without looking back at Belinda, who seated herself in the front porch rocker, her dress pulled down on one side. The sight of it would haunt him for the remainder of the day, so he kept his sights on the road. No doubt she was an ample girl. He figured by the time she hit her twenty-fifth birthday, she'd have breasts reaching to her knees.

~

Maynard had collected his newspaper and a cup of coffee and propped his body into a chair outside that teetered back against the jailhouse wall. "Morning, Reverend. Sorry I missed services last night. Some boys got into some liquor and decided to raise a ruckus down on the south side. Seems we been having a lot of that lately."

"Deputy, we have another situation on our hands."

"I heard you took in another youngen. Ain't you the cat's pajamas, as the young people say. Was it a little boy or a little girl? The one that told me didn't know for sure."

"I didn't take in the baby, as you say. Someone dropped her off and I can't care for her properly. I already spent half the grocery money paying off Belinda Tatum to wet-nurse a baby that's not mine."

"Shame what come of her. Good family. Can't say what led her astray," said Maynard.

"What I'm saying is that you're the law around here. Dropping off a baby can't be legal. I need you to do something about it." Jeb took the chair next to him. He stared straight ahead for a while, folding his arms, crossing and uncrossing his legs, fidgeting.

"You want me to put the little thing in jail, Reverend?"

"You're funny, Maynard. I'm saying that I can't take care of this girl baby. I already know for a fact that I don't have a way with girl children. Ask Angel."

"Seems to me the Almighty done decided you was awfully good at it."

"On top of that, I got the whole Tatum clan parked out on my front doorstep, as though I didn't have enough youngens underfoot. I have to leave my own house just to get some peace and quiet and study for my sermons. Imagine trying to read and study with Belinda Tatum jawing about her milk production while her kids hang from the light fixture. Something about it is plain uncomely for a man of my standing."

"Problem is everybody's got it hard. Families around here have already taken in more kin than they can feed. On top of that, I heard it was a colored child."

"She's the color of a human. She's a baby, that's all."

"Have you been to Tempest's Bog?"

"Already did that. I didn't find what I was looking for, that's for sure."

"I can keep an eye out, Reverend. That's all I can do. You know I got this sudden crime wave going on here in Nazareth. Keeps me up nights just trying to figure out what I'm going to have to do to keep this town safe. We got the mystery of a bloody shirt down on the apple pickers' path and drunkenness down on the south side. If I didn't know better, I'd say the world was going to hell on a rail."

"Will you send a telegraph to Little Rock and see if they know of some family that can take in a baby?"

"I can try."

Jeb came to his feet. "I got to get back. No telling what the Tatums might do to the place with me being gone so long."

"You ought to ask Josie to come around ever so often and watch that baby for you. She's a nut about little ones."

"Josie. I forgot about her. She all but adopted Littlest. She's always had a way with Ida May that I couldn't explain."

"Josie's got the touch."

"I'll stop and see her before I go home. You take care, Maynard."

⤳

Jeb found Josie at home soaking her feet in salt water. She invited him through the screen door to come inside. She pulled her feet out of the bowl and dried them as she spoke to him. "What brings you by today?" she asked.

"Because you are so highly recommended when it comes to advice about caring for the little lambs of the flock," said Jeb.

"How is that sweet Idy May? She's still my favorite," said Josie.

"The child can't stop chattering about Mrs. Hipps this and Mrs. Hipps that."

"Go on! The minute I laid eyes on that little girl, I just saw so much of my own baby girl. You know she went on to be with the Lord back in '27."

"I do know, and I hope Ida May has been a comfort to you."

"Oh, she has, Reverend. No other child can steal my heart like that one."

She lifted the bowl from the floor and carried it to the sink. "I've got to keep my feet from drying out. But you didn't come here to hear about such things."

"Actually I do have a mission in visiting you here today."

"Just say it, Reverend. You know I'll help out however it's humanly possible."

"You've heard about the visitor dropped off on our doorstep, I suppose?"

"Visitor? I haven't stuck my nose out, what with the influenza going around. How was the Wednesday service, by the way?"

"A real humdinger, Miz Josie. So you haven't heard of the little girl left on our doorstep?"

"No one tells me anything. You know I stay out of the town's gossip. You've another little girl? Praise be, that's good news, Reverend. Boys is a whole lot worse trouble."

"I've hired a wet nurse to come and feed the orphan girl."

"Only one I know about."

"Belinda Tatum. But I can't leave the baby in her care."

"Heavens no, I don't blame you a bit for that, Reverend."

"So I'm paying you a visit today to see if you could help out days with this baby while I assume my duties as the preacher of Church in the Dell."

Josie hesitated and then said, "Take care of a little girl again? Well, I can't think of another thing I'd rather do."

"Just until I can find the child a proper family."

"A baby girl. What is her name and her age?"

"Myrtle and she is a newborn."

"A newborn. That's a handful, Reverend, and me approaching middle age."

"I would have taken you for late twenties."

Josie laughed.

"Not every person could care for her like she should be cared for. That's why I came to you."

"Does she fuss before your wet nurse shows up?"

"Belinda comes twice a day. In between times Myrtle does grow fussy."

"Newborns have to eat more than that. This Belinda knows better."

"I'm paying all I can pay for twice a day."

"That poor baby. I'll go and see about her right now. Is Belinda with her now?"

"She is, but she wants me back soon."

"I heard bad things about that girl. It's too bad you don't have another girl to hire."

"If you can see about Myrtle now, then I can go into town and handle church errands."

Josie fished around in her closet for a jacket. "I got some blankets left over from when mine was small. Myrtle must be such a sweet baby."

"She has a way about her."

$$\sim$$

"Reverend, no one's expecting you to take care of a baby and preach three times a week on top of that. You got to go and take her to some family," said Will.

Jeb sighed. "Will, you act like I have a choice in the matter. What you want me to do, leave her on your wife's doorstep tonight like what was done to me?"

"I can't take in a baby, not with rheumatoid arthritis," Freda yelled from the back of the store.

"It's not rheumatoid arthritis," Will said like a whisper. "It's gout. Her daddy had it and she don't want to deal with it."

"The thing is, I do have Belinda helping out. And now Josie is on her way over to check on Myrtle and keep Belinda straight."

"Did you tell Josie about this baby?"

"Will, she's on her way over to my place now. Of course she knows."

"So it doesn't bother her about the baby's sitchyashun?"

"I'm sure she's as bothered as I am."

"Reverend, you going to make me say it?"

"Say what?"

"That baby's a Nigra baby. The town ladies won't want to have no dealings with her. It could cause trouble in Nazareth."

"Myrtle's too young to be making trouble."

"You know that when Reverend Gracie recommended you to take his place that we knew those Welby children came with the deal. But this baby is not part of the package."

"I didn't know this was a community decision, Will."

"You're not just a man trying to decide what you should do for yourself. You have to make decisions based on how it will affect Nazareth and Church in the Dell."

"Not that it changes anything, but how does Myrtle affect Church in the Dell?"

"She's a bad dream."

"She doesn't smile like a bad dream."

"She ain't your problem."

"Listen to you."

"Will, I need you to sweep the back room." Freda tried to place a broom in Will's hands, but he wouldn't take it.

"Reverend, you keep that baby and you'll lose half the church or more."

"That's a sorry thing to say."

"Will, you're fighting with the minister in front of the whole town." Freda pulled on Will's arm.

Will glanced around at the sets of eyes peering over the

tops of canned goods and flour sacks. "If you'll excuse me, Reverend, I've got some work to do for the missus." He stomped to the back of the store without telling Jeb good-bye.

Jeb walked out of Honeysack's without his list of supplies filled.

6

BELINDA'S SMOKE RINGS COULD BE SEEN FROM the road, like circled messages lifting from beneath a tribal blanket. She leaned against the porch railing, palms down, with her cigarette poised like a fine fountain pen between two stout fingers. Her boys played beside the parsonage, bent over something like a bird they had stoned, or something else from nature they could observe in a motionless state.

Will Honeysack's words kept raking over Jeb's thoughts until he found himself rehearsing what he should have said and rewriting how Will should have responded.

He glanced around the churchyard as he wheeled around and parked in front of the parsonage. He did not see Josie Hipps's rusted Ford parked anywhere in sight.

Belinda rose from her slouch when she saw him and then disappeared inside the house. Her boys did not glance up, except to see who came walking into the yard and then they returned to dissect their prey.

Angel would not be home with her brother and sister for another ten minutes. Jeb would spend the time studying. Belinda had left the front door open. Part of him half-expected to find her stripping down for another feeding. He kept his eyes on the floor.

"Preacher, that woman you sent over was rude." Belinda waited for him in the parlor like she was loaded for bear.

"She came to help."

"She wasn't no help at all but a nuisance. I made her leave."

"Josie loves children. You could have left Myrtle with her and gone home for the day."

Belinda laughed. "You expect me to believe that?"

Jeb slumped down onto the sofa. "I'll apologize to her."

"Not so fast! I'll have you know she took one look at Myrtle and started giving first this excuse and then that one. I could see what she was about, so I told her just to get gone and stop wasting my time."

"That doesn't sound like Josie."

"You should have told her the baby weren't white."

"I didn't think it mattered."

"Not only that, but she gave me the once-over, like I was trash for nursing Myrtle. People around here start spreading stuff like that and my reputation will be ruined."

"Where is Myrtle?"

"Sleeping next to my Jonathan. They look like two little peas in a baby pod."

"Jeb, tell Willie that girls don't like boys to make bad pencil drawings of them with big body parts!" Angel stormed through the door, red-faced and holding up a lewd drawing.

"She stole it from my books. Besides, it's not you, so what do you care?" Willie tore the drawing from his sister's hand.

"It was quiet for a moment," said Jeb.

"Don't wake up your little sister," Belinda whispered.

"Sister?" Angel laughed and glanced at Jeb. "Willie's sweet on Tillie Whittington. If she saw how he drew her with giant—"

"Angel! Lower your tone. Babies are sleeping and we don't want to hear your ridiculous feud with Willie." Jeb yanked the drawing from Willie's hand. "That don't look like Tillie Whittington anyway."

"I'm hungry and I don't want cold corn bread neither," said Ida May.

"Have an apple and then go get on your studies," said Jeb.

"I put the babies in the kids' room. Maybe they can study in the kitchen," said Belinda.

"I study in the kitchen," Jeb whispered. Then he heard Myrtle cry out in the next room.

"I'm leaving you with it, Preacher. Got to get my brood home for a meal. My boyfriend's skinned a deer and we're having a get-together tonight. You're more than welcome to come, maybe bring a lady friend if you want. But it's not what you would call a church social."

He declined as politely as he knew how. "Does Myrtle need another feeding?"

"She should be fine. Doc gave me a can of evaporated milk for babies. It's not as good as momma's milk, but I poured it into a couple of bottles for you. They're in the icebox, so you can warm them in a pan of hot water. Not too hot, though. A bottle feeding should help you get her to sleep tonight."

Belinda retrieved her large bundle of baby boy and left for the night.

"You getting the hang of this baby business?" asked Angel.

"The next thing I'm expecting to hear is that my family was taken by a tornado and all eight of my nephews and nieces will be coming to live with me," said Jeb.

"We don't have enough beds," said Ida May.

Willie snatched his drawing out of Jeb's hands. "I think it looks just like Tilly. She could work in Hollywood if you ask me."

❧

Jeb took the rocker inside. What with the settling of cold upon the nights, rocking in the evening had fast lost its appeal. As the girls took turns passing Myrtle back and forth in the front parlor, they used the rocking chair to lull her into a stupor for at least a part of the evening so that Jeb could concentrate on his weekly study. Angel had borrowed some baby dresses from one of the girls at school who had filched them from her mother's grab bag of clothes. She and Ida May dressed and undressed Myrtle like a doll, deciding what clothes would fit and what they could put up for later.

Willie cracked open pecans with a hammer, trying to abide by Angel's request to store as many as possible for a good pie come Thanksgiving. But the temptation to partake of the fruit of his labor had thus far caused his yield to amount to only a handful of fresh shelled pecan nuts. He poured them into a jar with a newspaper funnel.

"Whoever give us this baby didn't give us enough clothes to outfit a termite," said Ida May.

"Her curls is getting long around her face. Wonder how long until I can tie up her hair in a ribbon?" asked Angel.

Jeb sat forward and lay his Bible in his lap. "It's quiet tonight."

"Starts getting colder and the toads go dormant," said Willie.

"Not a bird or anything, though, is making a sound." Jeb went back to his reading.

"I like it best when it snows and everything is softly quiet at night. If you look out the winder on a snowy night, it's like the Lord has rocked the earth to sleep," said Ida May.

"Lights up the sky at night almost," said Willie. "Like morning at midnight. Dog it, Ida May, you make me wish for winter."

Myrtle let out a sigh as gentle as a dropped thread.

That was when the glass broke, the small one at the top of the door, and shattered into triangles on the welcome rug.

"Get down!" Jeb yelled. "Facedown, all of you!" He crouched low and ran for his hunting rifle. He dragged it from under his bed and had to load it. He could hear Ida May crying and Angel trying to hush her. Myrtle wailed louder than the both of them.

By the time he reached the parlor and peeked through the window curtains beside the front door, he could see nothing at all.

"Someone shot out our winder glass!" Willie told him. "Look at the hole in the wall. Went clean through to the kitchen."

"What if that would have hit one of us?" asked Angel. She reached out and touched a shard of broken glass but didn't pick it up.

Jeb threw open the door and pointed the rifle straight out into the darkness. He could see car lights cascading over the woods and back up the road. He jumped in his truck to follow it, but by the time the old truck engine had cranked and rattled out to the main road in front of the church, not an automobile or human was in sight.

Angel peered through the open door holding Myrtle against her shoulder, jiggling her to try and comfort her. It made Myrtle's cry sound rhythmic and it bounced off the night air like a distress signal.

When Jeb returned to the house, he saw a note dropped on the top step of the porch. He picked it up and read it to himself. It said, "Get rid of it!"

༈

Angel woke up and, seeing Jeb still up and reading, joined him on the sofa. Myrtle slept between them, her face smashed into the blanket as though she were melting. "The baby's not safe. We can't keep her here, Jeb."

"I've never tried so hard to get rid of something."

"You're sure no one in Tempest's Bog wants her?"

"It's not safe to leave her in Tempest's Bog."

"It's not safe here."

"I'd almost think someone is messing with me. You know, like hanging out in the woods, watching to see what I do next. But who would do that?"

"God maybe."

"Tomorrow night is Wednesday church meeting. I'll give a call from the pulpit to see if anyone wants to help out this orphan baby. Kindness has surely not gone out of style."

"Kindness is for your own kind, that's what it seems like," said Angel.

"Myrtle sure carries a world of trouble with her wherever she goes."

"It don't make sense."

Jeb stroked Myrtle's head. She was soft to the touch, like mink. "I suppose I could bring my things in here and sleep next to her. It'd be a shame to move her. She's sleeping so good."

"You go to bed, Jeb. I'll sleep next to her."

Jeb checked the front-door locks again and the cloth taping up the broken window. "I'd rather you be in your own bed, Angel. I'll keep watch for Myrtle tonight."

꒰꒱

Jeb left Myrtle with Belinda an hour before the Wednesday-night service.

The sun had gone and left only the pale residue of tarnished sky, the only light left besides the clouded-over moon. Jeb lit lanterns around the church and then swept the floor and the large rug donated last summer by Florence Bernard.

The chapel was chilled, so he stuffed some of the firewood into the potbellied stove. Will had chopped and stacked the wood on the far wall Monday afternoon to save Jeb the work. The wood kindled fast. The stove helped take the bite out of the air.

He heard a couple of car doors slam, so he left his notes on the lectern and went to the entrance to greet the early arrivals.

The door opened. Oz Mills bristled past.

"Evening, Oz," said Jeb. Behind Oz walked three young men, fellows Jeb had seen hanging out at the bank drumming up work. "Haven't seen you in church in a while."

Another car pulled up and then another as the families arrived for the Wednesday church meeting. Jeb greeted each respective family and then waved at Will and Freda. She met up with two friends and they walked into the church, but not so talkative.

Jeb asked Will to take his spot greeting folks so that he

could return to the platform and gather his notes. It would be a brief service, but a good message from the New Testament.

"I hear you've taken in some trouble, Parson," said Oz.

"Depends on how you describe trouble."

"Folks are starting to wonder if you'll ever get the hang of this job."

"The truth is that she was dropped off without my consent. But I have her now. So I have to see to her needs."

"You might want to remember the needs of those who pay your biscuit-and-coffee tab every week at Beulah's."

Jeb made a fist at his side.

"My opinion? You're a fool for not dropping the kid off in Tempest's Bog," said Oz.

"Maybe she's better off with me. Who are you to say?" He stepped toward Oz.

Oz held up both hands in mock surrender. "None of my business, Parson. Let's go stand by the fire, boys. It's cold on this side of the room."

Fern came through the door holding Ida May by the hand. Behind her, Angel stared hard into a worn pink bunting, like the contents might break if she so much as sneezed.

Jeb brought his right hand into his left. He came two shakes from pummeling Oz Mills two feet from the altar. He took a breath and mounted the platform.

Some of the women gathered around Angel when she showed up holding a baby. Mellie Fogarty asked to see the child. Angel said, "She's sleeping. She just had her supper," and then walked away from the ladies. Ida May led the way to a pew one seat behind Fern.

Fern smiled up at Jeb, but his thoughts wandered back to what he was about to say.

Oz and the young banking clerks took a seat in Fern's row, right next to the schoolteacher.

Jeb opened with prayer and then said, "My children and I received a precious package on our doorstep this week. For those of you who don't know, someone dropped a baby off with us. Her name is Myrtle."

Some of the women craned their necks to see Angel's package.

"Being as how I don't have a wife at my side, it don't seem fitting that I try and take care of another child. Especially a newborn baby."

Many of the women cooed at the mention of a newborn.

Then from the middle of the church, Josie came to her feet and said, "You forgot to mention that baby's not white, Reverend." She floated back down, quiet.

Each woman's smile faded, like lilies losing their blush. Their eyes strayed from Jeb, no longer held spellbound by the news of their minister. The church building held silence as well as it held music, but the silence paralyzed Jeb in a manner that caused him to want to toss away the evening's sermon. Finally he cleared his throat and said, "I guess the good Lord's given her to me then. Pray then that I won't allow harm to come her way. Ask God to give me grace if he won't give me a wife."

His last comment caused some of the women and the men to laugh. Fern laughed without opening her mouth.

Jeb waited for her eyes to connect with his. He wanted to come down from the platform, take her by the hand, and walk away from this troublesome place. But instead he opened his Bible and began to read.

7

SCHOOL HAD BEEN OUT FOR TWO HOURS AND
Fern's automobile sat parked in front of her cottage. Jeb
paced, treading out a one-by-three-foot path in front of her
doorway before he announced his arrival. Wednesday night
after church, Oz had walked her out to her car.

The moon's high and yellow mark beyond the paper
shell pecan trees was too good a light to waste on Oz Mills.
Oz had given her a peck on the cheek, but it was too dark to
tell if Fern liked it or not.

Today Jeb wanted answers from Fern once and for all.

Jeb rapped against the weathering frame of her screen
door. Fern opened the door and Jeb said, "Fern, I think it's
time we had a talk."

She invited him inside. A stack of bedsheets and kitchen
towels sat next to her sofa, where she had knelt folding linens.

Jeb nudged them to the side and then took a seat on her sofa, tossing his hat onto the seat next to him.

Fern sat across from him in an overstuffed chair the color of ripe apples. "You look flush, Jeb. You want coffee?"

Looking at her in her green cotton dress, like a girl cut out of *Sears and Roebuck,* Jeb nearly lost all thoughts of Oz and what he had planned to say.

Fern poured coffee for both of them.

"Fern, I know you think you know me, but not in the way that I want you to know me."

Fern's cup froze right in front of her lips.

"That's the whole thing in a nutshell, if you catch my drift, that you've never known the real Jeb. I've been afraid of that more than anything. I know I've tried to prove to you that I'm a changed man, but somehow in proving it, you don't really see the real Jeb. I know I came into town lacking in social graces. I had to adjust my way of thinking about women and such, but I did adjust. Especially about a woman like you." Just to be safe, he added, "You're the top of the line where women are concerned. But you should know some things about me."

"You're getting at something, I can tell." The sweet place between her brows dented.

"I'm tired of playing patty-cake, or whatever it is that you expect of me." That didn't come out like he intended. "Or maybe that has been my expectations, I don't know. It may look as though I want a wife, someone to take care of all of these youngens I seem to be attracting. But the truth is that I'm miserable. I'm tired of juggling people and trying to please everyone but myself. You know what I really want?"

"I guess you'll tell me."

"I want a life with you in it. With or without this church, or all those kids, or any of these people in this town. Or all of them included, as long as you're in it."

"Jeb, I wish I had known." Fern took a breath and then cried like she'd come from a funeral.

"I've made you cry."

"It's just the situation in general."

Jeb came down to his knees and scooted across the hardwood of her floor. "Fern, here's the deal, the way I see it. Before you decide whether or not you're going to trust me again, in the way I want you to trust me, I want you to know me as I am. I want you to see me after I've been under the house and smelling like manure. I want you to know what I look like when I wake up in the morning." He pushed a strand of hair out of her eyes. "Come to think of it, I want to know what you look like before you comb your hair in the morning. I want to know that you're seeing me at my worst and yet still loving me." He took both of her wrists and pulled her next to him. Her softness and the way she looked at him caused him to breathe harder. "First off, I don't really ask permission to kiss." He kissed her, maybe too hard, but she didn't seem to dislike it. "I do it because I want to or because I don't know any better. But it's what I want, so I kiss you and that's that."

Fern didn't try to speak. She kissed him back, but another tear streamed down her face, dampening the faint line around her mouth.

"The truth is that I want to carry you back to that sweet bed of yours and give you everything of mine I have to give. It takes everything in me not to do that very thing." When she didn't act surprised, he said, "I want to love you and show you that I love you. But I want to do that with you as my wife." He pulled out his mother's old gold wedding band from the chain around his neck. After slipping it off the chain, he slid it onto her index finger.

"Jeb, wait, I—"

Jeb kissed her again, sliding his hands down her back and around her hips. "I love you, Fern." He pulled her against him. She felt like a part of him that had been missing.

Fern burst into tears. She sobbed so hard that Jeb reached for a handkerchief from her stack of white linens. He slipped it into her hand. She wiped her eyes and nose and then laughed as though a little embarrassed.

"I know I've hurt you beyond words."

"Jeb, I couldn't tell whether or not we were going to, well, be us. That is, a couple. So when a job offer came from Hope, I thought it wouldn't hurt to check things out, give the job a shot." She hesitated as though she were reading the pages of his life. "Stanton School has six teachers now here in Nazareth and Hope is desperate for teachers."

"Hope?" He sat back on his feet. "Oz Mills lives in Hope."

"I wasn't following him there, if that's what you mean."

"He had something to do with it, someway, somehow, he did."

"The letter came from the school committee in Hope, so I wouldn't know if Oz had a hand in it." She started sobbing again.

"You're not taking that job, Fern. I took my time with you because I thought that's what you wanted. I see now that I took too long. You're not leaving, Fern. I won't let you."

"They're desperate, Jeb. If you could see those poor kids' faces—"

"I don't care about the poor kids, Fern!" He grasped her shoulders.

"I think you do. I know that much about you."

"We can live somewhere in between. You teach in Hope and I'll preach here in Nazareth."

"Jeb, I want to say so much."

"Come here, girl. Say what you want to say."

"What if I say something I'll regret?" She looked at the ring on her finger.

He could not think of a single poetic phrase that would make things right. But the quiet between them seemed to have a good effect.

"I love you, Jeb." She wiped her eyes and then moved her face near his. They kissed and Fern stopped crying; she touched Jeb's face with her ring hand. Jeb pulled her onto the couch, where she could get to know him better.

᭝

Belinda nursed Myrtle out in the bright sunlight of afternoon. The sky blued better than a wash of ink, crisp and perfect without a single fold of cloud. The day was almost like summer, like a day full of kites and blankets spread out on the grass, the last dabble of warmth before winter.

Willie took his studies out onto the porch. Angel watched him from inside and then followed him out. His gaze followed the V of Belinda's open blouse. "Willard, I know what you're doing," she said through the open door.

"This baby's almost asleep. Can't the two of you fight somewhere else?" asked Belinda.

"I'm studying for my spelling test, that's all," said Willie.

"He ain't hurtin' nothin', Angel," said Belinda.

"Where's Jeb anyway?" asked Angel.

"Off doing his preacher chores, whatever they may be," said Belinda. "What is it preachers do anyway?"

Willie wrote down a word, then scratched it out, his eyes still trained on Belinda.

"Preachers go around town talking to everyone, kind of like he's making sure they're going to be in church on Sunday and such. You say he said he was doing errands?" Angel asked.

"He said he was headed to Long's Pond." Belinda popped Myrtle loose from her bulldog grip. Myrtle nuzzled next to Belinda, still asleep.

Angel glanced up the road. "Long's Pond. Miss Coulter lives out that way."

"I noticed he smelled good this morning. Washes up real purty, like no preacher I ever seen. He ever date anyone serious? Not that I'm asking for any reason. I have a boyfriend."

"He likes one of our teachers, Miss Coulter," said Willie. "But she's been a hard one to pin down on account of she's rich and he was nothing but a cotton picker."

"And a murderer." Ida May appeared at the doorway. "But not really."

"Willie, you don't know diddly squat about anything. Hand me your spelling words and I'll give them to you just to shut you up," said Angel.

"Yonder comes someone from up the road," said Belinda.

The old squad car from downtown Nazareth turned into the churchyard drive. Deputy Maynard drove past the church and around to the circular drive in front of the parsonage.

Belinda got up out of the rocker with Myrtle to take her inside. "I don't have no business with cops. Angel, you talk to him." She disappeared into the house before Maynard could reach the front porch. He walked less leisurely, like he had some business to address.

"You looking for Jeb, I guess?" Angel asked Maynard.

"Got some news about the apple orchard incident. Is he about?" Maynard stood at the foot of the steps with his hat in his hands.

"Not for another hour or so. I can give him a message."

"You're old enough, I reckon. He was interested, so I thought I'd let him know. The word out is that some high-school boys skinned a cat down in the orchard. So that bloody shirt was left behind by one of the boys that got the worst of the deal handling that cat."

"Who told you that?" asked Angel.

"One of those banker boys, Frank Pella. Said that he caught wind of it when a group of teenagers got drunk down on the lake. He was down on White Oak Lake with a date and heard the whole confession."

"I'll tell Jeb then," said Angel.

Maynard climbed back into his automobile and drove away.

"What was that all about?" Belinda appeared again, fully dressed and carrying her own baby on her hip.

"Boys been skinning cats down in the apple orchards, I guess," said Angel. "According to Frank Pella. Ain't he one of those college boys that runs with Oz Mills from Hope?"

"That's a lie if I ever heard it." Belinda called her two older boys to join her out front.

"Why you say that?" asked Willie.

"I went to school with Frank Pella. He wouldn't tell the truth if you tied him up and left him on the railroad tracks. Why would he care, anyway, if boys was skinning cats? It don't make no sense. I'm done, I reckon. Please ask Reverend Nubey to remember to pay me tomorrow. I owe a wad of money down at the Woolworth's. They can't hold my bill past Friday, they told me."

"You take care, Belinda," said Willie. He watched her drive away.

"You're sick in the head, Willie." Angel picked up a dropped baby blanket and went inside.

⌇

Jeb helped Fern peel off her sweater. She let it drop onto the rug. "Come here," she whispered, and then held out her arms.

Jeb ran his fingers down her arms and then leaned over her with one knee against the sofa. Fern kissed him and she tasted faintly like molasses, as though she had eaten some on bread before Jeb arrived. Jeb touched the buttons on the back of her dress and then touched his fingers to the strands of hair that hung over her shoulders. The tendrils were soft, like a woman's hair feels when it's washed in rose water. He pressed his lips against her neck and then nuzzled the locket that hung on the chain around her neck, lifting it with his nose and then kissing the spot where it had rested.

Fern kissed the crown of his head, and then proceeded to press her lips against his brow, the side of his face, and then his mouth.

Jeb finally confessed about the nights he had lain awake wanting to come to her house and wake her from sleep.

"You should have," she said.

They talked about how they had allowed too many nights to pass without spending them in the company of one another. Jeb's shirt fell open just as a loud knock shook the front of Fern's house.

She sighed and said, "Don't answer it."

The knocker persisted.

Jeb roused but reluctantly. "I'll get it, but you wait here just as you are." He kissed her once more as the pounding persisted. When he opened the door, his eyes locked with Oz Mills's. Oz glanced at Jeb's open shirt and then blurted out, "What's going on?"

Fern appeared in the doorway. She straightened her blouse and leaned against Jeb, pressing her face into his shoulder. One hand came up and clasped his upper arm. "We weren't expecting company."

Oz slapped what looked to be a telegram into the palm of his hand. "So it's like this, is it, Fern?"

"From now on," said Jeb. "May we help you?"

Oz snapped, "Fern has a telegram, if it's anything to you, preacher boy." He held it out and Fern took it. Jeb read over her shoulder. Fern's daddy had taken a turn for the worst and passed away.

Fern pressed her face into Jeb's chest and sobbed as though she had been orphaned. He could not hold her in the same manner he had for the last half hour. So he turned back into a minister. He rested the palms of his hands against her shoulder blades, let out a sigh, and said, "I'll help you pack."

᠅

Angel fixed a supper of boiled oats and a side of eggs with a piece of crisped bacon dropped into the skillet to add flavoring. She burned the toast and the fog from charred bread hung over the stove like a storm. Myrtle cried relentlessly from her bedroom. Angel finally let out a tidal sigh and told Ida May to either go and close the door or try and rock the baby into a stupor until Belinda showed up again for the evening feeding.

"I can't stand the screaming of that kid. Day and night she torments me like a crazy woman." Willie paced back and forth by the back door like he would run out of it any minute.

Ida May pulled a chair up to the stove and then climbed onto it. "I'll finish supper, how about, and you go and rock the baby," she said to Angel.

"Supper's finished. Willie, go for jam in the cellar. Ida May, bring her in here and lay her on a blanket. Maybe if she's where she can see all of us, she'll not feel so left out." Angel spooned eggs into the plates donated by the women's committee. The plates were plain and stamped with lettering that no one could decipher, but they were by far the best plates for keeping the food warm.

"Babies don't know if they're left out. That's the dumbest thing you've said yet," said Willie.

"Count us out four bowls, Willie," said Angel. "You want sugar in your oats, then it's best to keep your opinions to yourself when you're talking to the cook."

Ida May walked with measured steps when she carried Myrtle. Her shoulders were too small for carrying a baby over, so she cradled the little girl as though she might fold in two. "Willie, make us a little bed out of that blanket Angel left on the chair. Right h'yere on the floor, but not too close to the doorway." She talked to Myrtle the whole time in a whisper, as though the two of them carried on in a mutual language only they possessed. Myrtle let out a breathy "aaahhhh" when Ida May laid her in the blanket, the kind of sound made by hot-air balloons when they land.

The sound of the front door opening caused all of them to react with a common relief. "Jeb's finally home," said Willie, and he stepped toward the doorway to let Jeb know how bad Myrtle had been.

"Eggs again." Jeb could smell supper. He tossed some mail on a table in the parlor. "Does anyone care this place smells like an outhouse?"

"Myrtle filled her britches," said Ida May. She meandered around Willie and down the hall, muttering about some schoolwork to which she should attend.

"I don't clean up baby's messes," said Willie. He followed Ida May.

Angel called them back to supper and then said, "You look flush, Jeb. You all right?"

"Fern's leaving for Oklahoma. Did you make bread?"

"Not for good?"

"Her daddy passed away in the night. I don't want her driving alone. But she'll have to drive herself all the way to Ardmore."

"She must be sad." Angel yelled down the hallway again for Willie and Ida May.

"Maybe Florence Bernard and Josie could ride with her. That wouldn't be a bad idea."

"Josie's husband couldn't do without her." Angel served up the eggs and set a canister of salt on the table. "Maybe I could go," she said.

Jeb tried to imagine caring for Myrtle without Angel. The baby flailed and let out a yelp. "Maybe you should," he said.

8

YOU HAVE TO WATCH CAREFULLY. IT'S NOT LIKE it's a big deal. You have to take care of the whole diaper business like you're cleaning out the stove. Just hold your nose and get it done." Angel lectured Jeb, Willie, and Ida May while she showed all three of them how to change Myrtle's diaper, a task she labored over, shaking her head and sighing.

"I'm not standing for this," said Willie. "Me and the boys got ball games to think about. They'd never let me hear the end of it if they saw me taking diaper duty."

"Willie, you'll listen to your sister. Now the three of us together can handle this baby until Angel returns from Oklahoma." Jeb squared his shoulders and studied the matter like he would figure out the engine of a truck.

"I don't want you to go, Angel." Ida May teared up. "I'll be the only girl."

"Always use a warm, damp rag, and a clean one. You see all those towels and rags drying out on the clothesline? I do those up at least twice a day. If you pitch them in the can out back, you won't smell up the house so bad. That's bleach water I keep them soaking in. Boil the water before you wash them." She brushed drool away from Myrtle's mouth.

"Why don't I go to Ardmore and you stay and bleach baby butt rags?" Willie cupped his hands to his face.

"You'd get too behind in school. Miss Coulter will oversee my studies and I won't miss out on a thing," said Angel. She wrapped the diaper expertly around Myrtle's bottom. "Clean as a whistle."

Someone rapped against the new glass of the door window.

"It's Miss Coulter," said Willie.

Ida May ran to the door. She hugged Fern around the waist. "I'm sorry you're sad, Miss Coulter. I wish I could go with you."

"My daddy's with God, Ida May." Fern did not carry the conversation any further, as though to do so would unleash too much.

"Fern." Jeb took her in his arms and held her next to him. "I want to go with you too."

"I wish you could. It's unbelievable you're sending Angel. I know how badly you need her. Florence Bernard should be here shortly. Josie's dropping her off."

"Mrs. Hipps said she was jealous of me being your escort and all," said Angel.

"She was downright green. But her husband is too reliant on her on account of his bad leg," said Fern. She counted the bags of clothing Angel had placed by the door. "We can fit these in fine, Angel."

"You'll be gone for months," said Ida May.

"Only two weeks, Littlest." Fern took Ida May by the shoulders and spun her around to refashion her braids. "The thing of it is, I haven't been home in two years. This will give me some time with my brothers and our aunts and uncles. It's a shame that funerals are the only reunions we have anymore."

Jeb said, "Ida May and Angel made you ladies a basket of food and I have something else to give you." He led Fern away from the Welbys and into the kitchen. He pulled a pistol out of his pocket. "I think you should carry a firearm. That road to Oklahoma is known for attracting bad seed."

Fern sighed and stared at the pistol. "Big difference between hunting deer and shooting a man."

"Come out back and I'll give you a lesson. I'll not send off a bunch of women unarmed."

"I can't drive and shoot, now can I?"

"Please, Fern. I won't worry so much." He placed it back into her hands and closed her fingers over it.

She examined it.

"It's locked." He showed her how the device worked, even though she rolled her eyes. "Let's take it out back."

Angel yelled from the parlor, "Mrs. Bernard just pulled up."

Jeb led Fern out back past the clothesline with its colony of white flapping linens and over into a clearing. He showed Fern a tree he had used for target practice. "Hold your right arm straight and look down this sight with one eye. Then squeeze the trigger."

Fern lifted the pistol and aimed. When the gun fired, it

caused the children to pour out onto the back porch while Florence Bernard shouted, "My lands!"

Jeb stepped out the distance between Fern and the tree and then studied the fresh notch he found. "Wrong tree, but you did hit one."

"I might be a little rusty. Hand guns are different than rifles."

"It's like picking off possums in a tree hole, Miss Coulter," said Willie.

"Jeb's let me shoot it a few times, Miss Coulter. Don't worry. I'll take care of the Dillingers and you handle the driving," said Angel.

"That'd be a sight to see," said Willie.

ॐ

Angel watched through the car window as Jeb and Fern said their good-byes. Jeb kept moving a tendril of hair away from Fern's eyes, and then hugging her. Jeb finally walked Fern around to the side of their house, out of sight of all of them and, most likely, away from Florence Bernard's prying eyes.

"It seems that our minister's finally gained ground with the schoolteacher," said Florence. She already had her knitting out and worked on it from her cramped space in the rear of Fern's car. "Has he said anything about marriage, or can you say?"

"I can't say," said Angel.

Florence laughed. "I wouldn't be surprised if they hauled off and got married soon."

"Miss Coulter hasn't said one way or another. Jeb don't tell me anything. When he's not with her, he's got his head in a book."

"Reverend sure seems to be enamored of her. Here they come," said Florence.

Jeb walked Fern to her side of the automobile. He opened her door and helped her to get situated. "Angel, you take care with that pistol," he told her.

"It's hidden under my seat and the safety's on. I'm sure we won't need it," said Angel.

"God forbid." Florence never looked up from her knitting.

Fern and Jeb made a couple of sappy comments, in Angel's estimation, and then he closed her door.

Fern watched him walk all the way back to the front porch. "I miss him already," she said.

"We got tuna fish for lunch. I've never been to Oklahoma," said Angel.

"Is it pretty this time of year where your folks live?" asked Florence.

"Ardmore's a lot like here, only in the summer it's far more hot. This time of year, I'd say it's chilly of a morning and nice in the afternoon."

Angel watched the parsonage disappear into the woods. She worried for Myrtle and then for Willie and Ida May. But she worried more for Jeb, who seemed lost without the help of a woman.

᠀

Jeb drove Willie and Ida May to school. They missed the early bell, but promised they'd make up the time with their teachers. Before Ida May disappeared into the school building with her brother, Jeb noticed she wore bright red socks. He had seen Angel wearing them to bed on cold nights but never with her school dresses. Ida May must have dug them

out of her sister's things after she drove away. It was too late
to make her change now, and to worry after a girl's fashions
was not on his list of things to manage.

Myrtle slept quietly in her basket on the truck seat.
With the addition of the big laundry basket in the cab, Willie
and Ida May were forced to ride to school in the truck bed.
They most likely would not complain over that arrangement
until winter had come full-blown. By then, Jeb prayed that
the mother of this baby would show herself or at least that
someone would ask after her.

Wednesday night would be the second time he brought
Myrtle to prayer meeting and her third outing to Church in
the Dell. He prayed she would grow on some of the women.
She had a way about her, he thought, that made girls coo over
her. Willie laughed at her when she seemed to have smiled for
the first time and when she found her thumb. Her hair curled
jet black around her face, flashing like lightning when Angel
sunned with her out on the porch. She was a comely girl, if
not round at the cheeks and gaining weight fast like a boy
baby. She had grown on him.

ॐ

It seemed the whole day long to Jeb that he was hauling that
laundry basket full of baby first one place and then another.
Belinda had not shown up for the noon feeding and he had
resorted to giving Myrtle a bottle, which she did not take to.
Beulah saw him coming up the walk and opened the door for
him after which she laughed.

"Don't say a word, Beulah. Just pour me up a cup of your
worst." Jeb placed the basket behind him on an empty table-
top. He took his place on a stool, glad to have his hands free.

He took out a book he had tucked into the basket and used a pen to underline the phrases that jumped out at him.

"Biscuits are fresh made," said Beulah.

"Give me an order then, with some of that sausage gravy." Jeb dropped his hat on the stool next to him. He felt winded, as though he had climbed the Ouachitas.

"I hear you're without your good kitchen help. Shame about Fern's daddy too." She filled Jeb's cup.

"I'm not helpless, Beulah. I can manage without Angel in spite of what everyone thinks."

"I'll get your biscuits," she said.

"Mind if I join you?" Deputy Maynard took the stool on the other side of Jeb. "I'll venture to say you'll be seeing a lot of Beulah over the next couple of weeks."

Myrtle let out a cry.

Jeb stiffened and turned to see her flail one hand, which fell over her eye. She let out a spewing sigh and then fell back to sleep.

"When Nebula's away at her momma's, I practically live here at Beulah's."

The diner biscuits smelled like the fresh crispy-topped ones his grandma used to make. He reached for the jam and placed it in front of his coffee cup. "I make do."

"We're having meat loaf tonight," Beulah said through the open space from the kitchen. "Bring those children by and ol' Beulah will see they're fed."

"I guess your children told you I come by this week about that apple orchard bi'ness?" George creamed his coffee.

"What business?"

"They forgot, I guess. I think those banker boys from Hope went sparking down on White Oak Lake and heard some stuff. Apparently they heard some boys bragging about skinning cats down in the orchards. I didn't want to scare your kids, but them boys was up to no good, trying to weave spells from what I hear tell. Nonsense, but it give me the willies to hear it told."

"Oz Mills told you?"

"His buddy Frank Pella. He come down here sparking one of those girls from down in the holler and then dropped by the next morning to tell me what he'd heard."

"Sounds made up," said Jeb. Beulah delivered the biscuits to him with a bowl of gravy.

"Pella's ornery, but I figured he had nothing to gain by telling tales."

"If Oz has anything to do with it, it could skew the story." Jeb gave thanks over his food.

"Excuse me." A young man clad in a sweater and new trousers tapped Jeb on the shoulder.

Jeb recognized him vaguely. His daddy was a railroad man who had invested in land just outside of Nazareth. "May I help you?"

"That's a colored baby, ain't it?" he asked.

"She's with me," said Jeb.

"This is an eating establishment. You'd best take her out back to finish your vittles."

Jeb glanced at Maynard, who looked down at his hands. "That baby's not hurting you, fellow. Why don't you go on about your business?" He cleared his throat, hoping it would account for his heavy tone, the kind he used to use before he beat a man to a pulp.

"Beulah, it smells in here. You want Lepinsky's business, you best keep the trash out back."

Beulah came out with a puzzled look on her face. "Something wrong with somebody's food?" she asked.

"Lepinsky, that's the name. I know your daddy," said Jeb.

"Well, you should. You worked for my daddy once. He'd not hire you now, nigger lover."

Jeb whirled around on the stool and jumped down onto the floor. His fingers curled, hard as baseballs.

George grabbed him by the arm. "Calm yourself, Reverend. Wade Lepinsky, now you know Beulah keeps her place in right standing with the townspeople. Reverend Nubey here is a Good Samaritan is all. He and I had some business to attend to and we need to finish up. You tend to what you came in here for and he'll take the colored baby out the back way shortly."

"George!" Jeb shot out. Maynard's plump hands grabbed Jeb's. He sat back on the stool while Maynard eyed the youth into submission.

"I'll not eat a single thing in this place!" said Wade Lepinsky.

"Go on, then!" Beulah shooed Lepinsky out of the diner. She apologized to Jeb and filled his cup again.

"Things is going to heat up, Reverend," said George. "People get funny ideas about such things and they'll say and do things you can't imagine. I can't be around all the time to pull your foot out of the trap, so to speak. You got to find a home for this child."

"I did, George. She's with me."

❧

Florence Bernard started a song that was a round. She taught it to Angel and Fern, but they kept coming in on the wrong part of the song. "Not like that." She laughed and demonstrated the round again.

"I don't think we're ever going to get it, Florence," said Fern.

"How long we been driving?" asked Angel.

"Three hours. We ought to be coming up on the state border in the next couple of hours. We can cut across the corner of Texas and drive straight into Oklahoma. I vote we ladies find a nice inn for women and stay overnight. Get a fresh start. I promised Jeb we'd do as little night driving as possible." Fern read a road sign aloud that advertised home cooking.

"We've still got plenty of food if you both want to stop along the road and have a bite to eat," said Angel.

"What a good idea," said Fern. "Look at that sun setting. It looks like glass melting on those mountains. This stop will give me another chance to go over the map again too."

"I brought that apple pie. Let's eat it for supper," said Florence.

"I like the way you think." Angel pointed to a filling station. "We could gas up and then eat our supper beneath that tree."

"Apple pie supper sounds like heaven, doesn't it?" Fern turned the wheel and parked them next to the gas pump. "Angel, open your door and ask that filling-station attendant the name of this town. But don't tell him where we're going. I think it's best not to give out our destination."

"Fern, you're a smart cookie," said Florence. "I'm glad to be traveling with you."

Angel opened her door. The attendant looked to be about thirteen with a home-done haircut and a streak of grease across his jawline. Angel asked him the name of his town and he answered bashfully, "De Queen."

"About how far are we from Oklahoma?" Fern asked him.

"You almost there now," he said. "Next town after this is Broken Bow. But you won't find no gas after dark. It's good you're filling up now."

Angel shut the door.

"Ladies, we want to stop for the night in Broken Bow?" asked Fern.

"It'll be dark when we get there, Fern, but I'm up for it if you are," said Florence.

"I wonder how Jeb's doing?" Angel asked.

"If I know Jeb, he'll have the whole town lined out and a potluck organized or some such goings-on," said Fern.

"He's got his hands full," said Angel. She got out of the automobile to fetch the pie. It didn't do any good to worry, she decided. Jeb needed to learn a thing or two about what women went through to keep up a place. He was probably cooking up a pot of beans right this minute, she figured.

✧

"Reverend, is that you I see clambering around in the back room?" Beulah tied on a fresh apron for the evening.

"I came in the back way so as not to bring you any more trouble." He hefted the laundry basket through the doorway. Myrtle was screaming to high heaven. Willie and Ida May sidled in behind him.

"Three blue plate specials?" She pulled out her pad.

Jeb pulled up three chairs and closed the door to keep out the cold night air.

"Did he burn supper?" Beulah whispered to Ida May.

"Charred like something from hell," said Ida May.

9

CHICKASAW PLUMS HUNG ROUND AND RED-
dened by the October sun, which grew hotter in
Oklahoma than Arkansas, like God had turned up the burner
on the Okies. A cedar waxwing cried *sreee, sreee* in the lilting
limbs, hunting for berries and pinecones the size of blueberries.

Fern's Chevy coup careened around a dusty turn that followed the river.

Angel noticed how change came into the Red River
Valley as the mountain forests gave way to grassland, like the
earth had torn off her skirts to run naked in the sun. They
passed through places like Broken Bow and Idabel that
blended from one town into another, delineated only by a
hand-painted sign marking where the city limits commenced.
She counted more than one abandoned automobile along the
road, travelers driven by the need to leave the doldrums of the

south only to be taken as far as the last tank of gas would allow.

"I hope we find another filling station in the next town," said Angel.

"Stop, you're making me nervous." Florence had claimed the whole rear seat for herself, setting up a basket of crochet twine that spooled across her lap and fed into what looked to be a doily.

"I've never left Arkansas until now. It's different in Oklahoma. I never knew how different until now."

"It feels like home. You ever feel choked by going home?" Fern asked Florence.

"I like being at home. Never was much of a gadabout." Florence kept to her stitching.

Angel did not know how to define home. "How you mean 'choked'?"

"Back in Ardmore I'm one of Frances Coulter's children."

"I wouldn't mind it," said Angel.

"It's kind of a costly privilege."

"Home never had much meaning to me, least not until Jeb took us in. My home is wherever Willie and Ida May are, I reckon."

"You ought to remember that lots of youngens are going hungry nowadays," said Florence. "Jeb's done a good thing, taking in you and your brother and sister."

"My aunt Kate says she thinks my sister and her family moved into Oklahoma somewhere. What town, I don't know." Angel stared at a family gathered on a front porch.

"Oklahoma's kind of a scrubby place, isn't it?" Florence dropped a stitch. "Maybe everyplace has turned scrubby in this godawful Depression." When she rattled on so, her voice softened and she kept saying, "I don't know, I don't know."

The Chevy coup made a rattling noise. Fern floored the gas pedal. The car made one final clattering sound, then died.

The Red River meandered around Tyler Road, trickling slowly to stretch what was left of the river beneath a bridge. Rain had been in short supply in Oklahoma. So was a good filling-station mechanic.

"Look yonder," said Fern. "I see someone coming down the road."

ॐ

Jeb left Myrtle with Belinda, but felt as though he were leaving her with the influenza. Myrtle had cried from three until just before dawn. Willie escaped out the door with Ida May, choosing to walk to school instead of waiting for Jeb, whom Ida May called "the Devil hisself" since Miss Coulter had left for Oklahoma.

By the time Jeb walked up to the front steps of the church, a number of automobiles were parked around the front as though they had been left in various states of pursuit. Jeb reached for the doorknob, but the door opened. Greta Patton held the door for Jeb. Her eyes batted and she would not look at Jeb.

"Afternoon, Mrs. Patton," said Jeb. "What brings you around?"

"It's a delegation," was all she said.

Inside, several women and men either stood or sat around the altar at the front of the church. Jeb took off his hat and acknowledged each one, as best he could, with a nervous smile.

Will Honeysack stood up in the middle of the group and said, "Jeb, I was about to come and get you. I'm sorry we're springing this so sudden."

"It was my fault, Reverend," said Floyd Whittington. "I got late at the store. I was supposed to come and ask you to join us for this meeting early."

Jeb read the expressions of each one: Will and Freda, Arnell Ketcherside, although his wife was most likely cutting hair for Faith Bottoms at the Clip and Curl, Floyd and Evelene Whittington, and Sam and Greta Patton. "Board meeting," he whispered.

Jeb recalled the first time he had awakened to some of these faces the night he had taken refuge from a storm in the church.

"I brought coffee, Reverend," said Freda, "if you'd like a cup."

"Will, what's this all about?" asked Jeb.

"It's not my idea, Jeb," said Will. "Some of the church members are complaining about the Nigra baby you been keeping."

"She's a real handful, I'll admit. But no trouble to anyone else." Jeb tossed his hat on a pew and approached the elders' group.

"We're not sure about that," said Arnell. "Folks get funny ideas about whites mixing with coloreds."

"You make it sound like a cake batter, Arnell. Will, you know I've tried to find a home for Myrtle. I can't set her out with the garbage."

"It ain't right, Reverend. They have to keep to their own kind. Word is spreading that we're the mixed church." Greta moved closer to her husband.

"Isn't that good news, Greta?" asked Jeb.

"You'd best watch yourself, Reverend. Powerful people are watching." Sam kept his voice low.

"Sam, we can't let the church be a weapon against a child. I appreciate all of you coming by today, but we still haven't solved the problem of where Myrtle should go. Have any of you stopped to think that God laid her in our laps for a reason?"

"God is not full of mischief," said Evelene.

"Can't prove it by me. Evelene. You think this baby's not the handiwork of the Creator? Have you looked into her eyes?"

"Don't use this baby to tug on our heartstrings, Reverend," said Sam. "The last thing we need is guilt. I ain't responsible for the whole slave trade of the Civil War."

"God used the slave trade to bring the Nigra to Christ," said Greta.

"Or maybe he used the sins of our fathers to show us the blackness of our souls," said Jeb.

"Sounds like you're taking sides, Reverend," said Sam.

"Who created sides anyway? Not God," said Will.

"Two sides, Will, if you don't mind my interjecting," said Jeb. "Love and hate."

"I say this meeting has come to a close, Will. We can see where the minister stands." Arnell picked up his hat.

"Don't let it end this way," Freda pleaded. "We're not enemies. Reverend can't help that someone dropped this baby on his doorstep."

"Fellers, I'd like to say something," said Jeb. "I'm the minister of Church in the Dell, last I checked. I've got a little authority on these matters. Next time you want to call a meeting, mind asking me first, just so's we don't get the cart before the horse?"

"You start getting high and mighty, Reverend, and next thing you know, you'll be running people off. Folks has stood by you when other preachers would have been run oft." Sam's face turned red as cherries.

"Sam, you and all of these fine men along with Reverend Philemon Gracie installed me to lead this congregation. If I'm the lead horse, sometimes we won't agree on matters, but that doesn't mean I don't love you. I haven't committed a sin or a crime. Maybe God did give us Myrtle to show us what is in our hearts. Take this matter to God. See what he shows you."

"What you're committing is division," said Sam.

"Sam, let's go," Greta whispered.

Jeb watched them leave, all but Will, who stayed behind and asked Freda to wait in the car.

Will waited quietly in the center aisle, his head down, holding his hat in his hands.

Jeb turned on another lantern.

"Jeb, this wasn't handled right. I owe you an apology. What started as a simple talk outside my store grew into this monster. If you think you ought to keep that baby for a while, then I'll stand by you. But what Greta said was right. People are watching. We got to keep our heads about us, that's all I'm saying."

Jeb stuck out his hand. "I love you, Will. Your friendship means everything."

"Go with God, Jeb. Maybe this will all go away soon."

Will left. Jeb swept out the church and wiped down the pews. It seemed he had done a lot of cleaning by supper time. Still, the church had a dirty feel to it.

Angel waved down the oncoming automobile. It was a newer model Ford, red with chrome that shone silvery in the afternoon light. The car slowed and Angel moved to the side of the road.

A woman, small and kind of plain to look at, rolled down her window and said, "Any of you ladies have a map?"

"I got a map," said Angel.

"We're having engine trouble." Fern had drawn back the hood and was looking into it as though she might know how to fix it.

The woman turned and spoke to the driver, a man whose face was darkened by a tan fedora. She turned back and said, "Clyde here's good with engines. If I could take a look at your map, he'll take a look at your engine."

Fern sighed a big amount of relief. "We're obliged. Thank you."

Clyde stepped from the Ford, paused to wipe dust from the chrome of the grill of his car, and then proceeded to look into Fern's engine. He asked her a few things that Angel could not decipher. She opened the map and handed it to the woman. "Where you headed, ma'am?"

The woman took the map. She studied it and made some markings on a piece of notepaper. "We took a wrong turn at Idabel, Clyde."

"I see your trouble, lady." Clyde reached into the engine, made an adjustment, then told Fern, "Turn the crank."

Fern climbed into her car. She turned on the ignition and the engine gunned, shot out a sound like a shotgun, and then hummed nicely again.

"I don't know how to thank you, Mr.—"

"Bonnie, you found where we're going now or not?" Clyde asked.

"We're set now. Here's your map, girl." Bonnie handed the map back to Angel.

As they drove away, the women sat in the car for a while without moving. Finally Angel said, "You think it's them? I mean, the real *them*."

"They'll never believe this back home," said Florence. "Bonnie and Clyde, in the flesh."

"They've gotten a ways ahead of us now," said Angel. "They're headed down Texas-way, not Ardmore like us."

"I feel a little dizzy," said Fern.

"Drive, honey," said Florence. "It's best to keep moving on this road before it gets dark."

ॐ

After supper Jeb decided to take his anger out on a pile of wood beside the church. The air was cold, like a candle had gone out in hell. The sun disappeared behind gray clouds at five and never came back again.

He came down wrong on the wood and knocked the fool out of his elbow. The ax dropped and he slumped onto the ground. A pair of shoes appeared, old leather that had never known a sheen. Jeb looked up. A man smiled at him with a face as dark as good dirt, but smooth and dewy. "You ought not to be so mean to the wood. You only hurt yourself."

"Evening to you," said Jeb.

The man extended a hand and helped him to his feet. "Are you Reverend Nubey?" he asked.

"I'm he."

"Name's Reverend Louie Williamson. I heard you was looking for help with a Negro baby."

"You know the momma?"

"I know of help for you, and that's all." Reverend Williamson turned and motioned for a girl hiding back behind his wagon to come forward.

"What church you pastor, Reverend?" asked Jeb.

"Mount Zion, up around Hope."

"You drove your wagon all the way from Hope?"

"I drove longer distances than that to help a sojourning Christian. Lucky, come over here and meet this preacher. I ain't got all day, girl."

The girl was thin but rather tall, with a round face. Her cheeks sat like peaches above a cleft chin and she was brown as olives. She held out her hand to Jeb. "I'm Lucky."

"I'll bet you are." Jeb laughed.

She looked at the Negro minister, who had delivered her to him. "I got to take this white man's jokes about my name?"

"He ain't made fun of you, have you, Reverend?"

"I like your name, that's all. Never met a Lucky before." Jeb held on to her hand. "How'd you come to hear about our baby?"

The girl looked at Reverend Williamson.

"Let's say for now that word spreads like a field fire from here to Hope. I told Lucky that if she'd come and work for you, that you'd give her room and board. You got a place for her to sleep?"

"How old are you?" asked Jeb.

"Fourteen."

"What about your schooling?"

"I know my books already."

"She's smart, Reverend. I seen grown people that couldn't keep up with this girl."

"Myrtle's the baby's name. She'll keep you up all night if she feels like it." Jeb studied her features as though he expected her to turn and bolt.

"I can keep up with a baby. I took care of my auntie's babies for a long time."

"Your folks don't mind?" he asked.

"Her folks put her out with her sister. Only her sister don't have no way to take care of her. When I put two and two together, I figured she needed you. You need her. Hand of God."

"I already got three big children in the room with the baby. For now, you can take Angel's bed. She's away. When she comes back, we'll have to find you a bed."

"You goin' to let me stay?" She looked surprised.

"I am." Jeb turned to Reverend Williamson and said, "How can I get in touch with you if this don't turn out?"

"I 'spect it will, Reverend. But I'll be in touch. I'll come and check on Lucky from time to time." He nudged Lucky forward. "I'll send your sister with the rest of your things."

Lucky held on to Louie Williamson until he pried her loose. "You wanted this, so now you have what you wanted. Go and be a servant, girl. Be Jesus-like and it will all turn out."

"Ardmore City Limits. I'm home," said Fern.

"Took all day," said Angel, "but we're here. You sure your momma's got room for all of us?"

"My brothers have all gotten married and moved out. She has more room than she knows what to do with."

Ardmore's streetlights led them through downtown. The shops were all dark except for one bar that was lit up. As they drove away from downtown, the night was blacker than the bottom of a lake. After several turns that seemed to lead them around in a circle, Fern saw the lights of her mother's house. "We're home."

As they pulled up, several men spilled out onto the porch. She identified them as her brothers. Her sister appeared and Fern leaped from the car to run and meet her. Angel and Florence followed Fern up the drive. Fern's mother treated them like family and invited them inside to make coffee and talk about tomorrow's funeral.

Over cake and berries, Angel nearly fell asleep with her head against a padded floral sofa back. She could hear the soft droning of Fern catching her family up on her life in Nazareth.

"So do you think he's really the one?" Fern's sister asked.

"I think I've been in love with Jeb from the minute I first laid eyes on him," said Fern.

Angel let out a sigh and fell asleep. At least Fern had not gushed about Jeb all the way to Ardmore.

10

IDA MAY DREW PUMPKINS AND AN OCTOBER moon the color of wheat. In a few days she and Willie would go out begging for pennies for All Soul's Day.

Willie yelled for the last time for her to walk with him to school.

"My drawing is going to win the art show," she said. "No one draws as good as me."

"Ida May, don't make your brother late for school," said Jeb. He held the door open and glanced out at the morning and its stillness. He worried over three women driving to Oklahoma.

The clouds overhead made rows like cattle waiting in paddocks for slaughter. He followed Ida May and Willie to the end of the drive. The morning's quiet languished without a birdcall, or even a friendly ripple of thunder. Only clouds, empty; limbs baring to all the giving up of summer, and it was a brown surrender, what with the lack of rain to rosy up the autumn. Jeb walked toward the empty porch cleared of rocking chairs. The house begged for Fern and Angel to return. Or else that was Myrtle crying for her mother.

Jeb turned when he heard the *snap* and *pop* of rock under rubber tires. A faded black car slowed. Lucky ran out to meet her sister. The door opened and Lucky accepted the bundle handed to her. She stepped away and watched the car drive out of sight.

Lucky Blessed smiled at Jeb for the first time. "You have kind eyes," she said. She appeared thinner this morning as though the fabric of her soul had shrunk on the wash line.

Jeb walked her back to the house. "I believe with Reverend Louie that God brought you to us. I don't know what to do with babies. They don't seem to like me much."

Lucky aimed an exasperated sigh at Jeb. Myrtle was cradled in blankets a few feet from the stove, where Willie and Ida May had made a bed for her. "I see a dish of milk out by the walk. You keep a cat?"

"The girls run after this stray—"

"It's a bad thing to keep a cat around a baby. They try to steal a baby's breath, so they lay on its face when the master ain't looking and smother it." She lifted Myrtle from the hive of blankets. She bounced her, slowly nodding, bending her knees and humming. "Baby's hungry."

"Belinda's late. She's late a lot on account of she has her own to feed."

"White woman don't mind feeding a colored baby?"

"Have you had breakfast? We have some left over from the kids' breakfast."

Lucky ate all of the leftovers, the biscuits, and even the

cold eggs, eating with one hand but never losing her grip on Myrtle. She had a way with her.

"I think she likes you," said Jeb.

Lucky looked at Jeb as though he had slept for a while and then awakened to find the world had changed. "You go on about your business, Reverend. Me and 'is baby will be fine."

⸙

Fern's daddy was laid to rest on the hill where he had practiced his drives. Fern's brothers and uncles acted as pallbearers. Angel had never seen quite so big a turnout for a man's funeral. He had known a lot of people, obviously.

Fern held her momma's hand as they huddled around the grave, each family member taking turns tossing dirt onto the casket. Angel and Florence each held a flower given to them by one of Fern's many nieces. They offered their flowers to Mrs. Coulter and she in turn dropped them as a farewell bouquet on top of her husband's final resting place.

The Coulters gathered around their mother to console her with words of remembrance about the family patron. It seemed a sin to covet a scene like theirs. Angel wondered who would come and see her off if she kicked the bucket. Not a lot, it seemed. Not like this.

"I think we're about to go back to the house," said Florence. She kept wiping her eyes. Her husband had left her without a trace, years back. She had not mentioned him at all on this trip, yet it seemed the thought of him might be running through her mind.

Angel wiped her own eyes, once for Fern and Mrs. Coulter, and once for Florence. "I made a good chocolate meringue pie," she said to Florence. "I'll cut you a slice when we get back."

Florence took her hand and they followed the Coulters back to their automobiles. Fern invited Angel and Florence to join her in the family car while the boys joined their wives.

They all made small talk about the beautiful service. The older women conversed about how well laid-out Mr. Coulter had been. Angel refrained from talk about the dead. It didn't seem right.

"I wonder how Jeb is making out with Myrtle," she said. "I can't imagine him washing out diapers."

"I'm fretting about the same thing," said Fern. "Ladies, what say we join my family for a big lunch and then head back to Nazareth?"

"Fern, you can't leave," said her mother. "Besides, I want you to think about talking to the school here in Ardmore. They've a teacher leaving to have a baby in the fall." Fern's mother did not miss a beat.

"I wish I could be both places, Mother," said Fern. She handed her mother a fresh handkerchief. "But Stanton School is stretched thin this year. They've got a student's mother taking my place while I'm gone and I've got my students in the middle of a term paper."

"And then there's Jeb," Angel said.

"Most of all, there's Jeb." Fern's brows lifted in surprise.

๛

Belinda scarcely looked at Lucky before leaving. Lucky had taken it upon herself to give Belinda a piece of her mind for her late timekeeping. Then they went round two over Belinda smoking while she nursed Myrtle.

"She's all we got, Lucky. You can't run her off." Jeb had come in from seeing a sick family and found them arguing.

"What kind of wet nurse hauls off feeding a baby with her smokes anyway? I seen girls having they kids younger than me that can take care of a child better than her." Lucky washed Myrtle's mouth with a damp cloth as though she had been contaminated by Belinda's feeding.

"She'll be back for the evening feeding, so you better get used to seeing her. I'm glad you're taking such an interest, though. You're better company for her than me."

"What you feed her in between times?"

"Angel put together some formula. You'll find it in the icebox. We warm the bottles in a pan of hot water over the stove." Jeb noticed a scar on her arm.

"Folks around here mind you having coloreds living with you?"

"I'm more concerned about where you'll sleep when Angel comes home."

"How you come by all these youngens?"

"Fate."

"We heard you was the preacher that took in stray children."

"Apparently so did someone else. How did you come to hear about me?"

"Church people talk about everything."

"You nailed that right. I'm worried about you not attending school, Lucky."

"I got pulled out of school long time ago to help my auntie. Ever since, I been working to help bring up her babies. All I know is bringing up babies."

"What's your auntie's name?"

Lucky gazed to the right. "We call her Auntie."

"She must miss having you around."

"Too many mouths to feed."

"Willie and Ida May will be home soon. Get to know them. I've got a load of wood to deliver. You think you'll be all right here by yourself?"

"I do well by myself, Reverend. I can take care of myself fine."

"I believe it." Her name suited her.

❧

The sky darkened and Fern's oldest brother told her they should wait until morning to leave. Fern agreed but kept gathering up her belongings until they were nearly packed and waiting at the front door. "Ladies, we may as well leave. We can stay at that same inn if we get there before midnight."

"Take this food with you, honey. We have more than we can eat." Fern's mother had a tone of resignation.

"We'll not have to stop for food this go-around," said Florence.

"I want to pay for your gas," said Mrs. Coulter. She held out several bills.

"It's not necessary," said Fern.

"Let me do something, for goodness' sake! You always have to be so much like your father?"

"I love you, Mother." They kissed. Fern accepted the money.

"Angel, you can come and stay with me anytime. You're a perfect guest. You too, Mrs. Bernard."

Florence and Mrs. Coulter exchanged pleasantries. Angel and Fern loaded up the luggage. Fern's brother insisted on checking out Jeb's pistol, so Angel retrieved it for him. "I practice-shot it before," she said.

"You good with a revolver?" he asked. His name was Buddy.

"Not as good as my brother. But a lot better aim than Miss Coulter."

"That I believe. Sis was always better on the archery range."

"Your family has a nice house," said Angel. "Is that your wife?" She had had trouble matching up all of Fern's brothers with their women.

"Esther. We married six months ago. Otherwise I'd be setting my sights on a girl as pretty as you." He winked at Fern.

"You don't have to say that," said Angel.

"It's true. Fern, I sure wish you'd wait until morning. But I guess you'll be safe here with young Annie Oakley."

"She wasn't afraid of Bonnie and Clyde. I guess if we meet up with Dillinger, she'll stand up to him too," said Fern.

The Coulters all stared at one another.

"She's not lying," said Florence. "About Bonnie and Clyde."

"They seemed decent enough people, I thought," said Angel.

"Don't tell me anything else," said Mrs. Coulter. "Fern, you stay away from gangsters. My heart can't take much more."

Fern said her good-byes and ushered Angel and Florence off to her idling car. "Look at that streak of pink sunset breaking through. It'll be a pretty night for driving."

～

"That Nigra girl's sleeping in Angel's bed?" asked Willie.

"I could give her yours if your conscience is bothering

you." Jeb was tired from hauling wood. The families with enough cash for wood had almost bargained him out of business. "Ida May, go wash up the dishes. Don't leave Lucky to do all the work."

"You already got people griping about a little one; now you got a big girl from Tempest's Bog living here too," said Willie.

"She's not from Tempest's Bog."

"Not that I care."

"Of course you don't."

"Her family care that she's here?"

"I thought you didn't care."

"I don't. But where's her family anyway?"

"Hope. Her minister brought her here. You got any more questions?"

"When's Angel and Miss Coulter coming home?"

"Not that you care."

"I don't care."

"I miss them too. Women shouldn't be on the road without an escort in this day and age."

"Who'd want to mess with Angel? She ain't the best-looking girl and she's not bright or nothing."

"Willie, you got anything nice to say about anyone?"

"I got a B on my spelling test today."

"Jeb, Lucky is the same color as Myrtle." Ida May stood at the door wearing an apron that touched the floor.

"Thank you, Ida May. You finished with the dishes?" Jeb asked.

"I'm drying. Lucky is a good dishwasher." She turned and joined Lucky at the sink.

"When I grow up, I'm only going to have one child and give him all the attention he wants," said Willie.

"Sharing space makes you humble, Willie."

"It's dark out. Mind if I go and check my coon traps?"

"It's cold. Get on your coat." He watched through the window, watched Willie's waving lantern swinging back and forth through the woods. Willie was good on his own. He never worried over him like he did Angel.

It was black outside, and with the cloud cover, it was as though the sky had been erased.

Jeb pictured Fern and Angel seated around the Coulter piano singing silly songs that rich people liked to sing off-key. The thought of that kind of scene comforted him.

❧

"I know it's a long road, but it just seems this car's been behind us for a long time," said Angel. "After we stopped at that store for Cokes, I noticed it."

"Florence, can you read your watch?" asked Fern.

Florence held up her watch until the lights from behind them illuminated it. "It's quarter past eight. We still got several hours to go until we find that inn."

"They're speeding up. I'm getting the pistol, just in case." Angel pulled out the revolver.

"Put it away. It makes me nervous," said Florence. "How are we doing on fuel?"

"We're fine for now," said Fern. "Angel, I would feel better too if you'd put away the gun. It doesn't do us any good to get excited about nothing."

"Let's talk about what we've done so far," said Florence. "I like the fact that we've taken a trip on our own, no men telling us what to do. No one asking us to darn something or sew on a button."

"Not like that would do any good. I can't sew a stitch," said Fern. It made Florence laugh.

"If I have sons, they're going to sew on their own buttons," said Angel.

"Jeb does seem a little dependent on the mercy of women," said Fern.

"He's all right, I guess. Not a lot going on when he gets in the kitchen." Angel slipped her feet out of her shoes. Her toes had turned white at the tops like they did when she was outgrowing another pair of shoes.

"Angel, this car does seem to be shining its lights through our back glass."

"Speed up, Miss Coulter. See if they do anything."

Fern slowly pressed the gas pedal and increased the speed. "Don't look back," she said. "Stay forward. I can see them in the mirror."

"When my husband was home, it seemed to me that he was always needing me to fix this or that or clean a mess of squirrels. After he left me, I wondered if I had complained once too often."

"Don't blame yourself, Florence. Bad times can cause a man to do things he never thought he'd do. Ladies, we do have a car on our tail."

The automobile sped around Fern's car and then, after driving back in front of them, slowed.

Angel reached for the pistol again and slipped back into her shoes.

꒰꒱

"She still here?" Belinda asked it as though she expected Lucky to be gone.

"Lucky is living with us for now to help out with Myrtle," said Jeb. He handed Belinda her Friday pay.

"Why you come so late? This baby's apt to starve before you get here."

"Hand me the baby, girl, and go tend to your other chores."

"Myrtle is my chore."

"When I'm here, you best make yourself useful elsewhere. I won't abide a girl like you giving me grief every time I walk through this door. I was looking for a job when I found this one."

"Lucky, how about putting beans on to soak?" asked Jeb. When Lucky met him in the kitchen, he said, "Lucky, I can't have you running Belinda off. You keep causing problems and I'll have to ask Reverend Williamson to take you back to your folks."

"Don't, Reverend. They would put me out. It's too cold to be put out nights."

Jeb could not tell if she was lying or not. "I'm not threatening you, Lucky. But I'm stuck with Belinda."

"I won't say another word. But she don't care nothing for that baby. You ought to see her, the way she act when you leave. Once you're gone, she do whatever she please, smoke in your place, eat from your icebox without asking."

"I'll talk to her. But please leave the room when she walks in."

"You mean, stay in my place."

"That's not what I mean at all. I mean, do like boxers do.

Go to your corner and she'll go to hers and we'll all have some peace."

Myrtle let out a cry. Lucky came to her feet.

"I'll check on Myrtle. Will you kindly put on the beans to soak?"

Jeb found Belinda holding the baby out, arm's length.

"Tell that girl to come and change this baby. She's soiled herself and I ain't in the mood."

"Lucky, would you come and tend to Myrtle?"

Lucky took the baby and left the room without saying a word.

"How long you going to be able to tolerate her, Reverend? She's got a mouth on her. I'd slap her, if I was you."

Jeb took his Bible out onto the porch and called for Willie. He saw the lantern moving slowly up the path. Willie had trapped one raccoon.

"I heard a bobcat caterwauling, Jeb. I'm not going out at night again without my rifle."

"Well, you'd best get it before going inside. It's worse in there than it is out here."

※

Fern hit the brakes. The car had screeched to a stop, sliding sideways and blocking the road.

Angel felt like all the air had been squeezed from her gut. She removed the safety from the pistol.

"This can't be good," said Florence. Her voice was tinny, like she couldn't get a breath.

One man emerged from the driver's side of the vehicle and then the other door opened. Another man stepped out of the passenger side of the car. They were barely visible in Fern's automobile lights, wearing coveralls and old coats.

Fern hit the gas pedal. The car lurched. She hit the man from the driver's side and then slammed the brakes down. "Oh, sweet mother, I've killed him!"

"Run over him, Miss Coulter!" The pistol quivered in Angel's hand.

Fern's forehead slumped against the steering wheel. She kept muttering how she had killed a man.

The passenger threw open Angel's door. "Give me your handbags, ladies!"

"Back off, or I'll blow your head off and your friend's too!" Angel's arms stiffened and she took aim.

The man dropped a knife onto the ground. A third man leaped from their rear seat.

"Mercy, a third one!" Florence shrieked.

Angel cocked the pistol.

The second man ran and dragged his friend back to the car. They all jumped in and drove off.

Fern had not let go of the steering wheel for one second.

"Angel, you ran them off!" Florence said.

"You think I killed him?" Fern squeaked.

"Drive, Miss Coulter. You did the right thing. You did what anyone would do. Besides, they'll have to take their buddy and get him help. Maybe they'll leave us alone now."

"This has been a humdinger of a road trip, ladies!" said Florence.

II

WHILE SOME PEOPLE MIGHT BE FRIGHTENED
to stand in front of a large group, Jeb hated nothing
worse than a sparsely attended church service. It wasn't the
first time members had punished him for disagreeing with
them.

Ida May sat near Lucky in the rear of the church. Both
girls were good about tending to Myrtle whenever she let out
a whimper. She had slept through most of Jeb's message. The
tension in the air kept everyone else awake.

Lucky had asked to stay home. Jeb would not hear of it.

Willie sat with a group of his buddies on the far side of
the church, away from Lucky and the kind of trouble that had
followed her into the church.

Freda Honeysack left the building with Josie while Will

hung behind. Jeb could see the anguish in his face as he walked up the aisle. "I know what you're going to say," said Jeb.

"The church is split over the issue of their minister taking in coloreds," said Will.

"I know you're standing by me, Will," said Jeb.

"You're problem has doubled," said Will.

"Lucky's good with Myrtle. I can't take care of an infant and make my rounds. Plus the offerings are low and I've started cutting lumber to sell to make extra. I can't do that with arms full of baby girl." Jeb shook the Whittingtons' hands. Floyd and Evelene were at least polite. Sam and Greta Patton left the building without a glance his way.

"I agree with everything you're saying. We just have to find a home for those children, though, before this blows up all over us."

"You see the way Sam looked at me this morning? Like he wanted to have me hanged."

"This is not a light matter to some, Jeb."

Jeb saw a group of girls gathered around Lucky and Ida May as they showed off Myrtle. Several of the women came and pulled their daughters from Lucky's circle of admirers until the two of them stood alone again. "Will, I should go."

"Have you tried families outside of Nazareth? If you were anyone besides the minister, it wouldn't be so bad. But some of the families feel you're trying to make a statement of some sort."

"They think I planned this?"

"I'm doing the best I can to try and smooth things over." Will took a seat on the front pew. "I'm getting old, Jeb. My ticker's not so good these days. I been thinking that maybe you ought to get someone else to lead the deacon board."

"Will, you can't quit on me. I need you."

"You're the only minister I ever knew I considered my best friend, besides Freda, of course."

"I turn down your resignation."

"I thought you might. It was worth a shot."

"It doesn't look like I'm going to get any invitations to Sunday dinner, so it's best I get these kids home to start a meal."

"When are the ladies coming back from Oklahoma?"

"Fern couldn't say. I told her to take all the time she needed." He still regretted telling her that.

"You're a special man, aren't you?" Freda had come up behind Will. She laid her hands on her husband's shoulders and massaged his neck. "Will and I were just saying we never met no one like you, Reverend Nubey."

"Freda, you're a peach," said Jeb.

"I'll make you all dinner," she said. "Nothing fancy, but we got lots of corn and hash put up." Before Will could say anything, she said, "Don't look at me like that. I can fix Sunday dinner for my minister if I want."

"I'll hang behind for a bit so no one knows," said Jeb.

"I'll not have my pastor sneaking in the back door like he's done something wrong," said Freda. "You gather up your brood and bring them on."

"The woman's said her piece," said Will. "May as well do what she says."

⁂

"I see the Arkansas border straight ahead, ladies," said Fern.

Florence expressed her elation by breaking out a sack of sandwiches. "I liked to have never got to sleep last night. Even with that nice innkeeper and her husband in the house, I kept hearing noises and imagining those no-good men hiding out under the windows."

Angel had lain awake, thinking of Mrs. Coulter's house. It had a sense of order and her thoughts liked swimming through that order and classiness. Jeb would call her vain. But Mrs. Coulter was a Christian woman who had kept up with many things and arranged these things so beautifully that all Angel could think about was sitting inside that house and enjoying the orderliness and good tastes of its matron. She thought of arranging those things so much that they became a part of the parsonage, replacing the church castoffs of knitted doilies and other serviceable items. Mrs. Coulter had a way of arranging the possessions passed down to her in a manner that made them seem new. She was a regular whiz at placement.

Fern had grown up in that house and it had not affected her in the same way it touched Angel, who wondered why fate had not dropped her into that house instead of Fern, who did not appreciate elegance.

"Do we have to tell Jeb I ran over a man?" asked Fern. "It seems like a minor part of the trip, considering all we've done."

Florence let out a laugh.

"You're going to tell him, aren't you, Florence?"

"What do you take me for, Miss Coulter? A regular snitch?"

Angel inspected the pistol again for ammunition and slid it under the seat. "I won't tell him if you won't," she said.

"The last thing I need is Jeb holding it over my head."

"The next time you go home to Oklahoma, you can ask me to be your companion, if you want," said Angel.

"That's real benevolence, Angel. I know how bored you must have been poking around in my family's big old home. I always felt like I was growing up in a museum."

"Ladies, it's Sunday," said Florence.

"With all that's happened, it slipped right past me, Florence. You want to read something from the Psalms?" asked Fern.

Florence read as they traveled across the border and down toward Texarkana. They said a prayer for Jeb and the children. The sun came out. They were glad for the passing of night.

⁓

Jeb and Will walked down a path toward the Honeysacks' pond. Lucky and Myrtle had both fallen asleep on the sofa after dinner. Freda ran the men off to allow the children to rest.

"I'm wondering if I've missed out on something, Will."

"Missed out on hearing from the Almighty?"

"Last time I checked, I'm supposed to serve and love others. Just when did love get outlawed?"

"You got me on that count."

"Maybe I'm not doing what God wants. You think this is his way of getting rid of me?"

"Now who's quitting?"

"I mean it. You think God wants me to quit?"

"If Reverend Gracie were still here, what would he do?"

"He'd tell me that I shouldn't lay down the plow. How long do I stay, though, when so many want me gone?"

"I hate that change comes too slowly."

"What if nothing ever changes, Will? What if sixty years from now, love is still being rejected? Or what if eighty years from now, people still can't sit by others in church who don't look like them or talk like them?"

"God wouldn't let it go that long, would he?" Will asked.

"Surely not," said Jeb.

"We all sat with our feet under the same table today."

"Let it start with us, Will."

"So be it, my friend."

"I'm ready for coffee. I wonder what those women are doing right now? Probably talking about us."

❧

"Flat tire. I can't believe it." Fern examined the blown tire.

Angel was kind of glad. It would slow them down. She wasn't in the mood to hear Willie and Ida May's fighting and Myrtle's midnight tantrums. The trip to Oklahoma was making her feel like a regular person, not what some had made her out to be.

"Law, girl, I couldn't change a tire if you held a gun on me," said Florence.

"I can change a tire, ladies. I can't sew on a button, but growing up with brothers had its advantages. Angel, you help me with this spare."

"I watched my uncle change a tire once. How hard can it be?" Angel took off her coat and laid it on the car seat.

"The most help I can be is to make us up a supper," said Florence.

"That's a good idea. I'm starving." Fern pulled out the tire tools from under the rear seat.

Angel crouched next to Fern and helped her jack up the car. It took both of them pressing up and down on the lever to get it moving. After a half hour they were both exhausted.

"Let's don't stop now. We're almost there," said Fern.

"Fern, can I ask you about Jeb?"

"Go ahead."

"Do you love him?"

"He knows I love him. Here, you hold these, whatever these things are called that hold the tire on."

"Enough to marry him?"

Fern scratched her forehead. It left a streak of grease above her brow. She turned and nodded at Angel and then showed her the ring.

Angel stared, stunned. "He didn't tell me." She ran and asked Florence for a handkerchief and then brought it back to Fern. "I figured Jeb might have trouble getting a wife the way things are now. I guess he's lucky to have you."

"How you mean?"

"He's got so many kids. Most women want their own children."

"If Jeb wants me, I'll take him with all of his baggage from the past, all the Welby children in the world, and a baby on top of that. Help me squeeze this thing off the axle hub." The tire popped off and thudded to the road.

"I won't tell him you told me, if you don't want me to."

"I don't mind who knows. You should know." Fern and Angel lifted the spare and shoved it into place. A car loaded with college boys pulled up beside them.

Angel got up and found one of them smiling at her.

"You look sweet as berries, girl, even with grease on your chin," he said.

She wiped her chin. Before she could come up with a wisecrack, she gave the situation a thought and said, "We're not so great at fixing a tire. It seems that maybe one of you might be better." She smiled and the young man smiled back and clambered out of the car.

"Men show up just when all of the real work is over. Ever notice that?" asked Fern.

Angel smiled at the young men. "We thank you for stopping, fellers," she said.

The other boys piled out of the car and took the tools from the ladies. Angel asked them about college as though she would be attending soon.

Florence passed out the last of their food.

12

JEB LAID A DRESS ACROSS THE BED, WHERE Lucky had slept the last two nights. It was from the church rag bag, a cotton dress the color of faded persimmons. She had worn a dress on Sunday that bagged on her thin frame. She showed up looking like some girl dropped along the highway between Arkansas and Texas for whom no one would ever return.

Fern might be a better judge of girls' dresses, but when he pulled the dress out of the sack, it looked like something a girl like Lucky might appreciate.

Girl like Lucky.

The cotton hand-me-down needed a good pressing.

"Reverend, you need me for something? Willie said you called for me." Lucky had a clean diaper slung over her shoulder. "He took his sister off to school already."

"Ladies sometimes give us things at the church. I never know what to do with these things."

"You saying that dress is for me?"

"If you don't like it, you don't have to wear it."

She threw her arms around him. "You a good man, like I been saying."

He pulled away from her. She smelled of sweat and smoke. When she smiled, her teeth looked as though they could use a good cleaning. "You smell of snuff."

"Sometimes I dip."

"Girls ought not do that."

"So why men do it and we can't?"

"I don't do that stuff no more. It'll make your teeth go bad."

"My daddy griped at me all the time about snuff and beer. My brother gives me both, if I ask for it."

Her daddy had never come up before. "What's your daddy's name?"

"John Blessed. My mother's name is Vera."

"They serve God?"

"Big time. Daddy never sinned a day in his life."

"That's not true. I sin."

"He don't sin on the outside then."

"I hear it's worse on the inside."

"You sound like Reverend Louie. Why you give me this dress?"

"For Sunday."

"My clothes not good enough for your church?"

He said, while trying to watch the weight of his words, "This one's better. Look, Lucky, arguing with me is not going to do you any good."

"You want me to look good for the white people, don't you?"

"For yourself."

"I ain't your girl to show off."

"Fine. Give me back the dress."

"I want to try this on, if it's all right." She held up the dress.

Jeb backed out of the room.

"Belinda's here. She giving Myrtle her feeding in your room." Her brows lifted. She had remarked once already about Belinda's flirtations.

"My room? Thanks for the warning."

⋙

Jeb bypassed his room and left the parsonage. He would spend the morning cleaning out the belfry and painting the steeple. Near the east corner of the church, he spotted paint splatters on the lawn. It was odd for a painting project to be in progress without his knowledge. He rounded the corner and saw the reason. Graffiti spelled out the message of the perpetrators: NIGGER LOVERS DIE FOR THEIR SINS.

Phrases in gray and yellow were splattered over the front of the Church in the Dell. Even the church sign had been painted. Jeb's name had been covered over with another slur. A stick painting of a hangman's noose depicted Jeb strung by the neck.

Floyd Whittington pulled into the church drive. He rolled down his window and said, "Your boy, Willie, flagged me down and told me what had happened. I found him running down the road with his little sister running behind and crying. He's afraid."

"We can't let them bully us, Floyd!"

"I'm afraid bullying may turn ugly. Let's get some paint and get this covered up before prayer meeting."

Floyd drove Jeb down to the Woolworth's. Jeb waved down Deputy Maynard and reported the vandalism. George wrote down the details and said he would go and look at the damage before they got back with the paint.

"George, there's more to this than schoolboy pranks," said Jeb.

"Reverend, I'll do the best I can. The company you keep, though, ain't helping matters. It's hard for me to keep the peace, what with you bringing up matters some folks have already settled in their minds."

"George, I want a peaceful life the same as the next person. You know I didn't ask for any of this trouble. The fact is that we've got laws being violated."

George didn't respond.

"Who do you think did it?"

"Hard to say." George excused himself.

Jeb watched George as he walked across the street, acknowledged the two young men standing outside the Woolworth's, and turned to head for Beulah's. Jeb nodded toward the young men. "Floyd, is that Frank Pella and Wade Lepinsky outside your store?"

"It's them. We can go in the back way, Reverend." He held up his set of keys.

"I'd rather go through the front door, Floyd." Jeb approached Pella and Lepinsky. "Morning, boys."

The two of them talked with two young women. Neither of them spoke to Jeb.

"Morning, Reverend," said one of the girls.

"Daisy, Laverne," said Jeb.

"You girls ought to be careful about talking to characters," said Pella. "You'll get a bad name."

Jeb glanced down and saw a splatter of yellow on the sole of Pella's shoe. He lunged for him, but Floyd held him back. "Let's go inside, Reverend."

"A fighting preacher? I'll go a round if you want." Pella made a fist.

"You're headed for trouble, Frank," said Jeb. "You can stop your foolishness and go the other way."

"Go preach to your colored friends. I'll take my sermons nice and white."

Floyd led Jeb indoors, back to the aisle crowded with stacks of whitewash. He and Jeb counted out five cans. "No charge. I'll pick up the tab on this count, but you got to take it out the back way. You've got more than enough to cover up the damage."

Jeb carried the paint behind Floyd. Once they made their way out to the street, Pella and Lepinsky had disappeared. Jeb saw George Maynard taking his coffee into the station. Shop owners conversed out in front of the stores. Women wrangled over the cost of a bushel of corn.

It was a peaceful day.

ॐ

Jeb collapsed on the sofa. He had covered the graffiti alone. It took lots of whitewash, more than he had ever used painting the church. After the first coat the words bled through. He had to keep dropping the brush back into the bucket and covering the words one letter at a time, blocking over them until they were first illegible and then invisible. He kept walking out to the street to see if the slurs had disappeared from a distance. It seemed like they would never go away. He painted one last coat on the entire church front before dinner. After a night of drying, he would go back and see if the insults had indeed vanished.

Lucky fed Ida May grits. Willie had stayed over with a friend for the night.

The front door banged open. Jeb stumbled off the couch.

"Jeb, we're home!" Fern dropped Angel's bags at the door. She ran to him and threw her arms around him.

Her hair smelled like the wind. He held her, too afraid to let go.

"I'm home too," said Angel. She walked around them and then stood staring into the kitchen.

"You were gone too long. How's your momma?" While she answered about the funeral and how the tire blew out, Angel gazed at the girl who fed her little sister.

"How is that baby doing? Is she still with you?" asked Fern.

"Myrtle's fine. Lucky, you want to come here?" Jeb called.

Lucky's brow knitted together at the sight of Angel staring at her. "This your missus come home, Reverend? I thought you wasn't married."

"They're not married," said Angel. "Who are you?"

"Lucky has come to help with Myrtle." Jeb still had a tight grip on Fern.

"Where do you live?" Angel asked her.

"I stay here. Reverend, I'm going to finish up with your youngest and then get Myrtle cleaned up before her night feeding." Lucky returned to the kitchen.

"Jeb, we don't have enough beds," said Angel.

"If we can work out something, she's good with the baby. She keeps her all day while I make my runs around town."

"You've taken in another child?" Fern didn't hide her surprise.

Jeb wanted Fern to understand. "Lucky's almost grown. It's not like I have to look after her. Someone's got to see to the baby."

Angel walked past Jeb and out the front door.

Ida May gasped and ran to throw herself on Fern. "Dub's crabby when you're gone. I'm glad you're back."

"I see you got your own cook, Miss Ida May."

"Lucky's a good cook. Better than Dub. He burns supper a lot."

"Ida May, go wash out your supper dishes," said Jeb.

"I have an extra bed, Jeb. We can bring it over tomorrow if you want." Fern walked toward the door. "Maybe talking to Angel would be good now."

"I didn't think she would care, Fern."

"She's used to being the lady of the house."

Jeb took Fern and held her next to him. "I need you around."

"I see that. To cook your meals, keep you in the manner to which you are accustomed."

"That's not what I mean." He kissed her cheek. "I'll help Angel in with the rest of her things."

❧

"I liked Oklahoma." Angel pulled the rest of her things out of Fern's car. "The Coulters have it good. It's quiet and kept nice. Not like here."

"Angel, you're tired."

"You do things without talking to a body, like moving in more mouths to feed."

"We can talk about it now. Fern said you had some things happen on the trip that were upsetting."

"She can tell you. What's the point of us talking now?"

"Let's say that we're keeping them until we find them a home."

"That's what you said about us. Are you still trying to find us a home?"

"Your home is with me. Is that what this is about?"

"Lucky is only going to make matters worse. Our place is busting at the seams as it is."

"Lucky is miraculous."

"Can't you see the end of this? People at church are already raising sand about Myrtle. This ain't no kind of fix-it for things."

"If I worry about what everyone thinks, then it's the same as making no decision at all. Ministers have to make the hard choices at times."

"On top of it all, I come from a place where I'm treated with respect and come home to find you give away my bed." She heaved the heavy suitcase out of the car. "What do I care?"

"Why don't you say what's bothering you, Angel?"

"That girl acts all settled in, like she plans to stay a long time. She don't fool me none, Jeb."

"Would that be bad?"

"Are you saying this is as good as it's going to get?"

"Give me your suitcase. It's heavy."

"I don't know what Miss Coulter sees in Nazareth," said

Angel. "All that's waiting for you back here is another mouth to feed and no way to do it."

"Come inside, girl, and let me cook your supper." Lucky stood on the porch, listening to them. "If you don't like it, I'll sleep on the porch tonight." Instead of waiting for Angel's answer, she went back inside the parsonage.

Angel carried her bags through the door. "We're going to catch hell over this." She saw the paint splattered across his boots. "Something must have gotten you in the mood to paint. Where's the masterpiece?"

"We'll talk about that tomorrow."

The sun was finally setting. Jeb wanted night to come and to forget the way the day had started. In his sleep he had practiced a speech to Fern, about the two of them going away and leaving Nazareth, leaving the church with the problem of how to care for the cast-off children of the Depression. It seemed like the thing to do in his dream.

Fern had put on a pot of coffee to brew. "Look at you, Rembrandt. Take those things off and I'll soak them," she said. She told Lucky how much she liked her name. Fern always set things straight. She always made bad things seem right. When she walked into a room, the way seemed more lucid. With Fern around, Jeb was home.

13

THE DAY'S BLUENESS LOST ITS WARMTH AS
the day wore on. The cloudbanks along the mountains
outlined all that was left of the clear day with something that
smelled distantly of snow. Everyone said it was too early for
snow, but the clouds hovered like orphans while the old people wished them away.

Wednesday prayer meeting had lost some of its zeal, so
the numbers were down. What had started out in years past
as a prayer meeting had become another ritual of standing,
reciting, singing two songs, and then listening to a sermon
that should not go late if the minister knew what was best for
everyone.

Nonetheless, the meeting kept the name of prayer upon
it for the sake of tradition.

Jeb learned the ritual from Philemon Gracie. With the

sun going fast, though, he could not usher the congregants into the hall fast enough. In spite of a third coat of whitewash, the graffiti bled through. Two days of priming in the sun had done nothing to help hide it.

"Evening, Mr. and Mrs. Pearl," he said.

The Pearls stood next to the Smithfields, who stood next to the Pattons, who joined the row of faces looking up, squinty-eyed to read the faded slurs.

Angel pushed her way through the crowd and ran inside. Ida May dawdled staring up with all of the others while the sun went down and the cold moved in.

"Ring the bell, will you?" Jeb asked Angel.

She tolled it good and hard until the couples disbursed and entered the sanctuary.

"We can't have people driving by and seeing that," said Sophie Pearl. "They'll think we're rabble-rousers."

Sam Patton agreed. "Reverend, you can't leave the church in that state."

Angel gave another tug on the bell rope and received the desired *bong-bong-bong*.

"That's good, Angel." Jeb ushered her into the hall.

Will and Freda slipped in and shook Jeb's hand before taking their seats.

"Can't figure out why the whitewash didn't work," said Floyd. "Beats anything I've ever seen."

"Let's all gather into the Lord's house," said Jeb. He had heard Philemon say it so often in that soft, whispered manner that caused the church to fall silent, reverent. Jeb felt when he said it, that his words sounded more like stones of provocation.

"Here we go then," said Angel to Jeb. "Been a while since we seen a hanging."

Lucky, who had waited until the dead last minute to climb out of the front of Jeb's truck with the baby, entered and sat fast on one of the rear pews.

Several boys got up and moved away. Muttering rippled through the congregation.

Jeb took his place behind the lectern.

Fern led Ida May down the aisle. She was a brilliant smile in a bevy of frowns.

"Let's bow for prayer," said Jeb. He said one first, silently, just between him and God.

❧

Jeb pulled to a stop in front of Honeysack's General Store. A boy waved newspapers down on the corner. "You all stay put. I want to pick up a paper and I'll buy penny candies down at Fidel's."

Angel and Lucky took turns with Myrtle, crushed into the front seat. Willie and Ida May shared a blanket in the truck bed.

"Hurry, Dub, it's cold," said Ida May.

Angel shifted when Jeb got out and closed the door. "Looks like the Woolworth's got in new dresses. Want to go and window-shop?" she asked Lucky.

Lucky covered Myrtle's head. "Anything to get out of this truck. Reverend needing some new wheels in a bad way."

Angel crossed the street and Lucky followed, holding the baby's face against her shoulder.

"Mrs. Whittington has the best winter hats. About as good as the *Sears and Roebuck's*," said Angel. She pointed to a set of earrings and a necklace displayed at the mannequin's feet.

Lucky glanced up the street. "Sure hope Reverend hurries." She saw a group of young men gathered at the corner outside the drugstore. "Let's get back to the truck," she said.

"I'm going to ask Mrs. Whittington for a job so I can buy my own clothes. I get tired of the church rag bag dresses. Yours is nice, though. I didn't mean it wasn't."

"Angel, you don't have to explain everything to me."

"There's that Oz Mills and his banking swells. They think they own everything, but they don't own me," said Angel as she turned to cross the street toward the drugstore.

"Angel, that's Frank Pella. Don't go near him. He's a scary son of a gun."

"How you know Frank Pella? Oh, that's right. You're from Hope too."

"We don't run in the same bunch, but I know him. I'm headed back to the truck," said Lucky.

Angel reached down and picked up a nail dropped in front of the Woolworth's. "This is Frank's car parked right here in front of us. What would happen if this nail were to end up right through that tire of his?"

"Hey, back away from the wheels!" Pella saw them.

Lucky turned her back on the boys.

The sound of feet pounding pavement ensued.

"Lucky, run for the truck!" Angel pushed her from behind.

Before the girls could cross the street, the boys surrounded them.

Oz Mills remained on the corner talking to girls. He yelled at the boys but then returned to his conversation.

"Leave us alone, Frank!" said Angel.

Lucky buried her face in Myrtle's blankets.

"Who's the pretty Nigra?" Gordon Watts stroked one of Lucky's braids. "You like ol' Frankie's wheels, girl? You want to go take a turn in the backseat?"

Frank nudged Lucky with his hand. "Whose whore are you? Someone knock you up and give you a pup to play with?"

"Jeb's coming out of the drugstore any minute, Frank, and when he does, he'll kick your butt between your shoulders!" Angel tried to insinuate herself between Lucky and Frank.

Lucky reached for the truck door. But instead of opening it, she came around with a right hook and landed it right in the middle of Frank's face. Blood splattered onto the street and Myrtle's blanket. Myrtle wailed. Lucky never lost her grip on the baby.

Frank lunged at Lucky and she stood unflinching, as tall as Frank and drawing back another fist. Angel took Myrtle and covered her head with the blanket to quiet her.

George Maynard came running out of the station.

"You?" Frank's eyes met Lucky's. "This isn't your town! You can't stay here."

Lucky said nothing, even when George grabbed her by the arm and started to throw cuffs onto her wrists.

Angel took the baby out of her arms. "Deputy, you can't arrest her for self-defense!"

"I saw her hit Frank Pella," said Gordon. "He didn't do a thing to her. Toss her in the slammer, Maynard."

Oz Mills came running across the street. He swore at Frank and Gordon. When he saw Lucky in handcuffs, he said to Frank, "You sure you want to take it this far?"

Frank was shaken. "I guess not. Officer, you can let her go. Maybe I caused it."

Jeb came running down the walk. Penny candy scattered behind him as he ran.

"Can we go?" asked Angel. She stared at Frank, mystified.

Maynard pulled out his key and unlocked the cuffs. "You better watch your step, girl. Pella's daddy don't like his boy being messed with."

Jeb opened the truck door and let the girls inside.

Ida May had buried her face in Willie's chest, sobbing.

Maynard tapped at the window glass. "Keep that girl away from town, Jeb. She's trouble."

Lucky shook out her wrist and massaged her knuckles.

The sidewalks had filled up with the curious from the evening gatherings at Fidel's and Beulah's.

"That felt good," Lucky whispered.

Jeb drove them away. He didn't say a word to either girl.

ॐ

Come Sunday, the Church in the Dell had received a new coat of paint courtesy of Floyd Whittington and a group of boys he had gathered to hide the defacement.

Jeb looked out off the porch steps at the families staring up at the new paint job.

Floyd and Evelene sidled around Jeb and ducked inside. "Sorry, Reverend. Maybe after a day of drying, the paint will hide the damage."

Jeb rang the church bell and greeted each church member, craning his neck to see Fern. She strode up behind the Honeysacks. This time she held Myrtle. "I told Lucky to go up front and sit with the other girls. She's too young to be playing nursemaid every minute of the day. I think we need to talk about getting her some studies to do too. Do you know, can she read?"

Jeb shook another hand. "I don't know. But maybe it's best Lucky and Myrtle stay on the back pew. I don't want to drag you into any of this, Fern."

"I go where you go, Reverend." She carried Myrtle into the hall, right into a group of women. Jeb watched as each woman addressed Fern politely and then excused herself to join her husband and children.

"Reverend, I heard that girl from Tempest's Bog laid into Stanley Pella's boy late Wednesday," said Sam.

"Lucky is not from Tempest's Bog. She's from Hope. Apparently the Pella boy provoked Lucky and Angel. I don't recall your anger the last time Angel laid into a boy from school."

"The Pellas are society in Hope, Reverend. They won't take to this matter lightly. I'm surprised you haven't already been paid a visit from Stanley and Deborah. They're sending their son down here as a banking apprentice. It's not likely they want to get him back damaged by a loose-lipped Nigra."

"Lucky has a sense of passion, Sam, I'll give her that. But she's far from loose-lipped. She's got a pretty mean right hook for a girl too. Even you have to admit that."

"You can make light, Reverend, all you want. But you can't say I didn't warn you."

"Pella is Horace Mills's apprentice. If he has issues, he'll let me know," said Jeb. "But I doubt he'll get involved in the petty wars of a bunch of college sophomores. Even his nephew backed out of the issue and encouraged Frank to do the same." That had seemed strange to Jeb. But when he questioned Lucky about Pella's backing down, she had shrugged and called him a coward.

Jeb saw a group of churchmen gathered at the front. He excused himself to Sam, and as he moved around several families, he saw they were addressing Lucky. She stood, head bowed, and started working her way around the seated families on the second pew from the front.

Jeb stopped her halfway down the aisle and asked, "Where are you going? What did they say to you?"

"Nothing, Reverend. Don't cause no trouble," she said.

"I've a right to know what they said."

"They asked me if I had gotten lost finding my place in the church. When I said, 'I'm not lost,' they told me that I'd better find my place and be quick about it."

"Where are you going?"

"I'm going back to the parsonage. I'll take Myrtle and leave."

"You're not leaving, Lucky," said Jeb. He led her to Fern's pew. Fern scooted down and patted the seat next to her.

Lucky let out a sigh and sat next to Fern.

Jeb took the platform and called the meeting to order. "Morning. I was about to open in prayer. But before I do that, I'd like to ask you something. This church has a motto written on it out front. At least it did before all of that whitewash covered it. It said, 'All who are weary, come home.' That word 'all' means a whole lot of things. I'll leave that for you to ponder." He took a breath and continued. "But before I pray, I want to see a show of hands. Lucky is helping me care for a baby that no one wanted. She lives with us. If that is a problem, well, I know how to find the door. I've been shown it enough times."

A few laughed quietly.

"I'd like a show of hands this morning. If you'd like for me to resign as your minister, I'll do it now."

Fern's eyes were moist and her head shook slightly as if to beg him to stop.

"Then one of you can come forward and lead in a prayer to Christ our Savior. But knowing that my family has grown to include two more children that are in some ways not like me, but in many ways a whole lot like me, how would you have it? Show of hands; who wishes for me to remain in the pulpit?"

Will and Freda raised their hands along with Fern. Several other hands came up. Will stood and counted. He turned and said to Jeb, "Reverend, you have a majority of members who want you to remain as our shepherd. Can we please have that prayer now? My soul is needy."

Jeb bowed his head. The congregation was silent except for the sound of a whimpering baby. Lucky rocked Myrtle slowly, forward and back, never looking up.

ॐ

Election Day had a sense of change in the climate, like October giving way to November and autumn to winter. Fern took a turn between two of her classes to drive downtown and vote at the library.

The line into the voter booths was not so long. She bought herself a Coke at Fidel's and crossed the street to join the voting line.

"Fern, you look radiant as always." Oz Mills was dropping off mail for his uncle at Honeysack's General Store.

"I'm in a hurry," she said. "I'm just in town to vote. I have a class in thirty minutes."

"I guess I've lost you to that preacher. You know you gave up the best man for one who's likely to be run out of town."

"Oz, you've never been right about Jeb Nubey. Why try now?"

"Fern, I'm not a biased type. But I know that I have a place, and girls like Lucky Blessed have a place and she's stepping into places where she's not likely to make friends. You're blind to what's going on. I understand. Let me tell you something for the sake of your reputation, though. It's all over town your color is changing. You keep going in that direction and even I won't be able to take you back."

Fern slapped Oz across the cheek.

He backed away. "You're all class."

Fern walked away from him, regretting she had slapped him. When she asked the woman in front of her how fast the voting line was moving, the woman said, "I've been wanting to do that to my old man for thirty years. Go get him, sister!"

Fern hung her head.

༜

"What do you mean, you quit? You're all Myrtle has for food, Belinda." Jeb's stance on the porch left a three-yard gap between himself and Belinda, who stood holding her car door open.

"Lucky gives her a bottle. I've seen her do it."

"Doc Forrester says a baby has to have mother's milk or else get sick," said Jeb.

"She's a good ten weeks old. She's thriving. I can't come anymore."

"Who told you you couldn't come, Belinda?"

"I'm thinking of moving to Hot Springs. I won't be able to drop by anymore."

"You've family in Hot Springs?"

"Reverend, I've got to go. The baby's fussing and he's had me up all night. I'm at wits' end."

"This is kind of sudden."

"I told you I was sorry as can be, Reverend."

"Someone's said something to you."

"I had my car broken into. Someone threw in an ugly picture of you and a black baby."

"May I see it?"

"I threw it away, burned it. I was scared out of my wits. I can't take on that kind of trouble, Reverend. I felt funny all along nursing that kid. Then that big girl come along and she gives me the creeps, like she's watching everything I do. If I didn't know better, I'd say she was kin."

"Myrtle's kin?"

"I can't prove nothing. But I have to let this job go." She squeezed behind the wheel. "I've packed and left that house. I owe some rent, so keep it under your hat that you saw me. I'm starting new somewhere. Say a prayer for ol' Belinda when you think of it." Belinda drove away.

Lucky came out into the yard, holding Myrtle. "I'm glad she's gone. She was a ho if ever I saw one."

14

JEB AND FERN WALKED BEHIND THE CROWDS that had gathered up and down Front Street for the town parade. Armistice Day brought out the veterans of the Great War in full military regalia. Several clowns showed up and passed out balloons. Jeb stopped in Honeysack's to order new strings for his banjo. Then he and Fern headed out into the street.

"The mayor's set up the platform near the courthouse," said Fern. "I'll bet they'll have you join the veterans over there. I'm glad they've asked you to start the ceremony with prayer. I'm proud of you, Jeb."

"I'd do anything to impress you," he said. "Even stand next to a mayor whose politics I can't agree with. Here comes the high-school band."

The band passed with thundering drums and most of the brass section on key.

"We'd better make our way to the reviewing stand," said Fern. "This parade is never much longer than a chorus or two of 'The Star-Spangled Banner.'"

Jeb led Fern across the street between the last row of the Stanton High Band and the color guard.

He squeezed through a lemonade stand and a hot dog vendor until he spotted the mayor of Nazareth shaking hands with a retired lieutenant. "Mayor Fabrey, I'm glad I found you." Jeb pulled out his prayer in writing. "I kept it short like you asked."

"Oh, Reverend N-Nubey." He stammered over his words and then gestured for Jeb to follow him behind the platform.

Jeb read his expression, a haggard look. "Is there something wrong, Pony?" he asked.

"These are hard times, Reverend. You're one of the finest men of the cloth I've ever known, but I've got to calm things down around here. My office is getting complaints."

Jeb thought of the small room in front of Pony Fabrey's house that substituted for a mayoral office. A priest pulled back the canvas from up front and said, "The parade's coming to an end, Pony. Want me to begin?"

"One moment, Father," said Mayor Fabrey.

"You've replaced me with a priest from out of town?"

"He's my second cousin. It has nothing to do with matters. Listen, Reverend, come Fourth of July this will all be blown over and you'll be back where you belong opening the ceremonies."

"This is because of Lucky Blessed, isn't it?" asked Jeb.

Fern came to Jeb's side. "Don't let the bullies run our parade, Mayor," she said.

"Miss Coulter. Lovely to see you," said Fabrey.

"Mayor, we've got to commence." Sam Patton stuck his head around the corner. When he saw Jeb, he drew back.

"Sam Patton's in on this?" said Jeb. "He's one of our board members."

"Sam had nothing to do with it, Reverend. I've got to go." He stepped up the back way onto the platform.

Fern had not let go of Jeb's hand the entire time that Fabrey spoke. "This is wrong, Jeb. We can't let them do this."

"Let's go find the kids and take our picnic inside. It's too cold out here."

༄

"If you kids are too cold, you don't have to stay out on my porch," said Fern. The porch was screened around the perimeter. "My daddy put those picnic tables together last year. May as well make use of them."

"Miss Coulter made chicken, Jeb," said Willie. "And tater salad."

"I'll fix the tea," said Angel. "Seems funny having a picnic in November." She joined Fern in the kitchen. "Jeb, you want yours sugared or not."

"Sweet like everyone else," he said.

"I'm not going to let those men ruin my day," said Fern.

"It's getting kind of hard at school," said Angel. "Kids are calling us names, bad names like they call Lucky. It seems like someone's messing with us, don't it?"

"How you mean?" asked Jeb.

"A baby on the doorstep. Then another teenage girl gets dropped off. It's odd, ain't it?"

"More like an act of God," said Fern. "I can't imagine what would have happened to that little baby if she'd been dropped off on someone else's porch."

Lucky came inside. "Too cold for my blood. I'll take my chicken inside if it's all right with you, Miss Coulter."

"Lucky, what would your folks say if Myrtle had been dropped off on their porch?" Jeb asked.

Lucky shrugged.

"Can you say why they sent you away?" asked Fern. "If that's too personal, never mind."

"My father kicked me out. He gets mad about things. My mother said I should go to my sister Jewel's house. Only Jewel couldn't take me in, said she could barely feed herself. She keep men around anyway. I don't like none of the ones I met. They use my sister. That's the way I feel about it anyway. I talked to Reverend Williamson about it and he said he would work on the matter. A week passes and then he comes and takes me from Jewel's and brings me here. That's all I can say about it."

"Your sister don't mind you living with white people?"

"Jewel don't think like that, like who staying with who. Long's she don't have to pay more bills than she got on her own, nothing matters to her. At least nothing about me matters to her. She too much like Daddy, all mad about something all the time."

"Who is Reverend Williamson?" asked Fern.

"He the preacher of Mount Zion in Hope. I wish I had him for a daddy. But he old. His wife is getting on in her years. His daughter lives with them and takes care of her six. They got too many in that house like we do here."

~

The snow finally came, but it was a thin, icy layer that sugared the lanes turning to slush in open roadways and forming slick patches in the shade. The frigid wind turned the temperature too cold for the children to want to remain outside. A wet snow is what Fern called it, when the mixture of sleet and snow had sent them running for coats and some borrowed blankets for the cold truck ride home.

Jeb affixed new locks onto the church's doors, both on the front and back exits, once he had considered the assault on the building.

He could see Willie pass by the front parsonage window on occasion as if he hoped for the snow to turn into mounds of good sledding snow, which it didn't.

He yanked on the rear door's padlock, careful for the sleet that had already iced the porch, and in the turning away, he saw a movement at the wood's edge about sixty yards from the parsonage. The shadow might have been a dark bleeding of shade from woods to house with the hour of the day waning; but the movement, quick as a sprinter, left him with the impression of a man watching the house. Not wanting to start his quarry, Jeb made a casual move in the direction of the church's west side and performed the utilitarian gesture of moving a shovel from the side of the church to the shed that sat out a good twenty-five feet from the corner. He fumbled with the shed door's latch to stretch the task into a good two minutes of fiddling-around time. The metal had rusted and he took the time to closely examine the corresponding pieces that no longer snapped closed. He hammered the metal, causing orange dust particles to sprinkle the white ground with metal cinnamon. That chore gave him the slight view of the woods he needed.

The man was standing in the shadow of a copse of pines, his back against the trunk of a fifty-year-old spruce, and now he was watching Jeb.

Jeb turned and made a dash for the woods. The man ran too, and in the flurry his dark frame, like an eddy of night zigzagging over snowy hills, was palpably visible. Jeb slipped upon a shaded patch and slid into a bramble of naked azalea. Even if he had not fallen, the man would have outrun him. He was a savvy navigator owning the territory in front of him as though he had mapped it out in his sleep.

"Did you fall or have you decided to nap in the snow?" asked Angel. She had watched Jeb through the window and then ran out in her thin slippers and a housecoat.

"I thought I saw someone," he said.

"I saw him too, hiding behind that tree. He's fast, ain't he?"

"I never saw him before."

"I didn't tell Ida May or Willie. They won't sleep tonight. Maybe he wrote those things on the church house, you think?" She kept staring into the woods. "Like when robbers return to the scene of the crime."

Jeb came to his feet, his knees muddied through. "Keep a watch. Let me know if you see him again. I'm catching whoever did it."

"Lucky saw him too. She ain't afraid of anyone." Angel shuddered.

"Keep an eye on Lucky too."

"Don't you trust her?"

"The list of who I trust is growing thin."

"It's snowing harder. Let's go inside, Jeb. I feel like someone's watching."

◦⌒◦

Lucky had set up a checkerboard for Willie. Her long fingers moved the checkers almost without any wrist movement. Her knuckles were inked with some sort of drawings, in the shapes of eyes and mouths. With every move of a checker medallion, the eyes and mouths appeared to converse. Ida May watched her fingers, fascinated, as though the Sunday funnies had come to life and walked around in the game of checkers.

Jeb spied the woods through the window, reading a passage from a book, and then changing from the sofa to a chair to get a different view of the woods and to keep an eye on the front drive.

Only Angel showed awareness of his watchfulness. Lucky and Willie advanced to the crowning of kings. Their only glance outside indicated their satisfaction with the blanketing of snow upon the windowsills.

Jeb let out a long breath and asked Lucky, "Why did you draw on your hands?"

"I made a puppet show for Ida May." She jumped Willie and told him to king her again.

The smudged ink discolored her fingertips. He imagined the ink staining everything she touched. She ate from a plate of cold fried potatoes, licking her fingertips between each bite and cleaning under her nails with her front teeth.

"Lucky, go wash your hands," he said.

"After I finish eating, Reverend." She advanced another checker into Willie's territory.

The first time Lucky had stepped out of Reverend Williamson's car, she wore an ironed blouse, crisped at the sleeves and starched. The whiteness of the blouse and the smell of bleach defined her as fresh off the shelf, an unspoiled girl. Her first impression warranted the approval of anyone who looked at her. "Lucky, you need to keep yourself better," he said.

"I'll be back, Willie." She huffed, pushed away from the checkerboard, and sashayed into the kitchen, clanging around the kitchen sink, clattering and slapping her wet, soapy palms together. Before she walked into the parlor, she posed beneath the arched doorway, one foot in front of the other.

Jeb kept his eyes on his reading.

Lucky waltzed across the floor and then slumped belly first onto the rug near the checkerboard. "I clean enough for you, Reverend?"

Jeb blew out a breath and turned the page of his book.

"Maybe I won't ever be," she said. She picked up the plate of cold potatoes and ate until she emptied the dish.

∽

Myrtle cried long, screaming cries, more like bleating, like a lamb scrounging around in the dark for a slaughtered mother. Lucky rocked her in Jeb's room, moving back and forth in the dark on one of the chairs brought in from the porch. She sang and her voice undulated, rhythmic and reaching into the snowy sky for an ancient choir. She would not sing for anyone, only for Myrtle. The door to Angel's room creaked open;

Lucky's audience, now out of bed and sitting by the open door, listened without comment.

The baby's cry fell into a whimper and then silent.

Jeb reached for the radio dial. A Saturday-night orchestra played "Girl of My Dreams." Jeb turned down the sound to keep from disturbing Myrtle.

His bedroom door squeaked open. Lucky tiptoed down the hallway to make up her bed, the one given her by Fern.

"Lucky, mind coming in here?" he asked.

"I finally got her asleep. Like wrestling with a baby pig. Don't know if she's ever going to get over not having Belinda's teat to yank on nights." She let out a breath. "I hate to move her. She fell asleep in the middle of your bed."

"Have a seat."

"I'm in trouble?" She took the sofa, a good distance from Jeb.

"If I've been hard on you, I shouldn't have been. You're a fine young woman. You ever sing in church?"

She laughed from the back of her throat. "You apologizing to me, Reverend?"

"Not if you're going to make a big deal out of it."

"I accept. We ain't alike and it bothers you, I can tell."

"We're alike, Lucky. That's why we clash."

"What you want from me, Reverend?"

"Not from you. More what I want from me. I had this big idea that if I marched you and Myrtle up the church aisle, it would change people. I had this big vision of peace for Church in the Dell."

"Funny ideas you got. They crucified the Lord for that kind of thing."

"What I'm doing, it's not fair to you. If you want to stay home from church, I'll not be mad."

"I'm sorry you lost your place at the parade ceremony. I wish those men had your kind of guts."

"I don't have guts, or else I'd quit hiding behind my words. Like anything I say carries any weight. It doesn't, only in my imagination."

"Maybe I'll think about whether or not I'll go tomorrow. I don't mind sitting in the back with a crying baby. That's where all the mothers of little ones sit."

"It's a shame not to share your voice with the church."

"You're dreaming a big one now. Sweet dreams, Reverend." She got up to head off to bed, then paused. "I'm going to tell you something, but if you get mad, it will be the last secret I tell."

Jeb set down his coffee.

"That man you seen in the wood today, he's my brother. He don't agree with my father about kicking me out the house and all, so he looks after me. His name is Ruben."

"I'm glad you told me. Now I won't have to shoot him."

"Ruben is not like my sister, Jewel. The last thing he wants is trouble, but when it comes to me, he'll stand up, even if it means taking a lick for me." She glanced toward the bedroom where Myrtle slept. She nodded good-night to Jeb and went to bed.

Jeb turned up the radio dial. The dance music faded. A radio broadcaster announced the serial-styled news show *The American Dream*. The documentary dramatized real-life Americans who had risen above disaster or the crushing results of the Depression. Jeb dozed, half-thinking about the lost particles of his dream floating away, the tide of inequity running roughshod over reason.

The broadcaster introduced a man whose voice held a distinct elocution similar to Philemon Gracie's. The show's sponsor had assembled a group of backers to support an essay contest named after the show—*The American Dream.*

The winner would receive a modest prize and the chance to read the essay at a ceremony near the Lincoln monument.

Fern would cinch up a contest like that. He took on the assignment only for a snowy night's musing. He drew out a piece of paper and played with the theme of his loss, the reaching for things that cannot be, the hunger to break bread peaceably across the borders of Tempest's Bog and Nazareth, or between Mt. Zion Church and Church in the Dell.

He wrote until midnight. The snow finally ceased, fingerprinting the window glass with multifarious designs. He made his bed on the sofa. A child needed his pillow tonight. It was a small offering, but nothing big enough to matter. A better gift would reach further. Only heaven could see a pauper's benevolence.

15

JEB WOKE UP ON WEDNESDAY, THE DAY BEFORE Thanksgiving, his face flushed. By Wednesday evening's prayer service, which had dropped to twelve in attendance, his temples warmed hot to the touch and Fern told him she would come Thursday morning to the parsonage and prepare a Thanksgiving meal.

Angel let Fern in on Thursday morning and the three women—Fern, Angel, and Lucky—set to work clanking a kind of kitchen music, stirring pots and skillets until the house smelled of gravy and green beans.

For a week Willie manned a turkey blind, letting several birds pass as he waited for a fat wild turkey, its torn wattle hanging from its face, and that's how he described the bird to Jeb every evening until he had sacked the thing. He took the bird's head clean off with one shot.

Angel and Lucky had groused over plucking feathers and especially gutting the bird and removing the stub of head and its yellow feet protruding like starfish. The snow had not entirely melted in the backyard, so the feathered tufts clumped in bloodied mounds around the remaining banks.

Jeb curled on the sofa, fifteen again, Fern feeling his head and throwing another blanket over him. She fluffed the blanket out and it lighted on him and he liked the airy feeling as it settled over him. Her hand felt like she had warmed her skin first with lotion and then air-dried it, smooth with a hint of some summer flower, like something she grew on her kitchen sill. He wished that women had been trained to check fevers by lifting a shirt and touching the chest and he thought about that as she held her hand across his forehead and looked up as if the temperature of his skin were registering in her mind. She never saw the way he looked at her or if she did, she punished him by poking a glass thermometer into his mouth.

His mouth was parched and he hankered for something like a hot toddy, but he would settle for well-sugared tea, but not hot like women drink it. Cold-from-the-icebox tea.

"I want to get you something. Tell me what you want," she said.

He shook his head, forgetting what he wanted. Jeb felt bad for not asking Fern to marry him sooner. He kept projecting how it would happen and under better circumstances, when he had gotten rid of some of the baggage of so many children, when he had saved a little money in Mills's bank, and when the church returned to its better condition. He had a picture of Fern and him that he pieced together, a tidy life of quiet ministration, a rocking couple on the porch, Sunday afternoons spent making love, and children who bore names like Elizabeth Cassandra and Thomas Aquinas. He knew she thought like that and it kept him from asking her to put on his ring. He pulled out the copy of *Pensées* Fern had given him several years back. It had slid between him and the couch. His head hurt too bad to read.

"I think you might sleep better in your bedroom," she said.

Jeb thought of saying how he did not want to miss the way she walked into the room and the sight of her walking away. "I'm dozing, I think."

"You're not worrying over the church, are you? Because you shouldn't. They may not appreciate what you're trying to do now, but they will."

Jeb decided she smelled like begonias, red velvet petals that tug at your fingertips when you run your hand across them. "Is Willie's turkey fine?"

"We had to prop the stove closed with a chair. It's an ambitious feast. Your water glass is empty." She took the glass and went into the kitchen before Jeb could touch her and ask her if she could smell the begonias.

A song played on the radio and it sounded like a church choir. Jeb wanted to turn it off, to not think of religious singers and the way they frowned from hymnals when their minister had made them sad. But the fever made him close his eyes. When he opened them again, Fern had set up a table in front of him and the glass of water.

She laughed from the kitchen. It made him smile.

ༀ

By early evening wild turkey took over everything, the roasting juices steaming and overtaking the onions and the dressing made of corn bread. Jeb sat up and his arms came out of the blanket. The air cooled his skin. He could feel his head clearing, and when Ida May talked to him, her voice did not come from a can.

"Do you want to eat with us, Dub, or stay on the couch like a vegetable?"

"Ida May, don't wake him up," said Fern.

Jeb did not know what she saw when she looked at him, but when she smiled, her lips met on one side. "Ida May, get me my comb."

"We can bring the feast to you, Jeb," said Fern.

"That's too much trouble," he said. He imagined all of them sitting around the table, laughing, and he would miss the jokes and the chance that his knee might touch hers.

Ida May handed him the comb. "Fern turned off the radio," she said. "Can I turn it back on?"

"Keep it low," said Jeb.

He tucked in his shirttail and combed the hair out of his eyes. He left the sofa and blankets and went into the kitchen. Someone had created a centerpiece, a flower arrangement from paper. Lucky set plates on the table. Angel went behind her, adding utensils and cloth napkins Fern had brought from her kitchen.

"That's a pretty song. You can turn that up, Ida May," said Fern.

The table leaf had been added. The center displayed several green foods, like green beans, which he expected, and a salad and some round things that he most likely wouldn't try unless Fern plied him and then he would eat anything to keep her smiling.

Angel pulled a baked cake out of the oven and set it aside to cool.

"I'm glad you made the turnip greens, Lucky," said Fern. "Mine never look that good."

Angel looked less sullen. An abundance of food might have lifted her demeanor, but she sat next to Lucky, it seemed on purpose.

"You won, Dub," said Ida May. She came into the kitchen and climbed into the chair next to where Fern had just taken her seat.

"What did you win, Jeb?" asked Willie.

"The prize," said Ida May. "The radio prize. The man said your name."

"I think Ida May's telling tales," said Fern.

Jeb went into the parlor. The jingle was playing for *The American Dream*. A radio song played, spewing the virtues of Clabber Girl Baking Powder.

"Are you sure you heard my name, Ida May?" he asked.

"Your story about bread," she said. "It won."

"I didn't know you mailed in a story, Jeb. What was it about?" asked Fern.

"Did they say 'A Feast of Breakable Bread,' Ida May?" Jeb asked.

With all of them looking at Ida May, she pinched out her bottom lip and lifted her shoulders.

"Someone, give thanks," said Angel, "before we all blow away."

☙

The kids went back to school on Monday. Willie complained as he always did. Angel got to the end of the drive, but instead of leading Ida May up the road, she turned around and looked at the parsonage. Lucky, who had come out onto the porch, turned and took a step, as though she had been pacing and not watching them all leave for school. Angel lifted her fingers and let them move up and down like she was playing "Rise and Shine" on the schoolhouse piano. Lucky did not see her wave.

Angel had asked her about her school back in Hope. Lucky did not take to talking about school and books, so Angel asked her about her hair and how she braided it in so many braids. Angel's braids fell out. Lucky asked to fix her hair, but instead of braiding it, she combed it until Angel got tired of the combing.

"I forgot my lunch sack," said Ida May.

"It's here." Angel held it out to her.

"I feel sorry for Lucky," said Ida May.

"Not me. She gets to stay home and doesn't have to do arithmetic all night till her fingers bleed." Willie took off and left them. His friend from class had come out of the woods onto the road ahead.

Angel tolerated the morning, answering the teacher when she called on her. But she kept thinking about Lucky and Myrtle and how they came together like stars had joined them. By lunch bell the feeling of getting back into her school work had returned since the numbing Thanksgiving break. Through the classroom window she could see Ida May sitting on a rock, eating her mustard biscuit and wild turkey.

A boy tossed down a handful of marbles near her and two others joined him for a game. The girls that usually joined Ida May during the lunch hour played at the other end of the schoolyard. One of the boys said something to Ida May. She turned her back to him. The other two sat up, interested in whatever their buddy had started. Their skinny faces contorted and they took up where their friend had left off.

Ida May's head went down and her arms came up over her face.

Angel threw up the window glass. "You boys, what are you saying to my sister?"

The tallest boy, the marble proprietor, felt safe enough, a wall of window acting as a fortress between himself and Ida May's grown sister. He said, "We told her that her skin was going to turn dirty if she didn't stop hanging around those coloreds."

Angel picked up her books and left the classroom. She found Ida May on the playground alone and showing wet eyes. "Let's go home," she said. The boys had run off. Angel could throw a rock that far if she tried. "Let's go."

ॐ

Fern had gotten to the point of coming and going from the parsonage without knocking. She came through the front door, holding two sacks, the tops of two bread loaves hanging out. Her cheeks blushed from the cold. "Day-old bread from the Honeysacks and donuts and a canned ham. You want these in the kitchen?"

Before Jeb could answer, Lucky said, "I'll help you in with those things."

Ida May undressed a doll near the radio.

"I heard you came home early today, Ida May," said Fern. "Angel about?"

"Will sent a canned ham? It's not Christmas yet, is it?" asked Jeb.

"I threw in the ham."

"Donuts sounds good," said Lucky. She held Myrtle face out. The baby held up her head now.

Jeb called Angel from her room. She had not come out in two hours. Jeb saw the satchel under Fern's arm. "Schoolwork for truant children?"

"I don't blame the girls at all for leaving. These are a few assignments for Ida May. No need in allowing a few boys to interrupt her studies."

"You brought my arithmetic home?" asked Ida May.

"She's thrilled," said Jeb. He heard the sound of feet against the front porch. He opened the door.

A man dressed in a blue shirt and slacks asked, "Are you Mr. Jeb Nubey?" The man held out a telegram and an envelope. "Sign here and this stuff is all yours."

"Who is here?" Angel emerged.

Jeb thanked the man and brought in the telegram and envelope. He read the telegram while Fern worried over the delivery of bad news. "I won the essay contest." He pulled a check from the envelope. It was signed by the *American Dream* people in an amount large enough to buy a new set of truck tires.

⨍

Fern had been gone several hours. She had papers to grade and complained she had not slept well in over a week. Jeb had walked her to her car, but so had Ida May and Lucky.

Fern kissed his cheek and climbed into her car. Her smile did not come all the way across her face this time and that troubled Jeb. He felt like what he had asked of her had not been enough or too much and the pressure of those two poles tore at both of them. They had not been alone since Oz had found them at Fern's house, nearer to the consummation of their feelings than they had ever been.

He still did not know how Fern felt about that.

He sat on the couch with the *American Dream* check lying flat in his lap. He stared at the floor while the girls ran back and forth from the bedroom to the kitchen, sharing a glass of milk, and finishing the donuts until nothing was left but a bag gashed open and left empty on the kitchen table. Willie yelled at them to be quiet and finally, when Lucky took the baby into Jeb's room again for a peaceful rocking to sleep, the house grew silent.

The check gave Jeb a sense that certain possibilities ought to be considered. He could use the money to take Fern to Oklahoma and start off clean. If he paved the way with a letter from Philemon Gracie, then another church, perhaps one near the city, would hire him as pastor. He would allow men like Oz Mills and Frank Pella to take over Nazareth and let the smallness of the smaller minds drag it to the dogs.

A knock at the door startled him. He came to his feet, eager to quietly dismiss whoever had come at so late an hour before curiosity dragged four children into the quiet of his evening. He was surprised and opened the door. "Floyd and Evelene, do come in," he said.

Floyd folded his hat over so many times it would never return to its former shape. Neither he nor Evelene would take a seat.

The milk and donuts had disappeared, so Jeb apologized for having no refreshment to offer them.

"We're sorry to come so late, Reverend," said Floyd.

Evelene said nothing but kept looking through the door glass. They had left their automobile idling.

"Is this an official meeting?" Jeb asked, worn out from board member queries. He kept hoping Floyd would take a seat and stop shifting from one foot to the other.

"Evelene and I have been talking," said Floyd.

"Mostly Floyd's been talking. I've only been listening." She kept looking out the window and not at her husband.

When she talked and made that one statement, her inflection sounded pointed, although her voice never lost its gentility.

"What w-with all we have going on w-with the store and trying to k-keep our lives running throughout this Depression . . . ," he stammered, and that annoyed Evelene and she whispered about how she was sick of blaming things on the Depression.

Jeb took a seat even if Floyd wouldn't.

"I guess I have decided to resign from the elder board; that is, I'll give you some time to find a replacement."

"Reverend, I don't know about any of this," said Evelene.

"While we're at it, we're thinking of visiting the Lutheran church, up between here and Camden," said Floyd.

"We'd never fit in," said Evelene, but now she started sniffling and poking at her right eye as though she were trying to remove a speck.

"You're resigning, Floyd?" asked Jeb. "I understand. I also turn down your resignation."

"Oh, good." Evelene let out a big, satisfying sigh.

"It's the pressure of all that's going on, Reverend. You know all the board members got rocks throwed through the windows of our businesses. Next they'll be after our homes."

"Who is 'they,' Floyd? Do we know?" asked Jeb.

"I think it's that banking bunch, or at least the boys from Hope. I can't prove it, but even our own people don't like the reputation of our church being integrated."

"One teenage girl and a baby don't exactly constitute integration, Floyd."

"People get funny ideas."

"We help them get better ideas, Floyd."

"You can't change the way folks has been brought up. I

admit it. I don't like what you've done neither. I know what you're going to say, that what you're doing is Christlike. But things has been growing this direction in my head a long time. How can I change after all this time and feel good about it?"

"Sit down," said Jeb. He asked Evelene to go and turn off their idling engine.

Jeb excused himself. He went into the bedroom and took Myrtle from Lucky's arms. The baby had rocked Lucky to sleep.

Jeb walked Myrtle out to Floyd. Before Floyd could protest, he placed her in his arms. When Evelene came back inside, she laughed at her husband. "He won't even hold a grandchild yet, Reverend."

Jeb moved Floyd's hands in place and then back in place as he wobbled the baby around. "Look at her, Floyd. See, she's got a smile." Jeb pointed out her lashes, which were long and thick. He had Floyd count her fingers and then showed him her stomach and its soft, round arc. He handed Floyd a bottle and showed him how to feed her.

Myrtle turned toward Floyd and it made him flinch.

"She's reacting to your touch, human touch, Floyd. She hurts when she's lonesome, cries when her stomach is empty."

Myrtle latched onto the bottle nipple. She sucked a few times, batted her eyes, and then fell asleep.

Lucky slid out into the hallway. "Where's the baby?" She saw Floyd holding Myrtle.

"We'll put her to bed if that's okay with you, Lucky," said Evelene.

Lucky bid them a good-night.

"Change comes in strange ways, Floyd," said Jeb.

Floyd stroked the top of her head. "God forgive me," he whispered.

16

THE PARSONAGE HAD TOO MANY WINDOWS for winter. The wind seeped through and moisture gathered inside the glass, so much so that Willie made a game of breaking the ice off the parlor windows.

"You clean it up, Willie, or it'll melt on the floor!" said Angel.

"It gets dark too early," said Lucky. "I wish for longer days, don't you, Reverend?"

Jeb wrote in his sermon notebook and said, "Ten weeks of winter and then the days will come back to us." The winter had settled in too soon, but he would not complain in front of the kids. Meat had not been in the stew pot for a week and he worried over the cords of wood and whether they were too few.

Ida May's hair had grown to her waist, thin and silky like

a newborn colt's. Lucky braided it down her back and tied it pretty at the end with red silk. When she was done with the crafting of Ida May's hair, Lucky came to her feet, dragged a chair to the side window, and watched. If her brother had returned, Jeb had not seen him. She made no mention of him, but Jeb saw the way she craned her neck toward the woods, especially before sunset.

Angel glanced into the parlor, saw Lucky, but then pursed her lips, like she might consider something different to say. She folded her arms in front of her and then asked Ida May and Willie to take a turn at peeling potatoes.

Jeb scribbled another note in his notebook and sneezed into his handkerchief. He had not fully recovered since Thanksgiving, only good enough to maintain a steady course and hate the sight of daylight.

The falling sun, the deepening borders of sky weighing down the horizon, all of it seemed to pull Lucky down with it. She sighed. Jeb put down his pen and said, "I'd like to know something about Jewel. What are the differences in your ages?"

"Six years. Jewel is twenty and Ruben is eighteen. My mother said that she had them too close together, that Ruben took up her time and Jewel went wild," she said. "Everyone in the family knows that Jewel would go her own way no matter what. Momma likes to have things to blame, is all."

"Jewel dropped off your things that day. Has she ever been to Nazareth before?"

"Far as I know, it was her first time here. She don't have no business in Nazareth. Her business is where her men are."

"Her business, as in her work?"

"Her work is something else entirely." Lucky turned

around in the chair and faced Jeb. "You think I mean she sleeps with men for money. Her business is, you know, her life. She makes money keeping up laundry for rich ladies. Then she spends it all at bars."

"Did she know Frank Pella?"

"Why you want to talk about him? He no good. He don't have no business in Nazareth neither. He should stay back where he belong."

"How do you know him?"

Lucky turned back toward the window. "The sun's gone. You want me to fetch you a sweater, Reverend?" A slice of Willie's ice had hardened fast to the glass. She tried to scrape it with her nail.

"Frank is no good, you said."

"Not worth talking about."

"Enough about him, then."

Lucky got up and crossed the parlor to join the others in fixing supper.

ॐ

Jeb was relieved to finally hear out of both ears and to walk around without feeling as though his head would explode, especially during the Sunday sermon. He preached, went home, went to bed, and got up Monday, the first Monday since Thanksgiving that was clear of sleet pebbling the window.

Lucky stayed home with Myrtle and he dropped off the Welbys at school. He drove downtown to pick up a newspaper and drink Beulah's coffee, hotter than he could make it and, for his sore throat, a relief.

"I seen you coming, Reverend, and I got your cup ready," Beulah said. "God help those poor puffy eyes of yours."

Jeb took his cup and sat in a booth instead of at the bar. "Nothing to eat," he told her.

He read the front page of the *Nazareth Gazette,* a piece about how families celebrated Christmas in Europe next to an editorial about the rise of Germany's enigmatic leader, Adolf Hitler. The United States' sanctions imposed on foreign trade had been relegated to the back page.

Jeb pulled out a letter from his brother Charlie, learned that he was once again an uncle, only this time by their younger sister in Temple, Texas. He remembered to smile occasionally at Beulah to keep his coffee warmed.

The diner's quiet resonance could not be overcome, it seemed, even by the enticement of a Monday blue plate special advertised out on the sidewalk. Jeb read the sign before returning to his paper.

The clipped walk of the banker's nephew made him sigh. Oz Mills ferried the mail down the walk and in to Val Rodwyn, who kept the mail flowing in the Honeysack's General Store.

"I hear you won an essay contest." The voice came from behind Jeb, a man seated in the adjoining booth addressed him in a gentle manner.

Jeb turned and offered a handshake, polite and fast so he could return to the coffee and the news. "I surprise myself sometimes."

"Reverend Alexander, from the Lutheran church. We're on the other side of town from you."

Jeb fumbled through the paper, turning the pages.

"I read it in the Sunday paper from Hot Springs last week," he said. "Going to speak at the Lincoln Memorial, it said. Sounds 'big time.'"

"It's a modest event, I believe, and won't take place until the summer. Would you happen to have that newspaper on you?"

"Wife used it to line the garbage can." The Lutheran minister laughed. "You trying to fix the South, I hear."

"Not the whole South," said Jeb. "Not even a fixing of any kind." He invited the minister to join him at his booth, if only to keep the conversation private.

Reverend Alexander got up and took a seat across from Jeb.

"I've come by two more children that aren't mine. I'd be more interested in finding them a home than fixing anything. There's this girl that I'd like to marry and I have too many kids around."

The Lutheran laughed.

"I'm not much good at fixing matters, it seems. Not that I wouldn't wish I could."

"But you wrote an essay."

"I was mad, that's all."

"Apparently it got someone's attention."

Jeb wanted Alexander to lower his voice, but he didn't know him well enough to ask. He lowered his own voice. "If anyone around here knows about the essay, well, it wouldn't matter to them. I don't bring it up." He could not tell if the Lutheran comprehended what he was saying or not.

"You're stuck in the middle of something, not of your own making."

"That's it exactly."

"You'd rather be fishing."

"I would. I would."

"Is the girl pretty?"

"No one prettier. I think sometimes that I could just blow off this town and take her out of here."

"She wouldn't go?"

"Fern has too much character."

The Lutheran kept laughing, and every now and then, he would say how much he liked Jeb and the way he looked at things.

"Let me buy you coffee sometime, Alexander," said Jeb.

"I will. Beulah, bring him your biscuits. The man's stomach is talking."

Before Jeb could stop the biscuits, two lay on a hot plate in front of him. He didn't know he was hungry until he ate the first one. He thanked the minister.

The bell over the door tinkled. Oz Mills bellied up to the coffee bar. If he saw Jeb, he didn't say anything.

Jeb folded up the newspaper and gave his last biscuit to the Lutheran. "There's a man I need to see and that's him at the bar."

"You should pop the question, ask this Fern to marry you," said Alexander. "Maybe she'd say yes now."

Oz's head turned slightly, like his ear had picked up a radio wave.

"I'll see you around, Reverend," said Jeb. He rose from the booth and took several steps to sit one stool away from Oz. Their eyes met in the mirror above Beulah's workstation.

"Morning, Nubey," said Oz.

To the best of Jeb's recollection, Oz had never addressed him as Reverend. Jeb talked about the cold weather, his head cold, and, finally, the upcoming Christmas social at the church.

Oz let out a sigh.

Jeb moved to the next stool. "Oz, I know something's

gone on between the Blessed girls and that group of cronies you hang out with."

"I don't know the Blesseds."

"Jewel Blessed. From Hope."

Oz laid his money on the counter and thanked Beulah for the coffee.

"Something transpired the day that Frank Pella attacked Lucky Blessed."

"You have it backward and I don't run in those circles. I knew of the Blesseds. What can I say? They're not of my ilk."

"Has Frank Pella ever known Jewel Blessed, as in, has he ever had the chance to be alone with her? Has he ever obsessed over her?"

"You're headed downriver, Nubey. As usual, no paddle." Oz slid off the stool and pulled on his overcoat. Before he pushed the door open, he said, "Your church is falling apart. Maybe you ought to tend to things that you can fix."

᠅

Angel lay stomach down to write a school paper.

Lucky swept the floor, leaning into the broom to chase the dust from the floor cracks. She dabbed at the ceiling with the broom straw, executing a spider.

The sky marbled and the cold settled all around the parsonage, moaning through the attic. Angel buttoned her sweater up all the way to the neck. Lucky rubbed her arms and looked through the parlor window and up at the sky.

"Two more days and we're out of school. I guess you don't miss it," said Angel.

Lucky swept dust into a pan.

"I kind of like writing. Reading's my best subject. You ever think about reading?"

Lucky let out a breath.

"I taught Jeb to read."

"He know you tell people that?"

"Nothing wrong with saying it."

Lucky put the broom against the corner wall.

"I could teach you to read, if you want," said Angel.

"Maybe you think I'm dumber than a sack of hammers."

Angel stared at Lucky. She shifted from one foot to the other and then said, "I don't think that."

Lucky pulled a book out of Jeb's library. She threw open the book and slowly read from it:

As I walked through the wilderness of this world, I lighted on a certain place where was a den, and I laid me down in that place to sleep: and as I slept, I dreamed a dream. I dreamed, and behold, I saw a man clothed with rags, standing in a certain place, with his face from his own house, a book in his hand, and a great burden upon his back. I looked, and saw him open the book, and read therein; and as he read, he wept, and trembled; and, not being able longer to contain, he brake out with a lamentable cry, saying, "What shall I do?"

Angel lifted up off the floor with both hands, brought her feet forward, and came seated.

"Mr. Bunyan's got hisself a nice way with words." Lucky closed up the book and slid it back onto the shelf.

"Lucky, I'm sorry. I didn't know you could read."

"My father, in spite of his ways, made sure that his kids could read. But how you talk to other people, like the way you talk down to me, is not because you learned to read. It's from not knowing how others might see the world differently from you. I think they call that ignorance, but you can check the dictionary on that count." She spelled "ignorance."

Angel picked up her pencil.

Lucky picked up her broom and chased invisible things from the wall corners.

"I know I'm not perfect, Lucky."

"It's a good thing you know it. The way you hold your cup would make the queen turn whiter than she already is."

Angel laughed. "You know the queen?"

"We're chums, me and Queeny." Lucky waltzed into the kitchen and back out into the parlor. She turned on the radio. An orchestral piece played. "Come here," she told Angel. She held out her hands. "You got to move, one, two, three, without stepping on a boy's feet."

It was time to commence supper preparations. Instead, they danced.

༚

Ruben Blessed left his father's old Ford parked back in the woods. He had borrowed it saying that Jewel needed his help making all her laundry deliveries. Jewel let him make a delivery so it would not be a lie.

Ruben hung a lantern in the tree. He looked toward the minister's house and waited to see if Lucky would look out and see him. He could see movement through the window curtains. The moon hung high in the west, but not bright enough to give away his whereabouts.

A car slowed up at the main road. Ruben doused the lantern and stepped back into the woods. The sound of feet running, of limbs swishing, caught his breath. He went all the way down on the cold forest bed. Wet leaves soaked through his clothes.

He heard a voice like a young man's. Two young fellows ran past him. They stole a look into the parsonage window. Whoever had been moving around inside did not see the young men. The boys crouched down and crept back up the tree line all the way to the car.

Ruben saw a rope hanging from a tree. He untied it and retied it to the bottom of the trunk. He crouched down and his hand felt steel. He had brought his tire iron in case he ran into a dirty rat.

He could see inside the house past an opening through the window drapes. Lucky and some girl twirled around the room. The two of them laughed like girls do when they think they are alone.

The two young men ran back from the road. The moon shone off something one of them held, like polished metal. He was not sure about anything except that they aimed straight for the parsonage.

He saw the face of one as he ran past. He pulled the rope and the boys sprawled onto the forest bed, things clattering out of their hands.

"I know you," said Ruben. He took him out, laying the tire iron to the side of his head, his aim hitting sweet-as-you-please against his temple before the young man could react.

The other one ran for the road. He drove away and left his buddy lying on his face in the woods.

The curtains parted. The girls looked out, but they did not see Ruben. He was running back into the woods to find his daddy's old car and drive home.

17

JEB WAITED OUTSIDE THE LIBRARY, HAPPY THAT he had canceled the Sunday-evening service for Christmas. The librarian took both Christmas wreaths off the doors to take home on the eve of the holy day. His watch said a quarter after five, the time Fern said she would be finished at the library. She met the librarian, who was a friend of hers, to help her with some gifts for her family. Fern had hidden them at her house.

Loaded with ribboned boxes, the librarian came down the steps.

Fern had told Jeb that she would drop by the parsonage and help Angel and Lucky start the holiday dinner, like the pumpkin pie crusts and the special dishes that could be made up early.

Jeb told the girls to start the dough on their own, that he

would surprise Fern and pick her up at the library. He had Evelene Whittington wrap a locket for her in her better Christmas wrap. He wanted to give it to her without the pack looking on.

The door opened and Oz Mills came out the door, walking backward and talking. Fern followed him out.

Jeb stared, not able to breathe or move.

Oz kept touching her arm. He said something that made her laugh.

Jeb came to himself. He turned to head back to Front Street, where he had left the truck parked. He had gone a half block when he heard Fern call his name. He stopped halfway between Front Street and the library, right outside Lincoln's Barbershop.

"I thought that was you."

By the time he turned around, Oz was nowhere in sight. He wanted to tell her that he had come to surprise her and that he obviously had caught her by surprise. But the sight of her made him forget altogether what he was thinking of saying. She wore something red and the skirt of the thing blew around her knees, exposing her kneecaps. The cold made her stand funny, like her kneecaps almost faced one another. She crouched a bit, bending, and her bottom stuck out.

"You look pretty," he said.

"Oz Mills was here."

"What do you have to say about that?"

"All of my Christmas stuff, the presents, the things I want to cook for you, that's all in my car. We can come back for your truck?" She held out her keys like she knew Jeb would come and take the keys from her and drive her back to his place. He opened the door for her and she sidled in and he shut the door on her red skirt. She opened it and fixed her dress and looked up at him and laughed. She closed her own door.

Jeb climbed into the driver's seat. "It's noisy back at my place," he said.

"If we go to my place, I'll want to—"

When she stopped, Jeb said, "I want to too."

Fern came across the seat. "Happy Christmas, honey." She kissed Jeb.

He slid out from under the steering wheel. "Oz didn't kiss you or anything, did he?"

She drew back enough to say, "He met a woman. They want to elope." She pulled Jeb's arms around her.

"Did you tell him he should do that?"

"I told him not to come to me anymore for my approval."

"I love you, Fern. Let's go to your place and do what we shouldn't do."

Her face pulled away from his. "Drive, Jeb."

Jeb turned on the ignition and drove past the bank, circled back, and headed for Marvelous Crossing.

Fern's head lay against his shoulder. She kept rubbing his leg and talking about how long she had waited for them to be together. The moon looked like a disk, a pendulum hung in the air for Christmas Eve.

"I'll have you all to myself." She laughed. "Look, Nazareth, Jeb and Fern, finally together! Let's give them something to gossip about. You and me and no one to stop us."

"You and me," said Jeb. Her words "all to myself" stuck inside him like an ax in a stump. The headlights shone across the bridge ahead. His foot came off the gas pedal. The car slowed. He braked and stopped them right in the middle of Marvelous Crossing Bridge.

"What's wrong?" she asked.

The picture of Fern and him overflowed with too many other faces. Erasing all but two was hopeless. "You and me, Fern, and a hungry baby," he said. He waited for her to respond, but her smile thinned and she kept quiet. "Plus two teenage girls, a young girl, and a boy who wants to grow up to be like a dad who abandoned him."

Fern turned and looked out over the water. White Oak Lake reflected the moon in pieces, a winter wind blowing ripples across the disk and slicing it up.

"I can't give you anything you ask, Fern. Not a place of our own or time for just the two of us."

"I don't think I've asked for a thing." She stroked his arm.

Both of them stared into the dark waters.

He started up the engine. "This is not the life I want for us, Fern. We can't be alone, not really. The thing of it is, I want you all to myself too." He turned the wheel after passing over the bridge and drove past Long's Pond and her cottage and toward the parsonage.

Fern cried.

Jeb never knew how to tend to Fern's tears. He drove them to the parsonage and parked. He climbed out and yelled for Willie and Ida May to come out into the yard. "Come bring in Miss Coulter's Christmas bags," he told them.

Fern reached down into the floor to fidget with some invisible object and to hide her wet eyes. She kept her head down until Willie and Ida May ran back inside, hugging her bags. When her head came up, she banged it against the dashboard.

Jeb opened her door and held his hand out to her. "Are you all right?"

She got out on her own. She walked past him.

"I made you mad."

"You did the right thing, didn't you?" She stopped at the foot of the steps. "Don't you always do the right thing, Jeb Nubey?" She went inside.

The moon had not dimmed or even clouded over. Jeb hated the sight of it. He grabbed the last bag and felt against his trousers' pocket for her keys. His fingers struck against a small package. He had forgotten to give her the box with the locket.

Fern lingered dutifully. She finished pies and made sweet potatoes and put them in the icebox to keep for Christmas Day.

Jeb waited in the kitchen for some moment when she might incline her ear to allow him to explain what happened out on the bridge.

Angel and Lucky never left the kitchen at the same time. The evening gave plenty of reason for levity, a reason to test food and eat sugar cookie batter and tease Ida May about St. Nick.

"I heard Frank Pella was at the bank sometime this week and someone bashed his face," said Angel. "I'd like to have seen it for myself."

"Someone got tired of that boy and give him what he needed." Lucky rolled out the cookie dough. "You got any gumdrops?"

"On the table," said Fern.

"Why you hate him so much?" asked Angel.

"You going to ruin Christmas with that kind of talk." Lucky rolled out the gumdrops and cut them into shapes.

"I never seen that done," said Angel. Lucky demonstrated how her grandmother had taught her to roll gumdrops out for cookie decorations.

Fern gazed into the cake batter, not as much interested as staring beyond it.

"Miss Coulter has to give me a ride back to my truck, girls. You keep up the work and I'll be back."

Fern looked surprised. "I thought we would go after the truck tomorrow."

"Tonight's better."

"I think I'd rather go home tonight. Today's worn me out."

Jeb saw how she wouldn't look at him. He got up and put on his coat. "Wouldn't want to bother you with a trip into town Christmas Day, Fern."

"He wants to get Miss Coulter alone, like lovers," said Willie.

Lucky said "whoo-ooo!" while Angel told Willie to shut up.

Fern pulled her coat off the chair back and finally looked at Jeb, her face not as smooth and happy as when she came out of the library. The silent stroll from the kitchen, across the parlor, and out into the cold yard made it even harder for Jeb to speak. Fern asked for her keys.

"You going to leave me standing here, stranded?" Jeb asked.

"I feel like driving, that's all. You can get in."

They rode down the church drive, driving the two miles to the lake, and over Marvelous Crossing.

Ice formed on the windshield.

"I guess I'm a fool for messing up our evening."

"You made me feel like I was throwing myself at you."

"I want you to throw yourself at me, that's the honest truth. It's all I think about. You probably think I sit around drumming up spiritual truths. I don't. I have to ask forgiveness for the things I think about you."

"You think about me all the time?"

"Only when I'm awake. Otherwise I just dream about you. I think about how you watch me from the pew and I'm careful not to mangle doctrine, because I know you'll know. I think of how you smell like clean linens drying in the sun and flowers on the windowsill, and I don't know how you do that in the winter," he said.

Fern trembled.

"I remember how you taught me to think about things that I hadn't thought about before. When I write, I find myself rewording every sentence because when you read it, I want it to sound just right on your lips. You make me better than I should be. I like me better when I see me through your eyes. I hate me worse when I make you cry."

She parked behind his truck.

"Hold on." He ran around to her side of the car. He looked up at the moon. Clouds covered all but a thin slice of silver. Jeb opened her door.

Fern's feet came out, one at a time, and she got out. Jeb pulled out the box. "This is not the big gift, the one I want to give you when all of this chaos goes away."

Fern held out her hand. "It's snowing."

Jeb handed her the box.

"You have to know things about me, Jeb. I love you in the middle of the chaos. When I'm with you, the chaos goes away. In the middle of all of the clatter, you sing. I can welcome a bad day because of you." She opened the rear door and pulled out a heavy box. "Mine's not the big gift either."

Jeb hefted the box. "It feels like books."

"For your library."

He set the gift on the street.

"I don't care what's inside my box," she said. "You've already given me what I wanted." She looked at her ring, kissed Jeb, and the snow fell. The night had lost its moon. Snow cast its own net for lovers. They sought warmth, one against the other.

※

The last week of December did not bring any better weather along with it. Angel caught the next cold and prayed God to take it from her, but it lingered, settling in her throat and lungs.

Fern moved Angel to her place to get well on hot soup and tea with honey. Angel allowed it, along with Fern's steady attention to a chest poultice while maintaining her own usual posture of pride.

Two days before New Year's Eve, Jeb restrung his banjo. He had nearly played it to death over Christmas. The picking soothed Myrtle, quieting her before Lucky took her to bed.

Lucky let Myrtle fall asleep in the middle of the floor, the center bloom of an old quilt. Frost formed all over the windows in the shape of winter flakes. The baby lay sprawled, holding a spoon in one hand, like she fell asleep waiting for dinner.

Lucky went out back to take a dip of snuff.

Someone knocked at the door.

Myrtle's spoon hand fidgeted. Her lips pursed, shiny, as though she anticipated that Belinda might descend in her dreams to bring succor from heaven.

Jeb opened the door in as quiet a manner as possible. "Reverend Williamson, come in."

"I come to check on Lucky and that baby." His voice quavered at the end of his sentences.

"Baby's growing in spite of the fact our wet nurse quit on us. She had bigger fish to fry, according to her."

"I expect so."

"Some of us are getting over sickness, what with the wet weather."

"I hate all this snow and sleet. You better keep that baby inside. Children is coming down with awful things these days." The preacher saw Myrtle and he grinned. "Lucky anywhere's around?"

"She'll be in soon."

"Has she told you anything about her family, Reverend Nubey?"

"Told me about her sister, Jewel, and Ruben. I think he drops by, but he doesn't come in," said Jeb.

"Her brother has a thing about whites. I don't think he approves of her living among the whites, not that he has anything against you. Ruben's had run-ins and not all of them his fault entirely."

The kitchen door slammed closed.

"Ruben's welcome in our home, same as Lucky."

Lucky peered from the kitchen, and then she disappeared. The sound of water running in the kitchen ensued.

Jeb told her that her minister had dropped by. "She's getting some water," he said to the minister.

Lucky ran into the parlor and grabbed Williamson around the shoulders. He hugged her back and she pulled up a chair next to him.

"You keeping yourself well, girl. Your folks will have to climb a ladder to kiss you if you get much taller."

"Baby's holding up her head and smiling when you look at her."

"They do that, don't they?" said Williamson.

Unlike most girls, Lucky spent the entire conversation talking about the baby instead of herself. Williamson answered and asked her further questions and she talked like she was the baby expert. In the parsonage that would be true.

"I brought fresh salt pork for your New Year's dinner." Williamson held up a sack.

"Black-eyed peas and salt pork. Why everybody cook that on the first of the year anyway?" asked Lucky.

"Luck," said Jeb.

"Reverend is right," said Williamson.

Lucky took the sack into the kitchen.

Jeb leaned toward Williamson and said, "Any reason to believe Jewel Blessed has any ties to this baby?"

"You sharp as a tack, Preacher Nubey."

Lucky came back.

Jeb waited while Williamson and Lucky said their goodbyes.

"We'll talk again soon?" Jeb wanted him to stay.

"Come see me at my church. We'll talk some more."

He put on his hat and said farewell to Jeb. "You an agent of the Lord, Reverend Nubey."

જી

"I can't believe it's another year gone past us," said Fern. She sliced the salt pork and dropped it into the pot of peas.

Jeb gave her everything for the dinner. Angel sat up on Fern's couch now. The pink circles under her eyes gave her the look of a rabbit.

Will and Freda pulled up outside. Freda carried sweet rolls through the front door. Freda had invited her neighbors to come and wanted to know if that was all right.

"More the merrier, Freda," said Fern. She took Freda's rolls.

"They'll be another few minutes or so," said Freda. "They've made up a mess of catfish."

Jeb helped them off with their coats.

"That baby's almost as big as you, Ida May," said Freda.

Ida May rocked Myrtle while the others cooked.

"She's only three months, come the tenth," said Lucky. "I think she'll be getting her teeth soon."

"What's her birthday again, Lucky?" asked Jeb.

"October tenth."

Freda helped Fern cut up the corn bread for cooling.

Jeb stared at Lucky. She turned and left the room.

18

Jeb waited for Lucky to make up the bottles for the day on Friday. She needed enough formula to feed Myrtle until he could return in the evening with more of Doctor Forrester's special formula. He told her only that he would be gone for the day and to see to supper. He took along his banjo to see if the new strings he ordered at Honeysack's store would work.

Lucky did not ask him why he would be gone all day. She watched him leave without saying a whole lot of anything.

Jeb drove out of Nazareth. The morning chill never left the inside of the truck cab, even after he had been driving for thirty minutes. A big sign shaped like a watermelon and painted red and green advertised a farmer's market from at least two seasons ago. The red had turned pale pink in the sun and the black seeds had grayed. The watermelon fields grayed too, swirls of dust ghosting through the fields, with nothing rising unless it had first met a disintegrated state.

Jeb drove past a boarded-up church. A child's bicycle frame lay out in front of the church, the tires taken some time ago. Someone had painted across a board: ASHES TO ASHES AND DUST TO DUST, HEADED FOR CALIFORNY OR BUST.

The Hope City Limits sign had a skirt of grass grown up around the post.

He made a stop to feed his truck with a little more gas. He asked the filling-station attendant how to go about finding Mt. Zion Church. The man told him to stay on the highway and take a right on a street named Lowell. "Go right on that road into colored town and you'll see their church on the left."

Jeb followed the highway and turned on Lowell. The neighborhood had taken a beating. Tin replaced roof shingles. One building's architecture suggested it started out as a house, but the sign nailed on the front said MT. ZION CHURCH, and underneath it read MERCY FOR THE DOWNTRODDEN.

Mt. Zion Church bloomed at the culverts of those dried fields.

A ladies' choir rehearsed a song about heaven. Jeb wanted to march, but, as a guest, he kept his feet still. They might take offense. A soloist led the women and they echoed her chorus, a rising and falling of voices of an oceanic quality. Her blue sleeves rose and fell along with the undulating vocals, the sound coming out of the choir was like strings pulled by her fingertips. The ladies' mouths formed into faultless, open ovals. The ladies' swaying gave the choir loft a tidal feeling, a swelling from the bottom octave rising into the eaves. The chief singer clapped her hands and those women stopped, not moving so much as a toenail.

"Mister, you looking for someone?" she said to Jeb.

"Reverend Williamson, if I'm in the right place."

A woman whose cotton-white hair pillowed around her temples and cheeks laughed.

"Sister Williamson, you want to tell this man where he can find your dear husband," said the choir director.

The cotton-haired woman pointed way left and Jeb followed her signal into a short corridor. At the end of the hall, a sign read MINISTER'S STUDY. Jeb knocked in a gentle manner. The door came open a hair.

A row of candles lighted along a primitive altar blazed in front of Reverend Williamson. He prayed in that light facedown. His shoulders shuddered.

Jeb removed his hat. He took a chair a few feet away from the minister to wait for him to finish his morning prayers.

"Father, help my people. They going through some business that I can't fix for them." Williamson spoke trancelike, his voice coming from the floor like a man hunkered down in a trench. "Evil is dwelling in our land. We don't know which way to turn, so we turn to you, Savior." His fingers stroked the threads on the rug as though he gathered scattered grain into his palms. "Help us to forgive them who throw stones at our children. Show mercy to men who torch our houses and take our little girls for evil deeds." His left arm stretched out behind him. His fingers waved in Jeb's direction like a man giving the all clear.

Jeb bowed his head. He came down on one knee and then knee-walked until he reached Williamson's altar. He felt like the new man crawling into the trench, dumb to yesterday's blood on the ground; still, he whispered, "God, you made your life breakable so that we could eat from its bread. Make us breakable bread and then show us how to feed others."

"Yes. Make our life a feast for hungry lives," said Williamson.

Jeb prayed for God to give his people more love. Williamson prayed for God to give his people more grace.

Williamson's hand rested on top of Jeb's hand.

Jeb cried. Williamson slid him a handkerchief. Jeb didn't care if he knew.

ᘒ

"I'd fix your coffee for you, but Louie says I don't cream his enough," said Jaunice Williamson. She gave both men black coffee. "You got to hear our women's chorus, Reverend Nubey. We got a nice sound, don't we?"

Jeb told her, "I might have joined you, but you would've asked me to quit, right off."

Jaunice had changed from her better dress into a house-dress. "I hope you don't mind fried chicken legs. We out of the other." She retied her apron. "Our daughter and her six live with us, and we run clean out of food by the weekend."

"You got that dough rising, Jaunice. Make him up some bread. He's our guest," said Williamson. "She cooks all the time. Company gives her a way to show off."

Jaunice halved boiled eggs over a dish and creamed the yolks with mustard and pickle relish.

"Call me Louie," he said. "We're both clergy."

"Of course, and call me Jeb. I hoped we could talk some more about the Blessed family."

"I knew that was coming," said Jaunice.

"Woman, keep to your kitchen chores," said Louie. He kept his voice to a tender level.

"You in my kitchen. You respect me, beloved." She could smile without moving her face.

"My apologies, dearest." Louie let out a breath. "Jeb, the Blesseds have pride, John especially. He's Lucky's daddy. Growing up black means you got to fight to hold on to things like self-respect. John takes it to degrees that is hard on a girl like Lucky. He held that little girl's feet to the fire so long, he might never get her back. Same with her sister, Jewel."

"Jewel lives in town."

"She and another girl rent a shack outside town. Jewel don't have the kind of money to get herself anything better. Worst of all, that place is only a mile up the road from the High Cotton Club."

Jaunice let out some kind of undefinable noise, like air seeping from a tire.

"It's not a real club like in the city, or one of them places operating over in Hot Springs. They high rollers over there. This is a small-potatoes club. Wayne Jackson took an old cotton house and put in a bar and a jukebox and named it a club. They got poker and gin. Lots of men looking for girls, like Jewel and her friend Colleen, who need a free meal and their beer paid for and a body to dance with."

"What did she do with Lucky nights?"

"That's the question of the hour, Jeb."

"Jewel left her sister and went honky-tonking," said Jaunice. "That's what!"

"I'll tell it, beloved. Lucky is a good girl. She is a lot like her mother, that one. Maybe that's why John and Lucky had so much trouble. Vera is strong-minded. Lucky and Jewel fought every night Jewel and Colleen went out that door."

Jaunice slid a plate in front of Jeb.

"Can't tell you the last time I had fried chicken and potato salad," said Jeb.

Jaunice gave them both a look of pure examination. "I'll eat mine in the parlor. You men about to get into some things, I can tell." Jaunice gave her husband a sideways glance.

"I'm not divulging, Jaunice, not what I can't divulge," he told her. "My pumpkin forgets she can trust me," Louie said to Jeb.

"I understand you feel a need to protect the Blessed girls," said Jeb. "What *can* you tell me?"

"How about I tell you how to get down to the High Cotton Club? Long about seven this evening, Wayne Jackson will bring in a live band. You play the banjo. If I was you, I'd act like I was there to meet the musicians."

"Banjo's in my truck."

"If you talk their talk, they'll give you a chair to listen. If you see a thin, pretty black girl, a scar on her left cheek, hair tied up with a flower, that's Jewel. She'll come prancing in, wearing a fur."

"It's fake fur." Jaunice leaned out of her chair to say it.

"Big gold earrings. Bangles all up and down her wrists. She knows how to get attention."

"Jewel might talk to me about Myrtle?"

Jaunice huffed. Both her feet lifted—heels down, toes up.

"See if she brings up the subject," said Louie. "I'm not saying she'll tell you everything. John Blessed still has control of his girls even if they're no longer under his roof. That family has its own code. Only way she'll ever tell you anything is by winning her trust."

"Code, my foot!" said Jaunice.

~

Daylight lingered, a pale blue January sky near the color of twilight. The moon's surface could almost be made out, a watery blue and pale. The lights of the High Cotton Club flickered like swamp mosquitoes against the sunset. The club's name shone in bright white letters on a blue background. Neon pink cursive spelled out Wayne Jackson's name above the club name and a silhouette of a cheek-to-cheek dancing couple hung off the sign, fastened by iron rings.

A guitar player swayed through a back door, hugging his instrument case. He and someone unseen clapped hands. Another fellow came right behind him, carrying two sets of drumsticks. Both men wore dark fedoras and the second wore a vest the color of orange rind.

Jeb picked up his banjo case and approached the door.

A man whose size filled the doorway raised his chin. He stared down at Jeb. "What you doing here?"

"Wayne Jackson hired a band, didn't he?" Jeb's face lost all feeling except for a tingling around his ears that reminded him of a beating he had taken as a boy.

"I'm Wayne Jackson." The voice came from behind Jeb. "But I don't know you."

The bouncer dislodged himself from the doorframe. "Want me to remove the white boy, Wayne?"

Wayne Jackson was dressed in dark trousers, something like navy blue but it could have been black. The blue shirt he wore covered his belly like a tent. No jacket off the rack could have fit those shoulders.

The guitar player stepped sideways into the doorway, twisting the keys, making eye contact with the white interloper. He looked Jeb up and down and then said something to one of the men inside.

Jeb wanted to send a signal to the guitar picker, a code shared by musicians, something that said that musicians don't let other musicians get dropped off a bridge or tied to a train track.

"Is that a banjo?" the guitar player asked.

Jeb fumbled for the case. He flipped open the latch and pulled the banjo out by the neck.

"Joe, we got us a banjo picker," he said.

The bouncer looked disappointed.

Wayne Jackson and the band leader, a guy everyone called Joe Geronimo, discussed the set. Jeb stuck out his hand and nearly inaudibly thanked the guitar player for saving his hide.

"Joe's been moaning about a banjo player. Here you show up. It was like magic." He introduced himself as Harry.

"Harry, I'm Jeb." Jeb could not add a lie on top of his arcane presence with a false name.

"We do dance numbers, at least that's what we do at the High Cotton Club. That's all these people want, at least. You trying out for the band?"

Jeb had not gotten up the nerve yet to talk to Joe, so he kept talking so that only Harry could hear. "I'm not really here to join the band."

"Don't tell that to Wayne Jackson."

"Do you know a girl named Jewel Blessed?"

"This is only my second time to play this club. Maybe ask Daniel. He's our drummer. He's from around here." Harry initiated their meeting, talking quietly to Daniel before backing up and allowing Jeb into their circle.

"Daniel, nice to meet you," said Jeb.

"Jeb, let me give you a one, two, three, and then, Harry, you do some riffs, and then banjo man here will take us into the night. Jeb, you do know jazz banjo, right?"

"I can pick some jazz," said Jeb. He felt idiotic trying to talk jazz with real musicians.

Daniel let out a whoop and tore into his drums like a man driving bats from the rafters.

Jeb picked up the key from Harry and hung with them on the song.

The waitresses listened outside the kitchen doors.

Wayne Jackson mouthed to Joe, *"White boy can play a'ight."*

Joe picked up the bass guitar and took a spot opposite Jeb.

Car lights flooded the front windows. Evening sunk the daylight into a corner pocket and the High Cotton Club opened for business.

Several women slinked in together, threads of purple and blue, grouped like fillies at auction and sharing lights off one another's cigarettes.

The club had yet to see the likes of Jewel Blessed.

৵

"Where'd you get him?" a young woman talked Joe up during the break. Her black dress and the amethyst jewelry around her throat gave her a starlinglike quality.

"Jeb, meet Colleen," said Joe.

Jeb set down his banjo and stuck out his hand.

She took hold of his fingers with both hands, like she planned to hold on for a while. "You play good banjo, Jeb," she said. "Want to buy me my very own glass of gin?"

"My money can't buy gin anymore," he said. "You live around the club, Colleen?"

"You're kind of fast, aren't you, already checking out where I stay?"

"Colleen, stop hitting on Jeb. This man's about to get hisself engaged," said Harry. "Ain't that right?"

"I've got a girl," said Jeb. "Pretty as they come."

"Better-looking than me?"

"You're at least as pretty. Too pretty to come here alone."

"You ain't my daddy and I ain't alone. My friend is parking the car. Hey, Wayne, you need to make more parking room. Jewel had to park halfway down the street," she told the owner. She turned back to Jeb and said, "That's her coming through the door now."

Jewel Blessed owned the floor. Two women turned away when she walked through the doorway, ladies who had danced every dance, but they made way when Jewel showed up. Jewel wore a fur, just like Louie had said. It fell open, revealing a green dress that shook with sequins and beads. Her neckline dipped and she let the coat fall off one shoulder so the dress could have its best showing.

"You, banjo man, take your break for this first set's opener," said Joe. "It's a slow number."

Jeb propped the banjo against the wall. "Colleen, introduce me to your friend."

"Why? You're engaged." Before she could walk away, Jeb took her by the arm. He pulled out some cash and put it in her hand.

"You're strange, aren't you?" Colleen smiled anyway and took the money. She led him to the table in the back of the room.

Jewel glanced at Colleen and then at Jeb. Part of Jewel's

hair fell across her face, Jeb figured, to hide the scar. She pushed the other side of her hair back with a flowered comb.

"This man wants to meet you, Jewel."

Jewel told Jeb right off, "I ain't no whore."

"Jewel, I'm Jeb Nubey."

Jewel waved Colleen away.

Jeb sat across from her. "I thought we could talk about Lucky."

"You give my sister room and board. She works for you. I don't have no say anymore in what she does."

"I visited your minister this afternoon," said Jeb.

"My mother's minister." She laughed. "I don't guess I have no minister. What's wrong anyway, is Lucky in trouble?"

"I hate to see her taking care of a baby at her age. Sure be nice to find the mother."

"What did Louie Williamson tell you?"

"Nothing. I told him I wanted to speak with you. He sent me here."

"Where I go is none of that man's business. He thinks he knows me."

"Maybe he does."

"He blames me for Lucky's problems. But I ain't the blame. Ruben, he's as much at fault as anyone."

"Your brother is Ruben. Where does Ruben live?"

"He stay at our mother and father's house. They spoil that boy."

"Why Ruben? Why is he to blame?"

"After Daddy made me leave, he thought he got rid of all the family trash. That's what he calls me. One night Ruben and Lucky stayed up late. Momma and Daddy went off to some church social or bingo night or whatever it is they do.

Lucky got into Ruben's stuff he keeps under his bed. Case of beer, maybe some whiskey."

Jeb acknowledged Harry, who waved him over.

"Daddy and Momma come home, they found Lucky sick. She was throwing up and drunk. She had messed up the house but good. Daddy screamed. Momma started crying. Ruben never said nothing. He didn't say where she got the stuff. They acted like I give it to her. I still hate him for it."

"So Lucky got kicked out of the house."

"Kicked herself out. Daddy whipped her. She got up and said things she says she can't remember. Daddy made Ruben drive her to my place. He dropped her off without telling me what happened or how I was going to support her. Lucky said that after a few days Daddy would send Ruben for her."

"Did he?"

"He might have. Things got worse, though. They're waving at you from the bandstand." Jewel pushed away from the table. "Reverend, I know you think you know some things about my family. Things is not how they seem, though, and that's all I can say."

"Is there anything else you want to say, Jewel?"

"Talk to Ruben. Not at my folks' place, though. They think Lucky's still with me. If you can help it, it's best you not cause us that kind of trouble." She walked away.

Jeb slipped around behind the bandstand and grabbed his banjo. "Harry, I've got to check on some things. Good playing with you." Jeb slipped out the back door.

19

J EB CAME TO THE BREAKFAST TABLE FEELING like he could read the inside of his eyelids. He had driven around Hope for an hour after he had left the club, until a deputy who saw him circling through the colored section of town stopped him and questioned him. The white cop didn't know of a John Blessed, and even if he did, he wouldn't give out that kind of information to a complete stranger. He told Jeb to go home.

Angel served eggs and toast to Ida May. Willie sat opposite Ida May and next to Lucky. Lucky wiped dried milk from Myrtle's face. None of them said a word to Jeb.

He poured a cup of coffee and asked Ida May to send the butter dish his way. His grits needed flavoring.

"We ate supper without you last night," said Willie.

Ida May stared at him.

"I had to call on some people," said Jeb.

"Church people, right, Jeb?" asked Willie.

Angel scraped the last of the eggs onto Jeb's plate. "It's none of our business."

"Angel thinks you've gone back to your old ways, Jeb," said Willie. "Tell her that's nonsense."

"That's nonsense," said Jeb. He wanted to crawl back into bed.

Ida May held her milk glass in front of her, licking the white off her upper lip.

"Someone want to tell me why you're all acting like you shot someone and buried them out back?" asked Jeb.

"Reverend, last night you came in smelling like my brother, Ruben," said Lucky.

"Meaning what?" asked Jeb.

"Ruben goes out playing poker and smoking cigars with his friends on Friday night."

"Did I smell like cigars?"

Ida May nodded.

"I shouldn't have to explain myself. I'm a grown man."

"If you slipped up, I won't tell Sister Bernard, Dub," said Ida May.

"I didn't slip up, all of you. Sometimes a preacher has to see folk and they aren't the kind of people we might see like everyday folk. Jesus hung out with the sinner and publican."

"You was with a Republican?" asked Willie.

"I went to see your sister, Lucky," Jeb told her.

"Friday night? That would be the High Cotton Club," said Lucky.

"Did you meet any floozies?" asked Willie.

"Is that a dog?" asked Ida May.

"I asked her about your family, Lucky. You live here, so I check on things for your sake."

"You spying on me, Reverend?"

"So, last night the Church in the Dell preacher went honky-tonking," said Angel. "That's a fine how-do-you-do."

"Don't you go spreading personal business, Angel," said Jeb.

"They got a band on Friday night," said Lucky.

"Gospel?" asked Willie.

"Jazz. R-really good jazz. Lucky, for the record, I wasn't spying." Jeb gave his eggs to Ida May.

"Miss Coulter came by to see you last night. We tried to tell her that you were probably out visiting sick people. She wanted to know what sick people," said Angel. "Willie said he didn't know of any sick, so I elbowed him. Miss Coulter might have been vexed when she left."

"In Sunday-school class Sister Bernard says that God gets vexed," said Ida May. "Is it over cigars and poker?"

Jeb said, "I'm going to clean up and go and see Miss Coulter. I don't want any of you talking out of turn to anybody about anything we've discussed over breakfast." Halfway down the hall he heard Ida May say, "Dub needs prayer. I'll write it on a slip of paper for Sister Bernard's prayer box. She says it's very private. No one reads the notes but her and God."

☙

"She said I was vexed?" Fern wiped down the inside door of her car. She swallowed and added, "I am curious about where you went."

"I have a hunch about Myrtle. I think the Blesseds know whose baby she is."

"Why would they hide it?"

"To protect the mother."

"You think it's Jewel Blessed."

"I can't prove it. She acted funny about the baby last night. Her father knows something and I think the girls' brother, Ruben, may know too."

"When will you talk to Ruben?"

"I hope Jewel tells him I came by. If I talk to John Blessed, it could cause trouble for the girls."

"I got a letter from my mother. She is lining me up a teaching position in Ardmore."

"You told her to do that?"

"Mother does these things on her own. She did tell me to bring you along."

"Is she lining up a job for me too?"

"Is that a yes?"

"Does she know how many children come with the package?"

Fern closed up her car and set the rags aside. "Jeb, I'm scared."

"You've never said that before."

"What's going to happen, Jeb? Is something going to take you away from me for good?"

"I'm not afraid, Fern."

Fern picked up a rock. She hefted it and then pitched it mean over the surface of Long's Pond. The stone skipped three times and dropped into the icy water. She kept staring at the place where it sank, like she willed the bitter depths to cough up what had been swallowed.

She could be packed for Ardmore in two shakes. She said it twice. They would be in Oklahoma by Tuesday.

Jeb listened. The slander would dry up and blow away. He would not have to look into the eyes of a disapproving congregation tomorrow, some forever insouciant while others questioned his stability as a minister. Both kinds made him want to throw off polite decorum and kick aside the petty notions that kept otherwise faithful people distant from one another, from others that could give them a different view of things. "I've a little more studying to finish. Sunday's coming," he said.

"I'm with you, my beloved."

✌

Jeb turned toward town instead of home. He drove past Beulah's and smelled the deep-oil-fried chicken livers, her Saturday special, seeping out of the cafe to entice hungry men to step inside and give up a half-dollar for crunchy poultry organs with a side of gravy-smothered potatoes.

His mother cooked like Beulah, knowing what would be served on any particular day of the week. Monday meat loaf. Tuesday turnip greens and salt pork. He had never noticed before the alphabetical connotation of his mother's cooking. Wednesday wieners and sauerkraut, her version of it anyway; cook cabbage until it melts into the substance of seaweed and then salt it to death.

He wondered if Nazareth would have a smell at all if Beulah closed up shop. Then the smell of popcorn wafted into the cab. Kids lined up downtown for the picture show; the Ritz always ran a month behind the rest of the country's moving-picture runs. He did not recognize the title, but un-

derneath it in straight black letters spelled out The Marx
Brothers.

Neither Willie nor Angel had asked for picture show
money in months, not since Myrtle and Lucky had come to
stay under their roof. Their habit of adjusting to change had
followed them all the way from Snow Hill.

Jeb drove past the Ritz and out of town. The sky grayed
and the only hint of remaining color streaked across the horizon like pale chalk, a long trail of faded pink followed by
splatters and dashes of clouds that were rosed underneath by
sinking daylight.

He followed the naked tree line over the railroad tracks,
past Belinda's old abandoned shack, and beyond the weathered Tempest's Bog sign. The cold had chased the old men's
spit-and-whittle club indoors. The evacuated railway terminal
looked even more weathered; the overhang posts leaned east-
ward, giving the building a look of listing in the wind.

Two cars and a wagon parked in a slanted row in front of
the church. A man with graying hair, full around the back and
thin on the top, stuck a key in the front door, turned the lock,
and then put on his hat. His eyes lifted and met with Jeb's.

Jeb parked the truck next to the wagon and met the man
at the foot of the church house steps. He introduced himself.

"Reverend Nubey, I'm Reverend Joe Cornell." He kept
walking toward his automobile as though he had no intention
of stopping to chat.

"Is this your church?"

"It's God's church. I oversee the flock as shepherd, if
that's what you're asking. Overseer and under shepherd, that's
who I am."

Jeb tried not to demonstrate impatience, so he lowered

his voice. "If I may walk you to your automobile, I'd like to ask you something."

"If it's not found in the Holy Scriptures, I don't have the answer. Who you see before you is nothing but a small instrument of the Lord. I am God's piccolo."

"I know that people talk, Reverend Cornell, and I've been trying to put together a mystery. It's been troubling me for some time."

"Take your troubles to the Lord, Reverend." He opened his car door.

"Have you heard any rumors about Lucky Blessed or her sister, Jewel, anything that has to do with a baby?"

Cornell lowered his body into the car, holding his back as though it would give out. Jeb helped him into the driver's seat. "If you know of anything at all that would help me find this baby's family, I'd be grateful."

"God give you a child. You ought to thank him."

"Myrtle is not mine to take."

"Reverend, the only thing I can give you is a little advice." His voice lost a trace of pulpit bravado and he looked into Jeb's eyes. "You keep looking in my backyard, Tempest's Bog's backyard, for the answer. I say as kindly as I know how that you should try your own backyard. The answer is waiting to be found."

Cornell held the door out only so that Jeb could move aside. He closed the door and gunned the engine. The car backfired. Cornell closed his eyes and smiled. He patted the steering wheel like a man coaxing life from an old dog, threw the car into reverse, and drove away.

20

ANGEL SEWED SEVEN NEW BUTTONS DOWN THE front of a dress. The dress was a printed yellow-and-green pattern, so the blue buttons replacing the old wooden ones gave it a new look. She tried it on and looked at herself in front of the parlor mirror. The dress was made for spring and suited for Sunday, not a winter garment, but worth salvaging from the rag bag for the first warm day. Even in the dead days of winter, those warm days cropped up, even if few. Angel smoothed the seams around her waist and hips and then smiled at the way it fit her, the snug waistline hugging her slender middle.

Lucky stood behind her with her arms folded. "It's not your size and it's for an older girl anyway."

"Maybe you think it's your size, Lucky."

"Might be my size, but it's too big for you. Look how it

hangs off your shoulders. My mother was good at fitting dresses to me and my sister. We never had to go around with our things too big for us."

The girl working for Freda at Woolworth's might lose her job if her husband took a job out of town, so Angel wanted to be the first in line to ask about it and this dress had the look of that shop clerk, the smart look of a *Sears and Roebuck Catalog* girl. "I'll need shoes to go with it." Her hair had grown past her shoulders and browned darker in the winter. She pulled it up in back and held it until the length disappeared. "Maybe I'll crop my hair."

This made Lucky laugh. She plopped into Jeb's chair, scooting aside his pen and paper with the ragged toe of her shoe.

Angel pulled her hair around and examined the ends that split into soft, fine strands. "If I get a job at Woolworth's, I'll save a little so I can go for a real haircut at the Clip and Curl."

"I'll cut your hair. Why do white girls always complain about their hair, like if it's long, they want it short, or if they cut it off, they want to grow it back long?"

"Can you cut hair?"

"I'll give it a try."

"Lucky, either you know how or you don't."

"I'll cut it off if you want and you can pay me by giving me that dress, since it's too big anyway."

Angel unbuttoned the dress and let it drop to the floor, where she gathered it up and straightened it out, tripping clumsily on the rug in her haste to keep it from Lucky's grasp. "You can go through the rag bag at the church whenever you like. I found this one, sewed new buttons on, so it's mine."

"That rag bag is only for poor white trash, not black.

When that lady, that Josie lady put her things in the bag, she saw me standing there and she picked it up and looked around until she saw you. She said, 'Oh, there's Angel!' and then she carried that bag over to you, like she didn't want me touching her castoffs. If she was going to give you the dress, I don't know why she didn't go on and give it to you. It's like she wants everyone to see her giving her things to charity."

"Poor white trash is not what Josie thinks of me! I think you're jealous."

"I ain't jealous of anything that woman gives away." Lucky kept rubbing the tip of a strand of her hair between her fingers, smoothing the ends and feeling the slapdash knots she had pinned around the crown of her head.

Angel pulled on the old blouse she had worn to school—faded blue cotton, long-sleeved and warm—buttoned it up, and slipped into her trousers. "So to make you happy, I should give you the dress and cut off my hair."

"I said I don't want nothing that belonged to Josie Hipps."

Angel pulled out a pair of scissors. "Cut my hair then." She dared her.

"I ain't afraid to cut off your hair. You spiting yourself?"

"I don't think you'll do it."

Lucky took the scissors from Angel's hand and opened them over a large hank of her hair.

"What are you two doing?" Jeb entered the house through the kitchen.

Lucky sliced through Angel's hair and handed the cut-off strand back to her. "Here's your hair then."

"Have you lost what good sense God gave you?" Jeb asked.

"You are jealous!" The strand dropped out of Angel's hand.

"Angel wanted her hair cut, so I cut it."

Angel stared into the mirror at the right side cut just below her ear. "I'm a freak."

"I'll cut the other side so both sides match," said Lucky.

Jeb kept looking at the small pile of brown hair on the floor and then at Lucky.

Lucky stopped laughing.

"I can't trust you, Lucky, not for a day," said Jeb, mad as a hornet. "This is what people expect, shenanigans like this, and here you go and give them the ammunition they've been wanting."

Lucky ran out of the house, around the east side, past the window, and disappeared into the woods.

Angel and Jeb followed her as far as the porch. Angel pulled on her coat. "That wasn't the thing to say, Jeb," she said. She gave the scissors to Jeb. "This is great, just great. I can't see her going too far. Lucky don't like those woods." She grabbed an extra coat and took off after her.

✥

Angel regretted not having brought the lantern, but the moonshine along the streambed led her a good ways. Lucky made enough noise to keep Angel moving not far behind; the *thump* of a stone kicked by her foot, the *swish* of brush. Angel had known that wood's path for so long, she followed it as well as the path from the kitchen to the outhouse. She heard tell of having the second sight and thought about how finding her way in the dark might be that gift. Her toe hit a boulder. She stumbled sideways and then, flailing her hands in front of her, scraped her hands in thorny shrubbery. She thought of calling out to Lucky to stop making her run after her in the dark. But if Lucky had thought about stopping to rest, then hearing a plea from Angel might give her reason to keep running for spite. Lucky had had her way for too long in Angel's family and it had spoiled her.

Angel came into the clearing not far from where Willie kept his trot line. He kept a trap out in these woods too, but where exactly she did not know. The moon shone down on a boulder as big as the cab of Jeb's truck. A bird called out, maybe a raven, but Willie knew his birdcalls better than she. The cold had not caused the stream to ice over and it had run hard all winter, too hard to ice. The only sound she picked up on was the raven, the stream, and a bristling wind that stung her ears. She brought her coat collar up over her ears and swore under her breath at Lucky. She peered out through the neck of the coat. The splendid dark hair moved slightly from across the stream, a flash of lightning near the water. "I see you, Lucky," she said.

"I don't give a care," said Lucky. Her head went down into her arms.

"Sit over on that rock and freeze then. I'm going back," said Angel. She came to her feet and turned away from the stream.

"I am freezing, if that makes you happy."

"I brought an extra coat. But if you don't want it, I'll take it back."

Lucky shifted and said, "You can bring me the coat."

Angel had to roll another boulder into the water to reach the middle stone.

Lucky rose and reached out both arms, two extensions reaching in the dark, thin but strong like a boy's arms.

Angel balanced her weight between the stepping-stones. "You got a long stride."

Lucky rolled another boulder into the water and pressed her left foot against it. She reached her right arm toward Angel and grabbed her. Angel leaped. Her right foot kicked sideways. The water bit her ankle, icy and stabbing cold. She felt her body pulled forward out of the stream. Lucky backed away, making room for them both on the bank. Angel staggered but took two more long strides until her feet felt sod again. She gave her the coat. "Your arms feel like ice. I can't believe we made it across in the dark."

"After a while, my eyes grow used to it."

"You're shivering. I'm glad the moon's out." Angel kept holding on to Lucky's arms, even after she slipped on the coat. She rubbed up and down on her arms, sure that any minute Lucky would jerk away, but she didn't.

"I'm not jealous of you, but I'm sorry I cut off your hair," said Lucky.

"Why'd you do it then?"

"You're always daring me, like you don't think I've got any gumption. I got as much as you, and more."

Angel hugged herself for warmth. "I was stupid to dare you."

Lucky smoothed the short strands of Angel's hair. "It surprised me when I cut off such a big hank. I didn't mean to do that."

"Maybe I'll cut it all short. It's the rage now."

"Sometimes I do things I wish I'd never done. It's not the first time."

"First time giving a haircut?"

"You know about that old hay shed back in those woods, the one you find if you go left down this path?"

"It's abandoned."

"It's a good place for telling things you don't want no one else to know."

"You about to tell me something no one else can know, Lucky?"

Lucky headed down the path. "Follow me."

⌒

Jeb fumbled his watch out of his trousers' pocket a fifth time.

Ida May poked a milk bottle into Myrtle's screaming mouth. "She won't take it, Jeb. She never takes it from me."

Jeb lifted the baby into his arms. He jostled her gently against his chest and stroked the top of her head like he had seen Lucky do on nights she had soothed her into slumber. Myrtle made a sound like sucking wind and then let out another cry, a long and drawn-out bawling scream that possessed a horrific pulse.

Willie put a pillow over his head and lay flat on the parlor floor.

"They should have been back by now," said Ida May. "This is torture!"

Jeb paced in front of the window, gazing into the woods, not seeing a light or the shadow of girls conversing in the moonlight. An hour had passed since Angel had run out after Lucky.

Willie got up and grabbed his coat and took the lantern off the kitchen peg. "Better to be lost in the woods than stuck in here listening to Myrtle cry like a bobcat."

"You're not going without me," said Jeb.

"I go all the time to check my traps, Jeb."

Jeb bundled Myrtle into Ida May's arms. "You're the woman of the house till we get back, Ida May."

"I am not," she said. "I'm not cut out for it."

"You are, you'll see." Jeb lay Myrtle's head against Ida May's shoulder, propped the bottle on a towel, and poked it into the baby's mouth.

"I know what you're up to," Ida May yelled after them. "You're scared of a diaper changing. At least I'm man enough to admit it!"

Jeb grabbed his rifle from the wall rack and slammed the door shut behind himself and Willie. "I think there's a Scripture about this," said Jeb.

"If not, we'll say there is," said Willie.

❧

Back inside the hayloft, the wind did not cut through as badly as it did down by the stream. Angel and Lucky sat against the wall, listening to nothing at all. Angel had not asked her anymore about what she wanted to tell her, but held her tongue so Lucky would tell her outright and not assess what she divulged on a dare.

"When that Belinda woman used to come and feed Myrtle, I'd sneak off, lay up here, and let the sun warm my legs. I never had no place to myself except for those times," said Lucky.

"I never had no place to myself. Wouldn't know what that was like. Fern's momma's the only one I ever knew who did, but her husband had to die for that to happen. You think she's lonely knocking around in that house, or you think after we all left, she threw off her clothes and danced naked all to herself?"

"If I had a big house like the one you said she has, I'd dance all over it."

"We always had a lot of kids back home in Snow Hill. But we had two older brothers die, one of the influenza, the other got drunk one night and got himself killed. Then my older sister Claudia met a man and took off with him. I'd never been looked on as the oldest until then. I miss Claudia."

"I don't miss my sister much. She caused me too many headaches."

"You must have fought then," said Angel.

"We fought, but she don't look out for no one but her own self. If she did, things wouldn't have gotten so bad."

Angel pushed on her stomach across the straw and then rolled over so that the moonlight fell across her face in a diagonal stripe.

"She went down to that High Cotton Club and left me on my own. I was thirteen. Didn't know nothing about nothing, like boys and the things they do, if you know what I mean."

"I like boys."

"They're no good." Lucky crawled out as far as Angel and slumped next to her. "Especially the kind come sniffing around after Jewel. One night she didn't come home. I heard a car pull up, a nice car like no one I knew drove. I figure it was all right to open the door to someone who drives a car like that. White shining fenders. A boy come up on our porch. Not young like me, but in his twenties. White and smiling. He wore these good clothes, like them boys who go to college out of state." Lucky turned her face from the moonlight. "He asked for Jewel, and when I told him she was still down at the club, he asked me if I was her sister, and I told him I was. He kept smiling. I hated that smile, like it made me want to run. He told me that if he couldn't see Jewel that I was as pretty as she was. I liked him telling me things I'd never heard before. He wanted to come inside and wait, he said, for Jewel to come home. I said he could if he'd let me see his car. He let me look inside his car and touch the seats. I never felt nothing so smooth as that leather."

"You don't have to tell me, if you don't want, Lucky."

"He said he'd give me a ride down to the corner and back, so I climbed inside." Lucky cried. She wiped her eyes with the back of her hand. "He didn't take me back like he said. He drove me down to some old house where no one lived. He dragged me inside, and when I cried, he slapped me and told me to keep my nigger mouth shut."

"When did Jewel come back?"

"Not until he had put himself all over me and took me and pushed me out of his car into Jewel's yard."

"Did you call the cops?"

"White cops don't listen to colored girls, Angel. That boy told me if I told anyone, he'd kill me, and that no one would care, so I'd best keep my mouth shut."

"You never told anyone."

"Not until my stomach started growing with that white boy's baby inside."

"Your daddy got mad at you, I guess?"

"Like it was all my fault. The only one that listened to me was Ruben. He wanted to go and kill him. Jewel begged him not to, said he would get hanged and nothing would happen to that white boy for what he done."

"What happened to the baby?"

"When I started having pains, I was scared. Daddy wouldn't let Momma come and help. Ruben was mad. He put me in his car and drove me to the church, only no one was around. He said the minister had told him about a preacher that took in children down in Nazareth. Ruben was crazy that night. He drove me into Nazareth. Things started happening and I started screaming. He drove us down into the apple orchard. That's where I had that baby. He wrapped it in his shirt. Then he took off through that orchard for the lights of some house. When he come back, he had stolen someone's laundry off their porch. We wrapped that baby the best we could in clean laundry and put her in that basket. Ruben told me that I was not to blame for what had happened, that the whites ought to take care of their own kind."

"You brought your baby to our porch?"

"Ruben knew better than to stop and ask how to find your church. We drove up and down roads all morning. Once he spotted your church, the Church in the Dell, and the house behind it, he told me that's where we would come that night and leave Myrtle. He wrote that note. I couldn't do it. I cried for her for days until Jewel was sick of me. The minute I laid eyes on her, I loved her. I named her Myrtle after an auntie who was good to me."

"You're Myrtle's momma, Lucky?"

"Did you hear that, like a clanking sound?" asked Lucky.

Angel brought her hand over Lucky's stomach and then up to her lips.

"Girls, we're waiting for you down here," said Jeb.

Angel and Lucky peeped out from the loft. Jeb waited below. A lantern flashed across the field as Willie marched along the dead grasses hunting for them.

"You been listening long, Reverend?" asked Lucky.

"Who did this to you, Lucky?" asked Jeb.

"No one listens to me, Reverend. It don't do no good for you to try and help."

"I want his name," said Jeb.

"The buddy of that banker boy. Frank Pella. Myrtle's his baby."

21

Oz Mills whacked a badminton birdie over a backyard net to a young girl, who, when she occasionally missed the flying shuttle, endured Oz's correction and his taunting comments, like "Bad for you, good for me, Cousin," or "Another point for your elder relation." Both Oz and the girl had donned white sweaters and, even in the brisk Saturday-afternoon air of January, their foreheads perspired, wetting their hair and causing the blonding strands to stick to their cheeks.

Oz's reputation for possessing vigorously pursued court skills would not be undermined even to lend confidence to a girl who looked every bit as old as fourteen. He slammed her last attempt to the ground. She spun her racket up, caught it, and then left him to boast alone on the wintering lawn.

Jeb seized the solitary moment. He stepped out from behind the row of cedars; not that he had hidden for the duration of the badminton game—he hadn't. He had parked too far down the winding path to Oz's newly purchased house, a small mansion outside Nazareth's town limits, and hiked a half mile before he realized the distance to the tree-shrouded home.

Oz's expression of small victory faded. "Afternoon, Nubey."

"Glad to see me?"

"Elated." Oz called to a woman inside the house, who brought him a towel and a drink before disappearing back into the house to tend to his young relative.

"Sorry to barge in. You beat the socks off your unwitting contender. Must feel good, I guess," said Jeb.

"What brings you out here?" Oz asked.

"A matter that may concern you, your bank."

"That's doubtful, isn't it?"

Jeb gestured to a lawn chair. Oz invited him to take it and sat across from him next to a table, where he placed his drink within a few inches of his wrist.

"The young man you employ from Hope, an apprentice named Pella, has come under scrutiny. I'm here to ask you about him," said Jeb.

"Whose scrutiny? God's, Nubey?"

"Maybe for now, my scrutiny until I make it someone else's."

"Pella's from a good family. You already know that, though. He works for me."

"You do know Frank, don't you? Know him well, I mean. Not too many things get past you, like the way he talked to that young girl downtown that day you called him off."

"I chided him for mingling," said Oz. "Girls like her tell too many lies."

"Mingling? Is that what you call it?"

"Get to it, why don't you?"

"Last year, last winter, a Negro girl only thirteen got dragged away from her sister's house in Hope and suffered things little girls shouldn't ought to endure. The white boy who took her innocence shut her up, told her he'd kill her if she breathed a word."

"You've been listening to the wrong voices, Nubey. I'm not surprised."

"Frank Pella raped Lucky Blessed. Her brother, Ruben, felt she ought not to be forced to bring up a baby half belonging to whites."

"She's a liar, like I said."

"So they gave her to me."

"No one will believe her. I don't."

"Our baby-in-the-basket, Myrtle Blessed, is the offspring of Frank Pella. He's going to jail, by the way."

"That's very doubtful."

"Don't doubt me, Oz. It's an annoying habit."

"Frank Pella, the accused? He's the son of Wallace and Justina Pella."

Jeb shrugged.

"They own a little piece of every pie in every town between Hope and Texarkana."

"I like pie."

"Now, you take the town of Hope. Wallace Pella holds the mortgage to a little place called the Church of Hope Eternal."

Jeb felt like a bit of lawn moved beneath him.

"Good Reverend Williamson neglected to tell you that, I'm judging by your rosy countenance."

"You saying Pella's daddy owns the Church of Hope Eternal's building?"

Oz got up and took his drink with him. "You keep saying that all the way back to your jalopy, Nubey." The back door opened and Oz walked inside.

The servant woman holding the door open asked Jeb if he was coming inside.

Jeb shook his head. He closed his eyes. It was a long prayer back to the truck.

∽

"You are implying I sacrificed this girl for the sake of my church building," said Louie Williamson. "Maybe I should have forced her to go to the law. I did tell her, but I knew she wouldn't go. I have known the law. It doesn't honor our kind, Reverend Nubey. Lucky Blessed's only covering is the blood Christ shed for her." He sat back on his chair and it groaned. "We know too well what it means to trust fully in God."

"You knew all along."

"I only suspected. She never gave me the name of the white boy that did this to her."

"She was protecting you."

"Maybe protecting all of us. Big load for a child. Think about it."

"Frank Pella is a monster."

"I'm not afraid of monsters, Reverend, only the men who bow to them."

Jeb came down on his knees, next to the shrunken candles where he and Louie had last prayed. "I want you to give a message to someone for me," he said. He handed him a note.

"I'll try my best," said Louie.

Jaunice had not switched out the old candles with new and the cold melted wax of penny candles failed to offer the same monastic elegance to Louie's sparse study as Jeb had observed during his last visit. "Tell me what to do, Louie."

Louie Williamson watched Jeb cry. Maybe he had already surrendered his daily portion of tears or it could have been he simply honored Jeb's right to cry with a fresh awareness of injustice. Louie possessed the look of a man well-practiced in wakefulness. Either way, he did not have to say much of anything.

Jeb figured out how to interpret the silence of a friend. It sheds its own light.

Deputy George Maynard stared out his window. He kept saying things like "Sure as the dickens, it's been a long winter" and "Some say another snow is headed our way."

Jeb said, "George, have you listened to anything I've said?"

"Girls like that Angel of yours and the little colored girl, they got fertile imaginations, Reverend. It don't bother girls like them any to tarnish a family name. It's good you came to me first. Careful where you carry such tales."

"Is that your advice?"

"They don't know the meaning of a good name, not that you haven't done charitable by both of them, and improved your own standing in town, Reverend."

"This isn't about me, my reputation, or my charitable works, George!"

"I think you've caught this child in her own shame. Strange that over a year passes before she comes up with a story. I know of the Pellas. They wouldn't stand for slander, I tell you the truth." George could not stop staring out the window; Jeb wished the snow would start and get it over with, so George could concentrate on the matter at hand.

"She told me that no one would believe her."

"Why should anyone believe her?"

Jeb felt the need to swear. He refrained, at least where George was concerned.

The jailhouse door came open. Will Honeysack carried a rock through the door. He showed it to Maynard. "You see this? Every elder sitting on the board of Church in the Dell got one just like it through the window of their business this morning, and you know it's not the first time. Nice how-do-you-do, as if we don't have enough to contend with."

Jeb took the rock, turned it over twice, and held it up to the sunlight coming through the window.

"What do you make of it, Reverend?" asked Maynard.

"Looks like the work of a fertile imagination," said Jeb.

"Jeb, this whole business has gone as far as I can take it," said Will. "I want you to know that even as your friend, I lose control of things when they go this far."

"I'm glad you still call me friend, Will."

Will took the rock from Jeb's hand and laid it on Maynard's desk. "I'm glad we ran into one another so I have the chance to tell you first, Jeb."

"What is it you need to tell me, Will?"

"I didn't call this meeting tonight. But as head deacon, I have no choice but to attend."

Jeb could not take his eyes off the rock. It held

Maynard's eyes too, and Will's—like they all waited for the thing to go off in their faces. Jeb raked the rock into the deputy's garbage pail. "It's a rock, boys, not a gun."

"They're calling this meeting private, like I'm not supposed to invite you, Jeb. I don't have to agree to that, and so I am inviting you. You come if you want and I'll make sure you have your say. After supper, say six, then?" Will left the jailhouse as though he dragged the entire hundred-year-old structure back to his store by a single rope.

Maynard retrieved the rock. "As evidence," he kept saying.

ॐ

Lucky twirled and looked at the dress in the parlor mirror and then touched each button, testing the threads' security. "Angel give it to me," she told Jeb. "That Josie lady better not say a word about it. It's not from her old things anyway, but Angel's."

Angel measured the distance from the hem to the floor. Faith Bottoms had evened out her hair quite well. It hung above her shoulders and made her look older.

Jeb picked up Ida May from the rocker and set her on the floor. Ida May had grown gangly over the winter. When he lifted her, her limbs hung long and thin, spidery. They alighted on the floor as though she weighed less than air. Jeb turned the chair away from the girls' modeling of rag bag dresses and stared through the front window. In one hour the automobile lights would flood through the tree trunks of the church lawn. Will Honeysack would call the meeting to order and Floyd Whittington would second it. Sam would rush into matters while Will staved him off and waited, in some manner hoping and not hoping the Church in the Dell minister would show.

Jeb rocked out of the chair and paced to the window, breathing out shallow streams of air, scratching at his chapped lips, and then returning to the rocker to rock some more. Angel and Lucky laughed and they were loud. Jeb inched the rocker farther away from them and thought he heard an automobile engine. A minute passed and he settled back into the rocker. He glanced up and found all three girls staring at him. He turned his back completely on them.

"Something's wrong with Dub," Ida May whispered.

"You like Lucky's dress, Jeb?" asked Angel. "It's a good fit."

Jeb gave Angel and Lucky an obligatory nod. Myrtle cried from the children's room. "I'll see to her," said Lucky.

Angel crawled on her knees and then sat back on her feet beside Jeb. She stared with him out the window. "What's going to happen?"

Jeb kept looking hard at the trees and the cold sky overhead and feeling little parts of him slipping away with the shortening winter day. "I couldn't say."

"I'm glad we know about Myrtle now, I mean, that we know that Lucky's her momma and all."

Jeb felt like an attempt to speak might stick in his throat, so he kept answering Angel with silent nods and short grunts. Several times he did that, until she blew out a breath. "I need some time to think," he told her.

"Last time you acted like this, you was about to get arrested," she said.

"Dub's not getting arrested," said Ida May.

Jeb told Ida May to go and help Lucky. She got up, but

her bottom lip quivered and she sniffled all the way down the hallway.

Jeb mouthed, *"I'm sorry, Ida May,"* but the words stayed cooped up inside him.

"Have you talked to Miss Coulter today? She might could help with whatever it is that's bothering you," said Angel.

"Fern can't help me. Don't know that anyone can."

"Except God, you mean."

Jeb did not answer right off. "God has either put me here or maybe the Devil," he said. It seemed cruel, no matter how he had arrived at this desolate situation. He did not know how to shepherd a flock that bit and butted at one another and at him. The Scriptures told him one thing—that we are many souls, but of one bread, one body—but the body led him to believe otherwise.

"Does Frank Pella have anything to do with it?" asked Angel.

"Frank Pella, Oz, Louie Williamson, Will Honeysack, George Maynard, people I've never met. The whole town, maybe." It came to him that he might be without the aid of any friend at all, not any one person who could right wrongs.

Lucky came into the room, bouncing Myrtle, laughing, and saying that Myrtle was beautiful and that she had never seen such a pretty child, and smart, she added. Lucky sat with her baby on the sofa, dressed in the newly buttoned dress that made her look older, her hair pulled back and making ringlets around the crown. She had made the leap from fourteen to womanhood without the help of a single person. "I'm going back to school somehow," she said. "I'm going to teach, I've decided." Since no one seemed to be paying her any mind, she told Myrtle of her plans, referring to herself as "your mother."

A tear slipped down Angel's cheek.

"I don't want you to cry," said Jeb. "Hold fast and it will all work out." He wanted to believe it.

***

The sanctuary had one electric light in the entry, a dim yellow light that cast long atticlike shadows from the front door to the pulpit. Jeb waited in the shadow of the lectern, not wanting to be the last girl to arrive at the party.

Sam Patton parked his Chevy next to the church sign. He took one draw on his cigarette and stomped it out on the stone walkway. He paced out front, looking down the church drive and toward the road. He finally tramped up the church steps, opening the door, and then stopping. He asked who was there and Jeb said, "Your minister, Sam."

Arnell Ketcherside parked and came in behind Sam. He said quietly to Sam, "I thought this was board members only."

"So did I," said Sam.

"Will informed me of this gathering."

Sam and Arnell made an awkward pair, waiting halfway inside and outside. Jeb bid them to come inside and they finally did, but they took a seat on the back pew. Will and Floyd arrived. Will entered slowly, like a man not wanting to enter a funeral parlor.

"Will, we agreed that we should meet first as a board only," said Sam.

"You agreed, Sam. Truth is, Jeb lives out back. How you going to explain all our vehicles parked out in front of the church?" asked Will.

"I guess he's right," said Arnell. He took off his hat and approached Jeb, his right hand extended.

Jeb thanked him and said, "Gracie always taught me that if I was to lead this flock, that I had to take the reins. You all swore me in by the laying on of hands. I'm entrusted to lead, so from now on, I lead these meetings."

"I second that motion," said Will.

"Now hold on, here. Will, he can't step in and take over," said Sam. "He don't follow rules of order or nothing of the like."

"I never saw a race horse running backward, led by its own flank," said Will. "Reverend, I'm all ears."

Jeb started out with a prayer. He offered Sam the first say.

Sam bristled. "Ever since you started trying to mix not only your own household, but this church, we've had nothing but harassment. It wasn't but just this morning that every board member each unlocked our business establishments to find vandals had attacked us in the night. None of this happened before. We have a right to lead quiet lives, like the Scriptures say."

"No such Scripture, Sam, but go on," said Jeb.

"Next thing you know, our young people will start losing the morals we've taught them and the whole town will go to the degenerates. You seen that dancing club outside of Hope, Cotton Club or some such?" Sam asked.

Jeb didn't say either way.

"Nazareth will go the way of reprobates if we don't get a handle on this now before it all falls into a kafuffle. That's all I have to say about matters," said Sam.

Jeb gave the floor to Arnell, who only agreed with Sam. "Floyd, you have the floor, if you like," said Jeb.

"Evelene and me have worked hard to keep the Woolworth's going throughout this Depression. When we found rocks through our windows this morning, it scared us both. I'm not afraid to admit I'm scared. It seems to me we have no choice but to live separate, keep to our kind, they keep to their own kind. If we upset the apple cart, here's proof of what happens; things get out of kilter. You can't upset the natural order, Reverend, or we all pay." He kept spinning the brim of his hat around his fingers. "I'm done, I guess."

Will said, "I'd like to give my time to Reverend Nubey."

Jeb invited the men to sit along the first and second pew. He said, "Floyd, mind explaining 'natural order'?"

"The way I see it, life is lived orderly, like God puts us where we belong. We get out of the natural order, then we blow everything to kingdom come," said Floyd.

"Makes sense," said Arnell.

"Floyd, you think the church people thought Christ was blowing everything to kingdom come, what with him going off and having dinner with people not of his own kind, mixing and mingling with—what was it you called those kind—'degenerates'?"

"Jesus was a peacemaker," said Floyd.

"*'Think not that I am come to send peace on earth: I came not to send peace, but a sword,'*" said Jeb.

"That's Shakespeare, right?" asked Arnell.

"Shut up, Arnell!" said Sam.

"If you're asking me to resign as your minister for taking in castaway kids, I can't. Show me my wrongdoing and I'll resign," said Jeb.

Will gave each man another opportunity to voice his opinion. He said to Jeb, "Let it be said that the elders of

Church in the Dell find no wrongdoing in the life of our minister."

Sam got up and left. Arnell followed him, asking Sam what had just happened. Floyd and Will shook Jeb's hand and Floyd left for home.

"If they want to find wrongdoing, Jeb, you know they will, don't you?" asked Will.

"All I wanted tonight was some time, Will." Jeb told him he would lock up and shut off the lights.

He went back to the parsonage and waited for each child to disappear down the hallway and fall quiet. He lay in bed, staring out the window after all the children had fallen asleep. He troubled over what he should do with his borrowed time.

22

THE SUNDAY CROWD HAD THINNED BY AT LEAST two families a week for the three weeks surrounding Christmas, but typically picked up again by mid January. No crop needed tending and the boredom of winter swept the every-other-Sunday-goers through the door, if for no other reason, but that of having nothing to do in the cold weather.

Jeb needed at least another half hour of study before opening his message. Myrtle screamed from five on, rousing the rest of the household. Willie, wrapped in a blanket, walked through the house with Ida May hunkering underneath the tail of the thing for warmth. Jeb fired up the coals in the potbellied parlor stove. Lucky stroked Myrtle's bottom lip with a warmed bottle nipple. She finally grunted and took it.

"I'm going in early," Jeb told Lucky. He kept a plain face,

not giving away any of his morning plan. "Wake Angel and be sure you're all to church early and not late."

"I wasn't going, though. You can't mean me," said Lucky.

"I do mean you and your baby too," said Jeb. "You got something new to wear. I call that without excuse."

He felt Lucky watching him cross the yard.

An hour skimmed by and the church filled up, all except for Sam and Greta Patton. Arnell and his missus came in with their sons, two of whom Jeb had baptized last summer in White Oak Lake. Will and Freda, Floyd and Evelene, all took a seat and then came Fern. She wore something new, but in her usual manner, she wore a pair of older sensible shoes. Red and blue flowers on white fabric gave her the look of one of the high-school girls who campaigned for Pony Fabrey during the last mayoral election. Not that the teens had given a flip about the mayor's election, but the young volunteers had enjoyed the benefits of the free lemonade and fried chicken at the summer picnic.

Angel walked in with Lucky, who held Myrtle. Lucky wore the dress she had finagled from Angel and had done up her hair in one of those knots that the women were all asking about down at the Clip and Curl. She held her baby close, allowing Myrtle's face to peek out of a pink blanket, not awkwardly mishandling her as she had done in the past, but assuredly, like a fourteen-year-old Mary who knows that her child was sent by angels. Her eyes and her mouth firm, dogged, looked wise and like a girl who knows things other people have yet to figure out.

The ladies parted and followed their husbands habitually to customary pews, and none of them greeted Lucky or made a fuss over the baby as they customarily made over infants. Lucky made eye contact with several women, smiling whether or not anyone reciprocated.

Angel scooted down next to Fern and Lucky sat next to Angel.

Jeb asked for every head to bow and every eye to close before thoughts melted like lard in a skillet, sizzling and popping with opinion.

He asked that attention be drawn to Mark 10, and talked about the Sons of Thunder, James and John, and of their desire to sit next to God in heaven. The rulers over the Gentiles, he said, lord it over them, and Jeb gave the definition of supremacy—the desire to dominate. Jeb read verses 44 and 45 and asked God to teach him the way of servanthood.

It did not thunder at that moment, but some later remembered it that way, even though the sky had blued better than any day in January.

The church doors opened and a timid woman came through. She wore a tall, wide-brimmed hat the color of daffodils and a thick band decorated with a couple of flowers, though fake, but that yellow hat gave her the look of blooming in the doorway. She led two others, two handsome young people, a young woman and a young man, who walked together and behind her.

Jeb's eyes lifted and he smiled and nodded at them. Lucky turned and silently mouthed, *"Momma."*

Before Lucky's mother could lead her two progeny to the last pew, Jeb came down onto the floor and walked down the aisle, where he met them.

Some of the faces changed from Sunday ecstasy to something not as lovely or fitting for a church face.

"Are you Vera Blessed?" Jeb asked.

Her timidity did not allow her to speak, not with all of those eyes on her. She looked up and down the aisle, and when her gaze met with Lucky's, she teetered back on her heels. She pointed at Myrtle. "My granddaughter?" she asked.

Lucky wiped her eyes and she nodded at her mother.

"Vera is a sister in Christ," said Jeb. "I invited her and her two children, Jewel and Ruben, as a sort of symbol of this morning's sermon." Jeb took Vera's hand, it was gloved in white, and led her up the aisle. Jeb invited Vera to take a seat in the front row. Lucky followed, holding Myrtle close. She sat next to her mother. Jewel and Ruben took up the remaining space on the pew next to their youngest sister.

Jeb kept to his sermon. As he finished Mark's text, he closed in prayer. Will and Freda came up front and knelt in silent prayer. Then they turned and Freda greeted Vera and told her what lovely children she had reared. Lucky sniffled. Her sister held out her hands and she took her niece in her arms for the first time.

Angel got up out of her seat and came to the front too. Floyd and Evelene came forward and exchanged pleasantries with Vera. Lucky and Angel hugged, even with all the better-looking boys calling them silly girls. They walked down the church aisle, showing off Myrtle to the churchwomen who were willing to speak.

Church dismissed on its own, but hardly anyone left.

Vera said to Jeb, "Reverend, remember to pray for my husband, John, that he'll forgive what's happened and let Lucky come home with our grandchild." She looked around the room until her eyes fell on her boy, Ruben. He walked out the church doors without saying much. "Pray for him too," she said. "Ruben's got lots of turmoil in his soul over Lucky."

"I know we're not over all this, Sister Blessed. I was hoping that today might start something better than what we had yesterday."

"I'd say it's some better," said Vera. She moved politely through the church folk in search of her little girl.

❧

Fern baptized Jeb with kisses up until late Sunday. "You did the right thing inviting the Blesseds to church."

Jeb walked her to her door. He said, "I want to come in."

"You ought to," she told him.

She put coffee on to brew. Jeb dropped his hat on a chair and followed her into the kitchen. Fern put her arms around him and kissed him again. Jeb stayed for coffee. "I'll see you tomorrow after school." He listened to the quiet of her house and thought of the ruckus going on back at the parsonage. "Maybe I'll stay a minute more."

He kissed Fern in the doorway, not noticing how bitter cold the night had gotten.

❧

Jeb woke up with the sun in his eyes and thoughts about Fern. That moment lasted long enough for thoughts to creep in about Church in the Dell. Good intentions could sour over a single night. Not everyone had accepted the Blesseds, of that he was certain.

"We are late, people!" Angel stumbled down the hall, jumping into her stockings. The noise she made set Ida May to wailing hopelessly.

"Finally it's the end of the world," said Willie. "I's afraid this'd be all there was to it."

"I forgot pencils." Ida May cried and laid her face on the kitchen table.

"Everyone, get in the truck and I'll see you get to school," said Jeb.

Lucky came out with her hair tied up in rags, something about her expressing her opinion of all of those with so little hope on a Monday morning. "Angel, you'd think you was losing a birthday or some such." She held out her hands to Ida May. "I got a pencil if you will put a sock in that alarm of yours."

Jeb covered his head with a hat and said, "Might you have coffee on the brew by the time I return?"

"You'd best strap on some galluses, Reverend, pull you on some trousers." Lucky covered her eyes with both hands.

Jeb had fallen asleep Sunday evening in his Sunday shirt and not a whole lot of anything else. What with Fern's scent lingering on the collar, it had seemed a shame to change out of it. "Meet me outside," he told Willie and Ida May. He gave Willie the truck key, since he had gotten good at warming up the Ford.

Angel stormed past, yelling that she had dibs on the front seat and saying, "Jeb, you'll catch your death!"

Jeb found his clothes by the door, his everyday trousers he had preached in on Sunday. He picked them up but nearly knocked Lucky down, running through the hall. "You're smiling this morning," he said.

"We had us a good Sunday, Reverend. I'd say things is looking up from now on."

Jeb chided his own thoughts. Here was Lucky already on Monday's good side and he'd gotten up troubling over subjects left unsaid yesterday, of those who did not come forward and greet Vera Blessed. "Coffee?"

"I'll make your coffee, Reverend. Black. Side of biscuits," she said.

"You're a good girl."

"That's what I've been saying."

Nazareth seemed to grow for an instant, like a wintered-over tract that had suddenly greened, life coming out of it and feeding lonesome souls.

～〉

Jeb returned to find a car parked out front that belonged to Louie Williamson, of that he felt certain. Both rear tire rims had rusted around the corners, red paint dabbed at the edges.

Louie sat at the kitchen table drinking coffee with one hand and holding Myrtle by his free arm. Lucky filled his cup and filled him in on all that had transpired on Sunday.

"Lucky's told you about Vera coming yesterday, I see," he said.

"Vera told me last night at prayer meeting. I'm surprised you're not roasting over an open fire, so to speak. So that note you had me pass to her, it was an invite. I didn't open it," said Louie.

Jeb took his seat across from Louie.

"I asked him if my daddy had anything to say about Momma's coming down and seeing me and Myrtle, but he said he didn't know," said Lucky. She pushed Jeb's full cup to his side of the table.

"John Blessed is prideful, that's all I got to say. If I say anything else, it's gossip. Your baby's giving back a little of her breakfast." Louie reached for a towel and wiped the baby's face. "Vera says you are a nice preacher and she is glad Lucky came to stay with you. I can tell she wants things back like they're supposed to be, though."

"Daddy's too hard on me, like he was too hard on Jewel. Jewel said yesterday that he won't talk to her still," said Lucky. "He blames Jewel for what happened to me, but I lay half the blame on him."

"If you go turning hard, then you and your father will never meet in the middle. One of you at least has to soften. It's more likely to be you."

Jeb told him, "John Blessed sounds like my daddy, hard-nosed and not able to get past his own laws so's he can reach into what's human, or humanly possible." Jeb's brother Charlie told him their father still thought of Jeb as the black sheep. "I hope John doesn't wait until he's too old to change." Jeb imagined his father turning to stone before he'd come to see him or ask for him. "My daddy sits out on his porch with all his thoughts of me frozen in time, as though I was still sixteen and stealing chewing tobacco."

"People change," said Louie.

"If he loved me, he would tell me, that's the way I feel," said Lucky. She picked up Myrtle and took her to Jeb's bedroom to change her.

Louie got up and carried the coffeepot back to the table. "Lucky's a strong girl. I wish her daddy saw in her what I see. Smart girl, and she says she's going to teach. I believe she'll do whatever she says she'll do. You take Jewel, now that girl will be dependent on whatever man drags her out of Hope. The kind of men she goes with, they don't stay around."

"What happened to Jewel's face?"

"Jewel's not really John's daughter, I didn't know if you knew that. Vera came to John with Jewel. She must have been three. That little girl's own daddy did that to her, I'm told, to spite Vera. Vera was what they call a natural beauty. Jewel's daddy, he imagined things about Vera that were not true. He came home drunk one night and accused Vera of seeing another man. Vera, she stood up to him. Jewel was hanging onto her momma's dress, crying, and that made that man so mad. He sliced her, cut that little girl. Vera left him after that. She met John in church. My daddy was the preacher back then, before he retired and I took over Church of Eternal Hope."

Jeb filled both their cups.

"John did well by Jewel, until Vera give him his first child, a son. You met Ruben."

"Ruben is John and Vera's only son?"

"One and only, and spoiled. He don't do wrong in the sight of his daddy. But Ruben has some goodness in him, so he looks after his sisters to make up for what John lacks, so to speak."

"Has anything, any words, ever passed between Ruben and Frank Pella?" asked Jeb.

"Frank runs with a rich crowd of young men, bright, but they run to trouble. A young man from our church was found beaten and tied to the railroad tracks, those tracks that run between Hope and Texas. If his brother hadn't have found him, the five-twenty A.M. might have ended things for that boy. Some people think that bunch that Pella runs with did it. But that boy never said, and who would have helped out if he would have spoken out?" Louie rubbed the top of his cup. "To answer your question, Ruben's not confronted Frank Pella. The matter troubles me some."

"I can see why it would," said Jeb.

"Ruben is not one to let matters drop. Jewel and Vera

begged him not to confront Pella, that Pella's bunch would not let it stop until it completely stopped."

"Ruben listens to his momma?"

"Like I said, he's got some goodness. But whether or not he still listens to his mother is a guess."

Ruben had not taken Myrtle into his arms the way Jewel had yesterday. He had come because his mother needed someone to drive her, and that was that. "I'd like to ask you to do one more thing, Louie, if you're up to it," said Jeb.

"Are you trying to raise a ruckus, Jeb?"

"Sometimes you have to raise a little dust to get to the better dirt. I'm plowing a new row, that's all."

"Like I told you before, I'm not afraid of monsters, Jeb."

23

THE SCENT OF MELTED WAX AND DUSTY rafters permeated the church, a smell like prayers and sin melting in the room, burning, dripping off, and then rising up and collecting on the ceiling, but not rising any farther. Jeb had not thought before of how often he had stared at those rafters the mornings and evenings he had prayed alone. Even after the congregation had collected under the roof and had sung until chasing the last particle of cold from the room, he imagined the rising of desire accumulating under the roof and then sinking back to the floor at the last amen.

Back in his bad-boy days, he had not thought much about prayer, but now it came to him that praying was like carrying heavy packs onto a battlefield, only to load heavy cannons with heavy artillery and then propel heavy weapons into the air. The war of prayer commenced by a few half-uttered phrases, the bowing of heads, closing of eyes had lost ground when good men had forgotten the war of it and the place of it.

He had cast his eyes outward for too long, thinking the battlefield smoldered far beyond the borders of his own hamlet, not acknowledging the inward place of desolation. *Oh, wretched heart!* he professed, *that you could see the hearts crushed and scattered along your journey!*

He desired to know how the inward places had fallen so deeply into neglect and he prodded heaven about the matter; if the love for human souls had been traded for the singing of songs, the uttering of the same words from the same prayer books, and the naming of external sins, then how might he awaken hearts to the distant drumming over the hill?

Or perhaps the soul found solace in collecting its sin into a row of tin soldiers—abstain from these things and you will be holy. Yes, that was it! Self-righteousness was born of tin and things easily conquered, the toy soldiers of the church. *We have settled for the war games of children, Father, and neglected the trenches of humanity.* He prayed God would show him the difference, allow him to smell the stench of his own neglect. *I am a rotting corpse, O God! Collect me now, my pile of bones into a heap and set fire to me. Make me a light on your hill. Let them see that from ashes, you rise!*

He stoked the fire inside the stove and the first family arrived for the midweek prayer meeting.

Fern came early, smelling like fresh air, like she had been out running in the cold.

Frank Pella's name was whispered more than once as several families bustled in out of the January air.

Jeb said to Fern, "I see Lucky and Angel coming up the steps with Myrtle. I don't want Lucky to hear all this talk."

"I'll see she's seated with me." Fern turned and met Lucky and Angel at the door and led them to her pew.

Willie and Ida May burst in and sat next to a family behind Angel and Lucky.

Jeb called the meeting to order and prayed. He checked his watch and glanced through the window. A small parade of car lights wound through the tree line. He took his place in front of the shepherd's bench while the congregants rose to sing.

かへ

Fortunes rise and fall on the backs of risk takers. *Like me,* Jeb thought. It seemed his fortune never amounted to much. He rolled his dice and let those things fly that festered inside him. With every eye seeming to look clean through to the back of his head as he read from the Book of Jeremiah, he told about the Balm in Gilead, yet how there had been no healing, no remedy. "I think some of us might believe when we read that text that God's people are at the end of their row when the Lord says, *'Thou art Gilead unto me, and the head of Lebanon: yet surely I will make thee a wilderness, and cities which are not inhabited . . . Woe unto him that buildeth his house by unrighteousness, and his chambers by wrong; that useth his neighbour's service without wages, and giveth him not for his work'"* Jeb turned to the next text and read, *"'Go up into Gilead, and take Balm . . . for thou shalt not be cured.'"*

A man cleared his throat from a middle pew.

"No healing for our towns, our communities, or our nation. We would be left in a bad way if it had not been for a newer Balm."

A sound like the fluttering of pages rippled through the pews, the women curious about the text.

"Because of God's plan of redemption, there is a Balm created for the healing of the nations. Through the suffering Christ, there is concocted a Balm. When hearts are torn and angry words are hurled, a Balm is made available. We may not see it for its healing elixir or its power to heal the poor, the lonely, and, yes, even the chasm between human differences; we may not realize that even if we render it powerless in our own heart, its power to heal is not diminished."

The sound of a choir lifted outside, ringing through the trees:

> *There is a Balm in Gilead*
> *to make the wounded whole.*
> *There is a Balm in Gilead*
> *to heal the sin-sick soul.*
>
> *Sometimes I feel discouraged,*
> *and think my work's in vain.*
> *But then the Holy Spirit*
> *revives my soul again.*

Two boys jumped up and ran to the window.

"'There is a Balm in Gilead,'" said Jeb. "'It makes our wounded whole. It heals my sin-sick soul.'"

The voices rose louder, drawing closer to Church in the Dell. Josie Hipps tapped Mellie Fogarty's shoulder. Freda Honeysack covered her mouth with her hand. Will closed his eyes and mouthed the words in silence.

"It is cold outside, my friends. Should we open our doors

and let strangers come into our warmth? Can wounded travelers find in this sanctuary the Balm of Gilead?"

Oz glared at Jeb. He sat in the rear of the church.

Greta and Sam Patton got up to leave.

Floyd Whittington said, "I think I get it." He got up and went to the back doors and opened both of them. "Come in, neighbors," he said quietly, "where it's warm."

Jaunice Williamson came through first, her white hair all swaying and moving as she led the choir down the aisle.

"Welcome, friends." Will came to his feet and bowed as the singers passed.

The members wore satin robes that gleamed from the overhead light, blue as the seas.

Angel and Lucky stared, mouths agape.

Louie entered holding a box of new candles. He gave them to Willie and told him he could pass them out. Willie gave one to each choir member and then walked up the aisle to hand one to Jeb.

Jeb lighted his at the altar and Louie did as he did, lighting his candle from the altar, and then they held out their candles while each church member and choir member came forward to light their light by the ministers'.

Oz ran out of the church and yelled out something that no one could understand. Floyd closed the doors and got in line to light his candle.

The door opened once more and Sam and Greta Patton slipped quietly out into the cold.

Jeb invited Reverend Louie to take a seat on the altar.

It was strange the way a chorus of opinion rippled through the church without anyone saying a word, like every sitting-down place had shifted and hearts had skipped a beat.

Jeb came down on one knee in front of Louie. Ida May and Willie, who no one had noticed had been waiting outside the back church door, opened the door all the way. Willie carried in a bowl of water and Ida May a towel that she handed to Jeb as he had instructed. Ida May smiled even though her teeth were chattering from waiting in the cold.

"Reverend, may I serve you?" Jeb asked.

Louie looked up and down the aisle until he made eye contact with his wife. Then he nodded at Jeb.

Jeb pulled off the minister's right shoe and sock and then his left. He washed his feet and then sat back. Will and Freda came up front and knelt. Freda greeted the minister and told him he had the best choir she had ever heard. Will washed Louie's feet and then handed the towel back to Jeb.

Jeb set the bowl aside and came to his feet. Louie came up too, standing on bare feet. He and Jeb embraced. Fern stood up and clapped. Angel joined her along with at least fifteen people and that caused everyone to at least stand.

Louie said, "I was wondering why you told me to wear my good socks."

Will laughed and that caused laughter to ripple through the congregation.

Jeb asked Louie to pray for Church in the Dell and Louie prayed. Some of the women sniffled. Louie asked Jeb to pray for the Church of Eternal Hope. Jeb blessed them and he took Louie's hand. "Sometimes we don't know what has slipped into our heart until God confronts us," he said. "My human nature hates confrontation. Hatred is a small thing that squeezes in through our narrow places, places not made big enough for love. It can poison us to truth and make us complacent, not wanting to deal with what is unfamiliar."

"I agree, my brother," said Louie. "My heart grows weary and angry and then complacent. I can be smug about myself, thinking I know it all, that I'm always right, and I forget about the neighbor who is suffering quietly while I show off my righteous rags."

A quiet rested on the congregants.

A woman from the Eternal Hope choir held up her thin hands and said, "I confess that I knew about the little Blessed girl and did nothing. She wasn't to blame for her pain, but I turned my back on her."

"We all did," said Will Honeysack.

The choir woman said, "My kids is grown and I got a room I use for sewing that can be put to better use. I want to say right now in front of all you good people, Lucky and her precious girl child can come and stay with me."

Freda cried. Josie kept her face in her hands.

Another woman from the back of the sanctuary offered a dress to Lucky, a man offered a crib for Myrtle.

"Wait, I have something to say."

Jeb looked back toward the entry for the one who spoke, but was unable to see for the throng down the aisle. "Sir, speak up."

"I'm John Blessed," he said. The choir members parted. John, Vera, and Jewel had slipped in during the prayers. John moved around the choir members until he arrived at the middle pew, where Lucky sat. He took Myrtle out of her arms and kissed the baby's face. He handed the baby girl to his wife and then threw his arms around his youngest daughter. "You look all grown-up." He cried.

Fern blubbered. She dug through her handbag and pulled out a handkerchief.

"I haven't thanked you, Reverend Nubey, for seeing after my baby and my grandbaby. It's time for them to come back home, though," said John.

The choir members clapped and laughed and then took to hugging one another. Will Honeysack, who could not sing on key, sang:

This little light of mine
I'm going to let it shine.

Much to everyone's relief, Louie joined him in a nice baritone, which enlisted everyone to sing:

I'm not going to make it shine.
I'm just going to let it shine,
hallelujah. . . .

❧

"It's colder than the dickens!" Jewel Blessed squeezed through the parsonage door with Lucky. The girls had come for Lucky's things.

Fern told John and Vera to come inside and she might be enticed to brew coffee. Vera wrapped her shoulders with a shawl and eased out of the Model T, a car that made fluttering sounds, like bats in an attic, for several seconds after John turned off the ignition. She wore a hat, blue straw with straw flowers attached to one side of the band, all of it matching the shawl and her gloves. "If I'd a known it was going to be so cold, I'd have put on Ruben's old woolens." She said other things to herself, such as the way that women outright froze in cold weather and how men got all of the good warm clothes. She covered Myrtle's face with her blanket and said to Fern, "Do I know you, honey?"

"I'm Jeb's friend."

Vera glanced around until Fern pointed to him as he held open the parsonage door. "Reverend is a good man," she said. Then she said to her husband, "I told Ruben he ought to come tonight. He's got too much pride, that's what."

Fern helped Vera and John settle on Jeb's couch and then went off for the coffee.

Angel coaxed Ida May into the kitchen to help make icing for cinnamon bread and told Jeb, "We're making up sweets for everyone." After Jeb gave her a look, she said, "We won't stay up late, I swear." Jewel followed the girls.

Lucky plopped down between her folks and said, "Look at some of these things Angel and I sewed up from the church rag bag."

John muttered about charity and Vera said, "That dress looks new. Funny what people throw away."

Jeb said, "You surprised me, the both of you. When I asked Reverend Williamson to bring his church choir by tonight, I didn't mention you, but I'm grateful you came."

"Reverend Williamson talked John into coming. Louie Williamson has the gift of persuasion," said Vera.

"He said if I didn't come, that it wouldn't do him no good to mention me in his morning prayers. He said if my soul was so locked up by pride, I may as well give my key to the Devil," said John.

"He didn't say it like that," said Vera.

Lucky laid her head on her mother's shoulder. "I can't wait to go home."

"I guess your son, Ruben, is surprised by all of this?" asked Jeb.

"Ruben's got a lot of hate built up," said Vera. "He'll be glad to see his sister, though. He looks after Lucky like no brother I ever saw."

Myrtle made bubbling sounds and drew her grandmother's attention.

"I see some of Ruben in this baby's face, around the eyes, and, see, that grin, John? That's Ruben all over. The idea of this child being born away from home still gives me chills to think of it. Was she born here at your place, Reverend?" Vera asked.

"Vera, I'll do my best to always tell you the truth. But I think your daughter ought to be the one to answer your question about Myrtle."

"Not here, Momma," said Lucky.

"Where, then?" she asked.

Willie walked through the parlor, drawn by the smell of cinnamon. "You mean you haven't heard the story? That there's the apple orchard baby." Willie disappeared into the kitchen.

"Nobody asked you, Willie," said Jeb.

"Ruben never said you had this baby in the apple orchard," said John. "What else do we not know?"

"I've been kind of curious about it myself, Lucky. What made Ruben drive you down into the apple orchard?" Jeb asked.

"Ruben never wanted no one to know," said Lucky.

"You may as well spit it out," said John. "You've carried it this far all by yourself."

Lucky touched her daughter's face and sopped the corner of her mouth with the edge of the blanket. "Ruben drove us straight into Nazareth. I told you, Reverend, he was acting crazy that night. My pains had started and I was crying. He drove downtown and stopped at that drugstore, Fidel's place, but it was closed. A group of young men had gathered out in front of the drugstore talking to girls. When they saw Ruben banging on the window, they yelled at him, called him 'nigger,' and asked him why he was banging on the drugstore window. Ruben, all of a sudden, got calm. He told them that he was bringing money to Frank Pella, that Pella would want to see him. One of the boys just blurted out big and easy, 'Why, you can find old Pella down in the apple orchard necking with his girlfriend.' That boy told Ruben how to find the orchard and that it wasn't far. I told Ruben not to go, but he drove straight into the apple orchard like he was going to kill Frank Pella. I cried and started screaming."

Jewel came and stood in the doorway, silent and listening to Lucky.

"Ruben saw Pella's car parked under an apple tree. He got out and yelled for Pella to come out of his car. Only Pella wasn't just with a girl. They was three boys in that car. They all got out and came at Ruben with tire tools. I laid in the backseat of that car, crying, but knowing if they found me, they'd hurt me and my baby. I put a rag in my mouth and bit it. I had her by myself while my brother took a beating. Ruben, he laid on the ground until the next morning. He crawled to the car and found me and Myrtle in the backseat. I thought I was dying and that Myrtle would die too.

"He drove us out of town, away from Nazareth, but not home either. We wound up in the yard of some old woman outside of town. Ruben drove until the car was flat out of gas.

This woman came out of her place and found us. She thought we were all dead. She dosed Ruben with some yarbs and he slept for three days. She took Myrtle and finished off what needed to be done after I birthed her. I couldn't have done none of that without her. She made me chicken soup and kept making me sip her tea until I had the strength to hold the cup myself. After Ruben came to himself, he told her that I was in trouble, that I needed someone to take my half-white child. I cried. I didn't want to give up my baby. I had never felt the way I did when I saw her face. It hurt, like I was breaking open inside. I knew I was too young to take care of her, but it didn't stop my wanting to try."

Jeb kept saying, "I'm so sorry."

"This woman told you about Reverend Nubey?" asked John.

"She told Ruben. Said that she heard of a preacher who took in kids and showed Ruben how to find Church in the Dell."

"What was her name?" asked Jeb.

"She called herself Toni, like a boy's name. That's all I know," said Lucky.

Vera cried. John rubbed Lucky's back as she spoke. When it seemed that she had finished her story, he said, "Life don't make no sense."

Jewel kept staring at the floor without saying a word.

"There I was mad at Ruben for staying gone for all those days. I could tell he'd been in a fight. I thought he'd gone off on a drinking binge or some such. He never told me," said Vera.

"Hot cinnamon bread and coffee," said Angel.

Jeb told the children they could stay up later than usual

to visit. The sound of children and a baby filled up the parsonage with good sounds. He told the story of how he came to be minister at Church in the Dell. John laughed and Vera plain did not believe him.

"I had him figured out when he preached that Paul wrote from the Isle of Patmos," said Fern.

"You never told me that," said Jeb.

John and Vera laughed some more, eating cinnamon bread until nothing remained but a plate of crumbs.

"You're place is nice and warm," said Vera. "I'm glad we stopped by."

24

On Friday morning, the second to the last Friday in January, Beulah broke from custom and set a kettle of stew to simmer on the back burner, a convenient leftovers' recipe using up the unsold portions of Thursday's flank steak. Her rhythmic chopping of ribs of celery, red potatoes, and the skinning of corn lent a cheery quality to the cafe. Jeb enjoyed his first cup of cafe coffee at the bar minus one baby in a laundry basket.

"If I'd have known you was going to have the Eternal Mansion chorus Wednesday night, I'd have been there. Shame I missed it," Beulah told Jeb.

"Eternal Hope."

"I say those people can sing better than any white choir." She filled his cup. "I guess your house is quieter now, what with that teenager and her baby gone home to be with their family. I always say it's best for children to be with kin, if possible, but if not, you are the darlingest man I ever knew to take in a stranger's kids."

A group of banking apprentices milled outside of Nazareth Bank and Trust.

Jeb pushed his cup toward Beulah and said, "Keep it warm for me, will you?" As he walked toward the men, he pulled his hat down, keeping his eyes to the town walk. He decided to cross the street corner, up a half block from the barbershop, and then walk past the Clip and Curl. He averted his eyes from Faith Bottoms, who fiddled with a window shade. Jeb increased his pace and nearly ran to the corner adjacent to the bank. "Frank Pella!" he yelled.

"Who wants to know?"

"You came back into town. Good to see you," said Jeb. He figured he had a few seconds before Frank bolted for his automobile or came at him with a tire tool.

"Someone's started rumors, Preacher. Good thing my father has an attorney. He has a way with preachers." Frank Pella's shirt look disheveled, slept in, creased in odd places at the shoulder and forearm.

"Your father know he's a grandfather?" asked Jeb.

"Let's adjourn our meeting indoors, gentlemen," said Frank.

None of the men broke away from the group or went inside.

"Fine. Stay out here and freeze," said Frank.

"Frank, I have a question for you," said Jeb.

"Not interested."

"It's about last October. Want to tell me what happened down in the apple orchard between you and Ruben Blessed?"

Two boys turned and went into the bank.

"I hear you always stand on the wrong side of the fence, Nubey," said Frank.

"While you and your friends there took out your meanness on Ruben, Lucky Blessed was in Ruben's car. She knows you beat him, saw your white face shining in the moonlight. That little girl laid in that car having your baby, Frank, while you beat her brother with a tire iron."

"Shut up!" Frank came at Jeb, his arms raised.

"Something wrong, boys?" Deputy Maynard walked up behind Frank.

"Lucky Blessed saw her brother beaten last October by Frank Pella and two of these young friends of his," said Jeb.

Maynard looked at the others.

"I'm not taking your blame, Frank!" one of the young men said. "It's not my business, Deputy. Talk to Wade and Gordon. They just went inside."

Maynard got his name and told him, "Harry Marsden. I heard them bragging about beating up the Negro down in the apple orchard."

"Keep your mouth shut, Harry!" said Frank.

"Frank, let's have us a talk down at my place. Come quietly. You can call your daddy," said Maynard. He took Frank by the upper arm.

Frank pulled away. "This lousy preacher's not ruining my life!" He clambered into his car.

Oz came running out of the bank and saw Frank jerk away from Maynard. "Don't, Frank! Go with George. He only wants to talk, right, George?"

"That's right. But you take off, boy, you can add resisting an officer to whatever else it is this Blessed girl thought she saw." Maynard held out his arms, palms out. "You can walk beside me back to the jailhouse, like we're having us a good-buddy chat."

Jeb knew that Frank Pella's father would have him out of jail by the time the lunch crowd gathered for stew at Beulah's. "I'll see you around," he said to George.

"Get me that little girl in my office, Reverend. I'll listen to what she's got to say."

Ruben Blessed's thick glasses gave him a scholarly appearance, like a college boy who wore lab coats and poured chemicals into beakers. He had driven from home and waited in the parsonage drive. He came up from his leaning stance against his daddy's car. "Reverend Nubey, I understand I owe you an apology." He stuck out his hand and Jeb shook it.

"Vera must be making you apologize, but don't do it on my account," said Jeb.

"My little sister. She says if she can forgive the man who did this to her, then so should I."

"I didn't know if you'd heard, Frank Pella was questioned for beating you today."

"And let go."

"Deputy Maynard asked me to bring in Lucky, to ask what she saw that night in October."

"His daddy got him a Little Rock attorney. He'll never see the inside of a jail, Reverend."

"Deputy got a confession out of one of his friends."

"What he did to Lucky was worse than what he did to me. What kind of justice slaps a man on the wrist for beating the brother of the girl he raped?" He looked around and then said, "I've wanted him dead for a while. I almost killed him one night too." He pointed into the woods. "I could have killed him right there under that big cedar. He was sneaking around with two of his friends, the ones who tore me up. They was watching Lucky through the window."

Jeb had wondered if Pella had been sneaking around the parsonage, since the church had been vandalized. "You had your chance."

"I knocked him smooth out. He lay there, looking like he was dead already. It scared me to think that I was turning into a monster. I realized I couldn't kill no one, not even Frank Pella. I went to the High Cotton Club that night and got so drunk, Jewel had to drag me home. Oh, by the way, she's told me about your debut at the club. You play good. She said the boys told her that at the club."

"No need to mention that to anyone, though."

"No, sir. I slept for the whole next day. I was afraid of myself. Then I looked at my own face in the mirror. I wasn't going to turn into Frank Pella, I decided."

"Lucky is proud of you, Ruben. When she talks about you, her whole face lights up," said Jeb.

"I never thought any of us could love that baby or give it our name. You ought to see my daddy bouncing that little girl on his knee, like she was his own."

"She is his own."

"Maybe she looks like me. I've taken to her, I'll say that. Anyway, it's getting dark and I promised my mother I'd be home to help her cook peas and ham. I got my own recipe." He laughed. "Someday I'm going to own my own restaurant."

Jeb remembered how Lucky said she wanted to teach. "John and Vera have done well with you and your sisters,

Ruben, in spite of what they think. I see the future when I look into your eyes."

"Don't get all soft, Reverend. You'll turn into Vera." He stuck out his hand again.

Jeb threw his arms around Ruben and hugged him.

～

Fern had left cookies on the table next to Jeb's bed along with a note that said, "I miss you so badly I could scream." Angel told him that Fern had waited at the parsonage an hour before going into his bedroom and then leaving.

He would go Saturday morning and wake her up at sunup, the worst part of the day in her estimation, but then he would make it the best time. He ate one of the cookies, not one of her better batches, but the vanilla scent reminded him of the first time he smelled her hair. He placed a cookie on his pillow and fell asleep.

Nothing could have awakened him, he decided, except something that might startle him out of his dream—something like a fire. Even from his bed he saw the flame shoot up. He did not know if the blaze had ignited the whole woods, seeing as how it flared up only for one astonishing moment that brought him upright, stumbling off the mattress and feeling in the dark for his trousers, notching up his galluses. He called out for Willie, but then he had to go and wake him, telling him not to wake up Ida May. Half-asleep, Willie followed him outside. He unquestioningly dragged a pail of water, as if he were carrying it out for a washtub full of laundry or a Saturday bath.

Jeb hefted two pails and ran into the woods, and it

seemed like a dream, like a foolish thing to do in the middle of the night.

"Where are we going?" Willie asked.

"Fire in the woods."

"It's cold. Woods are too wet."

He realized Willie was right, but he saw the orange glow and kept pressing through the brambling brush, snagging naked brown ivy until he came to the flaming tree, an oak flaming at the base. Jeb threw water onto the tree, and that is when he noticed the shape of a man.

The man seemed to be part of the tree, but the water caused his eyes to come open and he said gently, "I thought you'd come."

Jeb and Willie put out the fire and pulled Ruben Blessed away from the charred trunk. The ropes broke well off him and he was surprisingly light to carry.

Willie could not speak at all, not when Jeb told him to run and fetch Angel to bring balms from the kitchen, or when Angel came out of her room to ask him what was going on and what lay on the sofa that Jeb was crouched over, that thing that could not be a man, yet was. Angel cried. She had trouble keeping her balance, dashing back and forth from the kitchen, and then, when the cupboard ran bare of ointment, she said quietly, "I'm driving your truck to Fern's. Then we're going for Doc Forrester."

"Get Fern first, that's right," Jeb kept saying, even after she ran out of the parsonage in her nightgown.

Ida May tiptoed into the parlor, soft as a moth, and then slumped against the doorpost and wailed.

Fern used tweezers to peel strips of clothing from Ruben's skin. Angel kept burying her head in her hands; then she would sit up, like a girl coming to the surface of a pond for air, and help Fern strip Ruben's charred trousers from his legs.

Doc Forrester sent Willie and Ida May out of the room. He told Jeb, "It's really bad, Reverend."

"Do your best," said Jeb.

"My wife went for the boy's family. Fern here told us where they lived." Dr. Forrester knelt next to Ruben. "Reverend says you talked to him. Can you talk to me, Ruben? Can you hear me?"

"I hear good. My legs and hands feel like the pain is going out of them. You doing good by me, Doc."

"Who did this?" said Forrester.

"I think they followed me this evening from Reverend's place. I stopped for gas and that's when they grabbed me from behind. Can you hear me? My throat feels like it's on fire."

"We hear you, Ruben," said Jeb.

"My momma won't understand why I didn't get home in time for her cooking," he said.

"Who grabbed you, Ruben?" asked Jeb. "Was it Pella?"

"You know it was, Reverend. I made him mad, but when he tied me up, I told him that stocking over his face didn't help his looks none. I got to get home and make sure he doesn't get to Lucky. Can you help me up?"

"Your family is coming here to see you, Ruben," said Forrester. He told Fern to clean the burns on his legs with soapy water.

Fern kept swabbing, dropping cloths into a tub, wetting more clean cloths, and then she would push the hair out of her face and go to work on Ruben's legs.

"His left arm is broken," said Forrester. "I'll set it after we get you cleaned up," he told Ruben.

"I fought them off but good. They tried to throw me in the hull of Frank's car, but I fought them. If they hadn't broken my arm, they couldn't have tried getting me into that hull." He sucked in several breaths and said, "I hurt," like it surprised him.

"Pella's not getting away with it," said Jeb.

The sky lightened. Automobile lights searched through the woods and then shone into the parsonage windows.

Jeb opened the door. Vera Blessed ran for the front porch. Jeb met her on the steps. "Your son wants you, Vera."

"Tell me my child's going to live." She sobbed.

Jeb once promised Vera he'd always tell her the truth. "Come inside. It's cold out here."

25

O<small>N</small> M<small>ONDAY</small> <small>AFTERNOON</small> W<small>ILLIE</small> <small>SAID</small> <small>HE</small> thought he saw Ruben standing out in the garden. When he talked about it over supper, Angel said she thought she saw him too. They all decided Ruben had come to tell them good-bye.

The sun finally came out on Tuesday, warming the yellow sod, and it seemed like spring at the Hope Eternal Cemetery. Vera kept saying that Ruben could not wait for spring to come, that he had wanted to wet his line, and that this was his way of saying spring had come and he was the deliveryman.

Louie delivered the eulogy and then Jeb talked about Ruben's last words and forgiveness. John gave a word over the grave and then Vera and the girls each dropped a flower into the ground.

The ladies' choir sang a song that Ruben once sang in church, a hymn that set Vera to crying again.

Lucky and Angel walked across the cemetery, taking off their sweaters and singing the "Balm of Gilead" song. They found it catchy and kept singing it on the hill until the adults made them stop and come back for the meal at the church.

Someone had made peas and ham. Jeb ate from that bowl two or three times until he felt he might burst. Louie invited him into his study and they closed the door.

"I guess you know that Myrtle and Lucky have adjusted well to home."

"This is not the end, Louie. Frank Pella's not getting away," said Jeb.

"I can tell you're used to getting things your way. If I had your confidence, I'd run for mayor."

"We've been needing a new mayor. I know what you're thinking. Frank Pella is gone, nothing can be done about it. Pella's daddy may have snuck him out of town, but that only makes him look guilty."

"I don't want to sound pessimistic, Jeb, but not all people love the way you love," said Louie. "Not all come to justice. Not all come to the cross."

"The last thing I need is a sermon, Louie."

"Vera told me how you came to God. You're one of those Paul types—hard-to-come-along but then God slays you, and for the rest of your days, you follow him around like a mongrel pup. That is very satisfying to know."

"How God slew Jeb Nubey?"

"That you're going to mellow with time."

"I can't imagine it."

"Maybe you are a prophet?"

"What about you and the way you stand up to the monsters?"

"Stand and see the salvation of the *Lord*!" Louie laughed, and it was in an irritating manner that made him sound always right.

"You've given me a new view of redemption, Louie, I'll say that," said Jeb.

"I walk out on the sea of God's peace, Good Reverend, and as long as I keep walking, his peace sustains me. Whether I stand before a saint or a monster, I won't sink."

Jeb could not take his eyes off the altar. "Mind if I light those candles?"

"Long as you don't try and sing 'This Little Light of Mine.' You cannot sing, my brother."

"No need to get bigheaded, Louie. I'll only sing along with you. We sound good together."

"Long's you know I got the lead." He started the chorus out. They sang until Jaunice opened the door and said they were disturbing the sleeping babies.

"You can't wake babies," said Jeb. "They're unforgiving as the dickens." He had come to know a lot about children in spite of his days as a bachelor.

❧

Jeb waited outside the school on Wednesday. Cold air blew across the schoolyard, lifting like sheets, undulating and spitting crystal flakes across the grass.

Fern saw him through the window and came out to meet him. She tied her white woolen cap under her chin and said, "Willie is still quiet, but he pitched for stickball today. Don't tell me it's snowing again."

"Smells like snow, feels like it," he told her.

The air had that kind of frigid, whistling force, piercing through grab bag woolens. Fern moved closer, her posture suggesting, perhaps to curious students, that she only used Reverend Nubey to block the wind and sleet.

"Fern, I keep waiting for things to get better, you know, as in a good life. Something that I can offer you that you deserve."

She had gotten to where she listened without comment whenever he made this speech about waiting for the ship to dock.

"It came to me today that it might not ever get any better, that this Depression may never lift, that my house may always be full of another man's young." He spread his arms, looking more like a big rooster instead of a savior, he thought. "What I'm saying is, take a look at what you see and ask yourself if what you see is enough. I may never be perfect enough for us, Fern."

"I'm not perfect, Jeb. When you know that, you'll know that what we have is enough for us." She pulled his face close and they kissed.

Snow fell down and covered the ground, turning white and erasing the trees and turning the roofs white.

Fern told Jeb she loved him while snow collected on her lashes and brows, with her lips turning blue, and with students banging inside on the glass and taunting their teacher. "They say that all the heroes went into hiding in 1929, but I have seen a hero of a different nature, and I think that is the way of true heroes. We all find our ways of surviving hard times, but men like you use your life to hold the rest of us up. You make the rest of us poor slobs want to carry on, to not give up."

"My baby knows what to say." Jeb pressed his mouth

against her lips, not caring if what she had said was true, but knowing that if she believed it, he could believe that a cotton picker from Texas could fall asleep in jail and wake up in heaven. Fern did look like an angel in the snow.

She tapped an envelope sticking out of his pocket. "You got a letter?"

Jeb pulled it out and handed it to her. "I almost forgot. I got a letter from Washington, D.C."

"The president wants your advice," she said. "It's high time he asked."

"Read it." He handed her the letter.

She opened the letter and read it to herself. Her lashes lifted and she stared at Jeb, astonished.

༃

Cherry blossoms do fall like snow on the Washington Mall. The clusters hung heavily on the branches, waving in the March wind, scattering onto the heads of people and covering the ground.

The banner across the platform read THE AMERICAN DREAM and behind it Abe Lincoln looked down from his chair on his hill. The radio emcee Jerry Shaperi talked about Americans who dream, and how the suffering rise from the ashes of diminished hope. He talked about a minister from Arkansas who had climbed from past circumstances to become a hero to the hurting families of Nazareth, Arkansas. He quoted the Scriptures, saying, "'Can there any good thing come out of Nazareth?' Philip saith unto him, 'Come and see.'" He introduced Jeb while a group of two hundred or so applauded, including Florence Bernard and Angel, who watched from down front.

Jeb felt Fern's hand against his back as he stood up and then took his place on the taped X behind the *American Dream* lectern. "I can't imagine how out of all the essays submitted, a transplanted Texan's shabby version of hope got picked, but I'm grateful to you for asking me to come and read it to you."

The crowd laughed and then applauded again.

"I call my essay for *The American Dream*, 'A Feast of Breakable Bread.'" Jeb read:

I have come to know a people cut from raw substance; alone, a ragged lot of individuals, but who, when fit together, form a deep basket of human expectation. Expectation foments hope. We hope so well and see so far that we are renowned as giants of hope. But even legends can stumble.

When Americans dream, we come to believe that who we are, or who we might become, is so tightly woven into the material of dreams that when dreams fail, we faint for fear. But we are more than mere dreamers. Our reach can surpass even a grand expectation when we know that sweet secret that can take us farther and higher than one human can imagine. This great mystery of humanity, this elixir that can fill hungry stomachs and put tyrants out of business, holds the key to our success as a civilization. What is this secret that holds so much sway over the human condition, yet is so easily overlooked? How do we unearth what seems so deeply buried in human misery and suffering?

The weight of national failure is a heavy weight, but we cannot forget that weights are forged by time, and broken by fortitude and character. Failure is the opportunity to scrutinize what has weighed us down, admit our failures, and look for elements most often neglected, elements that corrupt our dreams and leave us as

outcasts in our own land, desperately sojourning again, as our an-
cestors sojourned, and seeking to climb again, to see again, to feel
the sun on our faces and read hope in our children's eyes.

Our humanity cries for justice and of wrongs being righted.
We long to be lifted up and made strong conquerors. But history
proves that conquerors fall, so we listen well, retool, and seek a bet-
ter dream. If we look deep, it is the one most inevitable, the one we
can rely upon and trust as our constant; that is in knowing that
when we are broken, like the bread from Christ's table, the whole
world is fed.

The sweet nectar of brotherhood is my reaching across the
fence to take the hand of the fallen neighbor. Or if both of us have
fallen, we hold tightly to one another and stand together, one
against the other. But we have both given and, as a result, we
have both received.

Here we stand broken, some of us fallen, of that we are certain.
We dislike this broken state of affairs. It makes us ill at ease and
gratefully we look for the morning when we will leave it behind.
But as we empty our hands of failure, we should also learn our les-
sons in knowing for what things we should reach. Remaining
breakable is not our natural desire, but in the forging of our plans,
it should be our driving mission. If we remain breakable, we are
no longer keeping what we know of freedom, ingenuity, and hap-
piness under the roofs of a few. If what we are producing within
our own heart is food for many, for others beside us, then we be-
come that feast, a banquet of liberty, love, peace, kindness, generos-
ity, humility, and a country for all men and women that is a
bottomless basket. That is not only how we feed the world, it is how
we feed ourselves.

When we cease to feed our brother, to make room for him at
our table, bitter corrosion will infect us all and we will find our-

selves once more beneath its weight. Greed is not a friend. Love for all is not our foe.

What is my American dream? To remain that breakable member of humanity who is no stranger to charity. I desire a language that is so fluent in generosity and compassion that all the world will beat a road to my door to learn new tongues. If I can know the fellowship of strangers, see that no orphan is homeless, and rise up to find that no mother is left to grieve over the treatment of her children, I have found my dream.

Perhaps I am a man of lost causes. But what man or woman is without an ancestor who has not known the bitter defeat of a lost cause, only to rise on that one glorious morning to discover their broken state has proliferated and given them back their land, their fertile condition, and to know that it emerged from brokenness?

Christ declared we are only one body, one bread. He showed us how by giving up our single purpose, laying down our isolated aims, that we could accomplish magnanimous feats. Such exploits are gotten through pain, but what ideal wrought beneath the beatific pain of selfless love has ever disappointed mankind?

When the self is told to stand down, what rises is the spirit. From spirit comes flight. Flying once again is our grand enticement. By unfolding our arms to reach into a brother's life, we are unfurling our wings to fly.

Who is my brother? He is like me, flesh and blood and soul and yearning.

What is the American dream? It is more than a dream. This laying down of the self is our mission. It is our calling and we offer it freely, our feast of breakable bread, to our brother and our neighbor and those who sojourn with us on this soil.

Jeb thanked them.

The crowd exploded with cheers while Jerry Shaperi presented Jeb with a plaque.

Fern came up behind Jeb and slid her arms around his waist. "I've found my dream too, Jeb," she whispered. "I dream of you."

➳

"It says that the reflecting pool is one-third mile long. I feel small here," said Fern, who read from a brochure. "This is what it feels like to be an ant." She glanced up and down the reflecting pool, from the Lincoln Memorial to the Washington Monument. "Where did Florence and Angel go?"

"Sightseeing. You think anyone in Nazareth heard me today?" he asked.

"The ones who wanted to hear heard you. In time I believe that all will hear."

"That's what I love about you, your optimism." Jeb took her hand and led her to the center of the west end. He knelt. "I'm sorry this has taken so long. You'd think that with my speech making I'd know exactly what to say at this moment."

Fern's cap blew off in the wind. Her hair blew around her face, as it had done the first time he saw her from the stream.

"I know there are women who are easy to know, easy to get. I've known them and they've known me. But only once have I met the one who I knew from the minute I laid eyes on her that she was the prize. I've had to fight to have you and lose those parts of myself that made me, at least in part, unworthy to even call you my friend. But I'm asking you now, Fern Coulter, to be my friend for life, with all these children in tow, with my life in a mess."

Fern cried. "I never really answered you, did I, Jeb?"

"Marry me, Fern, just as I am. I love you more than life."

"Jeb, you are my very best friend." She bent and kissed him. "I have watched you grow into a giant of a man, but I'll gladly stand in your shadow if it means that you will always be holding my hand. I will take you if it means living with twenty children not our own and dealing with a hundred towns like Nazareth. I think you should know that I'm not the perfect woman, though. I don't have a perfect past either. Over time I want you to know that about me, that my history is not as honorable as you believe. But if you still want me, yes, I want to marry you too."

"The past is the past, Fern." Jeb came to his feet and they kissed.

They walked beneath the Japanese cherry blossoms and it was spring, a time when heroes walked the streets again.

1. Jeb Nubey has assumed the full duties as pastor of Church in the Dell but the stresses of the ministry are beginning to weigh down his enthusiasm. His tendency to exemplify a savior style of ministry is central to his self-doubt. How does his need to fix the problems of his church complicate his life? How does it improve his abilities as a minister?

2. When a baby girl is dropped off on Jeb's doorstep, his attempts to find a home for the baby are hindered by her race. Would this situation create a conflict today? How have racial relations improved or worsened since 1930's America? Should the Church or can the Church take measures to improve racial harmony?

3. Jeb wrestles with the burden he feels he has placed on his relationship with Fern Coulter. He imagines a life with Fern free of the responsibility of the abandoned children he has taken into his home. Some believe that a life of faith equals a life of selfless service to others. Others consider a life of faith as one limited to personal

development. What sort of boundaries can a person of faith create that strikes a balance with personal goals and service to others?

4. When Jeb finally resigns himself to the fact that he is the only one willing to step up to the plate and care for Myrtle, he realizes he cannot shoulder the burden alone. He hires a woman considered amoral by the community to nurse the baby. Then he allows the young teen, Lucky, to move in and help with her care. His life grows steadily more complicated as he invites people from outside the church to help an orphaned baby. How might the people who were judging him for these choices have helped to simplify his decisions?

5. The church board members view Jeb's dilemma as one that a good leader can mend quickly. Some of them imply that Jeb is a weak leader because he is not responding fast enough to the demands of the church families. If you were to make a list of the qualities of a strong leader, what would those qualities be? Does Jeb possess some of the qualities on your list? Have you ever witnessed a leader being criticized for not responding quickly enough to the demands of those he is leading?

6. The various opinions and viewpoints that confront Jeb cause him to question his abilities. He discovers that maintaining his confidence in his abilities is an exercise in mental strength. Have you ever been criticized for making what you felt was the right choice? Is our society supportive of those who choose to make the harder ethical choices?

7. Reverend Louie Williamson makes reference to standing up against the monsters of his day. What does he

mean by standing up against the monsters? In what way does he take a stand?

8. Angel longs to be a part of Fern's family or at least live as the Coulters live with what she views as quiet security. Fern considers her family's background a burden and one from which she has seemingly run away. It is human nature to want a life different than what you already have. Is there a key to building a life in which you will know true contentment?

9. The Mt. Zion church choir makes an unexpected appearance singing for the Church in the Dell families. If Jeb had asked for a delegation from his church to visit the Mt. Zion Church, what might have been the response? If a minister were to make such a request today, what might be the response?

10. When Lucky's brother Ruben shows up to express to Jeb his desire to forgive his family's enemies, he is eager to see his life change. Then his life changes for the worse. Injustice makes us feel helpless. What are the positives that can follow an unjust act? Do the positives justify the injustice?

11. Jeb is driven by his frustration to write an essay for the *American Dream* contest. He wins and then is invited to deliver the message to a small group of people in Washington, D.C., far from Nazareth and far from the inequalities that have not been brought to justice. Does it make us feel frustrated or encouraged when a life that stands for right is handed a small if temporary platform?

12. Jeb Nubey becomes a symbol to Fern of what a true hero represents. Are most heroes recognized in their day and by their peers?

13. What small fragment of a community might be changed through one heroic act? What biographies might you recommend of those who through small heroic acts have ushered in a world of change?

Here are a few recommended biographical titles, but by no means an exhaustive list:

The Hiding Place by Corrie Ten Boom
Eric Liddell: Something Greater Than Gold by Janet Benge
A Chance to Die: The Life and Legacy of Amy Carmichael
    by Elisabeth Eliot
Jungle Pilot by Russell T. Hitt
Mary Slessor of Calabar by W.P. Livingstone
Now It Is Time by Lois Heathman Roberts
R.A. Torrey, Apostle of Certainty by Roger Martin
Into the Glory by Jamie Buckingham
William Carey by Basil Miller
The Legacy of William Carey by Vishal Mangalwadi
George Muller: The Guardian of Bristol's Orphans
    by Janet Binge
Gladys Aylward by Catherine Swift

Multi-biographical volumes:
Movers and Shapers—Singles Who Changed Their World
    by Harold Ivan Smith
Profiles in Evangelism by Dr. Fred Barlow
Molder of Dreams by Guy Doud (one man's story of how
    everyday people impacted his life)